"Zöe Willow Martin," Dean intoned.

"Such a beautiful name."

"Thank you, Dean," I said, shuddering. But I was smiling.

"I think if you consider the alternatives, you'll find you want to take off your panties, but leave everything else on, your skirt and your socks and shoes."

"That's probably the best course of action," I agreed. I reached under my skirt and got my underwear off and down around my ankles. I had to kick it a little to get it over my shoes, and it ripped, but that wasn't important. I'd been planning to get rid of most of my underwear anyway.

"I have something I'd like to try with you," Dean said. "It might help you to get more in touch with how you're feeling."

"Whatever you think would help," I said anxiously.

"Well, to start with, I'll need you to come here and sit on my knee, facing me. I'd like to get a good, close look at your eyes. They say the eyes are the windows to the soul." I nodded, coming over to him, lifting my skirt out of the way as I sat down.

Also recommended...

You may also enjoy these other ForbiddenFiction works:

Held in Dreams by Ava Burquette
Elaine is an ordinary human with ordinary dreams, maybe a little too shy for her own good. At least that's what she tells herself, until she is kidnapped off of a city bus by a strange and charismatic man named Ghalib who has come looking specifically for her. Ghalib definitely isn't ordinary. He isn't even human. He's a Dream Architect, one of the beings who create dreams for humanity. His world is the realm of passion, imagination and nightmares, where humans may be kept as pets or personal slaves. Ghalib is obsessed with Elaine, whose vivid, erotic dreams he finds irresistible. If Elaine is to contend with Ghalib on her own terms, she'll have to do more than let go of her shy, inhibited waking manner. She will have to realize her own dreams. (F/M, F/F, M/M)
http://forbiddenfiction.com/library/story/AB1-1.000093

Winner Takes Her by B.B. Anderson
Freddie de Ford is a successful magazine editor, but something is still missing from his life until he meets Melanie Matthews. She is intelligent and sweet but also, shockingly, a fighter groupie—a woman turned on by men who fight other men. Freddie is drawn into Melanie's increasingly perverse and violent world of illegal fighters and women who want them. Freddie will risk everything to satisfy them. (M/F+)
http://forbidden-fiction.com/library/story/BBA-1.000006

Deep Focus

M. L. Caufax

ForbiddenFiction
www.forbiddenfiction.com

an imprint of

Fantastic Fiction Publishing
www.fantasticfictionpublishing.com

DEEP FOCUS
A Forbidden Fiction book

Fantastic Fiction Publishing
Hayward, California

CREDITS
Editor: D.M. Atkins and P.R. Fancier
Cover Design: Siolnatine
Cover Art: Artem Merzlenko at Dreamstime, background from public domain and original art by Siolnatine
Production Editor: Erika L Firanc
Proofreading: Jae Knight

SKU: MLC-000124-02 FFP
ISBN: 978-1-62234-135-1

Published in the United States of America

DISCLAIMER

This book is a work of fiction which contains explicit erotic content; it is intended for mature readers. Do not read this if it's not legal for you.

All the characters, locations and events herein are fictional. While elements of existing locations or historical characters or events may be used fictitiously, any resemblance to actual people, places or events is coincidental.

This story depicts fictional BDSM; it is not intended to be used as an instruction manual. It contains descriptions of erotic acts that may be immoral, illegal, or unsafe. The characters are not models for the Safe, Sane and Consensual forms embraced by most current practitioners of BDSM. The author takes license with the use of BDSM for dramatic effect. Do not take the events in this story as proof of the plausibility or safety of any particular practice.

This book is for Max and Moe, the inner circle, with gratitude.

Contents

1. Viewfinder..1

2. A Matter of Perspective................................10

3. Bloody Thursday..19

4. Hindsight..25

5. The Confidence Man....................................34

6. Depth Perception 43

7. Looking Out for Number One 52

8. The Smell of Apricots 59

9. Wirewalker...69

10. Intervention..77

11. Revision 83

12. The Gift of Clear Sight..............................92

13. SOTY 100

14. Showtime...109

15. Puppet Play..116

16. Guys and Dolls.......................................125

17. Empathy 137

18. At the Gates...148

19. The Smell of Curry...................................155

20. Staredown 163

21. Breaking the Girl 170

22. Persistence of Vision.............................182
23. See No Evil...191

Author's Notes 199
About the Author....................................200
About the Publisher................................201

Chapter 1

Viewfinder

Dean

Eye contact.

Welcome, everyone. Thank you, Doctor Thornhill, for that very kind introduction. I also want to thank Al Barlow, our provost, and the distinguished members of our faculty, for joining us tonight on this momentous occasion.

I don't say that lightly. This is a momentous occasion indeed. You don't need me to tell you how fortunate you are to be sitting in this auditorium. You've read the articles. Your parents can probably recite the statistics in their sleep. The reputation of our university speaks for itself, and the fact that you were accepted out of the many, many thousands of worthy applicants... well, I believe that speaks for itself as well. There is no question that you are among the very brightest and most promising scholars in the country.

The question is not "Why are you here?" The question is, "What are you here to do?"

Pause.

I don't mean the name of your chosen field of study. I'm talking about your purpose in being here. What is it... that you are supposed to be doing with your life?

Pause.

If you don't know the answer yet, that's okay.

Pause for mid-range laughter. Check response levels.

What I can tell you now, with absolute certainty, is that you are going to find out the answer while you are here. That's what our university is all about. That's what we do. We help each other find our purpose. We help each other succeed.

See, you don't have to do it on your own. You can't do it on your own. In order to learn, you must turn to others for help. Scholars who have gone before you. Professors who guide your studies. Fellow students who strive as you do. Even humble counselors like myself.

Pause for mild laughter.

And of course there are your parents, who love you, and who write the checks. We mustn't forget them.

Pause for mid-range laughter.

I'm sure they'd love to be here tonight, but they're not invited. As you know, our opening ceremony is for students and faculty only. As you know, tonight marks the beginning of your immersion into our Deep Focus academic program, during which your social contact with the world outside our lovely campus will be strictly limited. Some people find that prospect intimidating. Others find it liberating. What no one can dispute... is that it works.

The reason it works so well, the reason we get results here, is that we teach our students how to focus. How to do only that which needs to be done, without being distracted by anything else.

If that sounds difficult, it isn't. It's easy.

It's easy, and I'm going to show you how.

Right now.

Please look into my eyes.

Pause for confirmation from security.

Thank you. Thank you all.

Let me tell you about what I do here.

I get to know people. That's my job. For instance, I have met every single one of you in this room. Isn't that something? If you are sitting here tonight, you have shaken my hand and looked me in the eye, and I have spoken your name. That's how committed I am to my job. My job is to know you.

In the weeks to come, I'll be getting to know you even better. We'll meet, we'll talk, and I will help you to understand your purpose. Whatever is troubling you now will cease to trouble you. Your fears, your heartaches, your embarrassments, all of these things will melt away. You will know how to focus on what matters, and forget everything else.

Forget everything else.

Raise your right hand above your head.

Pause for confirmation from security.

It's just that easy. You just do what you know you must do.

It comes from within you, this voice, and it is all that there is. It is the only thing that is real.

From this moment forward, you are under my command. I am the ultimate authority. All that I say, you will obey.

Lower your right hand.

Pause for confirmation from security.

Send thought for all to stand.

Send thought for all to sit.

Pause for confirmation from security.

Repeat this word: daisy.

Pause for repetition.

Very good. Now we're all on the same page.

Pause for major laughter lasting ten seconds. Confirmation from security.

I'm nearly finished here. Just a few more remarks. After I leave the stage, you will hear a recording of my voice reciting a list of commands, and explaining what those commands mean. You will remember these commands, and when you hear them spoken, you will obey them without hesitation.

Once the recording is finished, Mr. Barlow will take the podium here for a few minutes, then you'll all be dismissed to return to your residence halls. You'll finish unpacking, you'll settle in, and you'll prepare yourselves for the start of classes. And as you do, your memory of this assembly will fade into something vague and... trivial. Just an ordinary assembly. Nothing to write home about.

You will obey without remembering.

So, that's how it's done. As I said, it's easy to focus when you know how. Now, I'm sure you're all eager to get out of this auditorium and get started on your own lives, so let's get right to that recording. Listen closely, it's important.

I want to thank you all for your very kind attention. Remember, if you'd like some advice or just a friendly ear to listen to your troubles, I'm here for you. You can make an appointment at the health clinic or come directly to my office. Incidentally, I'm looking for a new receptionist. The last one graduated. If you're interested, let me know.

Thank you.

Zöe

"Hello there."

I looked up from the book I was reading. It was a bright fall afternoon, and most of the benches dotted about the campus lawns were occupied by students like myself, taking advantage of the warm weather to study, or not study, under the turning colors of the trees.

The man standing near the parking lot looked familiar to me, but I couldn't place him. "Yes?" I said.

"You're Zöe, right?"

"Right," I said.

"Zöe W. Martin," he said, taking a few steps toward me.

"Yes," I said. "Do I know you?"

"Not really," he said. "You probably saw me at the big assembly a few weeks ago."

"Oh, that's right," I said. "I knew I'd seen you somewhere. You're the school counselor, right?"

"You remember," he said with a smile. "Most kids don't. I'm sorry," he added without a break, "I shouldn't say 'kids.' That's condescending. How old are you, nineteen?"

"I will be in November. That's okay, really. I don't mind." He was kind of cute in an older guy sort of way, with a rumpled, collegiate look. Pretty classic, really. Patches on the elbows of his corduroy jacket. And his eyes were a startling blue.

"I recognize your face, but the name escapes me," I said.

"Oh, of course, how rude—" He crossed the verge of grass and the pathway in front of my bench, and put out his hand. "I'm Kevin Carlson, but everybody calls me Dean."

"Dean," I said, shaking his hand. Wow, those eyes. They were really a beautiful shade of blue, bright and deep and hard to look away from. "It's nice to meet you, Dean."

"Same here. Anyway, sorry to bother you. I see you're reading, so..."

"Not really, I'm just kind of leafing," I lied.

"Mmmn. That sounds about right for a fall afternoon." It took me a second, but then I caught the double entendre and laughed. He smiled, and all the little lines around his eyes crinkled up. My insides flip-flopped. "Do you mind if I join you?" he asked.

"No, go right ahead," I said, scooting over on the bench.

He came and sat down. "Thanks. Hey, nice view of the river. You've got a good seat."

Far down the valley, we could see a tiny coil of the Lashaqua River curling between the red and gold trees. Somewhere under all that foliage was the town of Ferngrove, which I'd barely seen before arriving on campus. There wasn't much to see, from what I'd heard; a general store, a post office and a combined police and fire station seemed to be about the extent of it. Ferngrove needed the university, not the other way around.

"I think all the seats are good," I said. "Is it always this beautiful here?"

"Always," said Dean.

I sighed and crossed my arms. "That's good," I said. "I think I'm going to like this place."

Dean inclined his head toward me. "I think so, too."

I could feel him watching me. I kept my eyes on the river. "I was nervous at first. Like everybody is, probably, even if they don't admit it. But I'm settling in–"

"Why were you nervous?"

I arched an eyebrow at him. "Are you kidding me? Do you know how hard it is to get into this place? Well, of course you do, you work here."

"Oh, I'm just another cog in the machine," Dean said, stretching his arms wide and lacing his fingers behind his head. "You, on the other hand, had grades through the roof last year, not to mention an unusually insightful essay on the application."

"You read that?" I asked.

"One of the best I've seen in years," he replied with an easy smile. I found myself smiling along with him, bashfully. "You've got nothing to be nervous about. You were meant for a place like this."

Why was I blushing? Was this suddenly a big deal? I didn't even know this guy, but here I was, my cheeks getting hot. "Thanks," I said.

He dropped his hands into his lap and sat forward. "What's the book?" he asked.

"Oh." I picked it up, turned it over. "*Pride and Prejudice*. It's for a class."

"Zeller?"

"Uh huh. I'm not really a big Jane Austen fan, she's a little too soap opera for me, but—you know—it's not bad."

He laughed. I liked his laugh; it made me feel strangely proud of myself, like the way I felt when I got an A on a test. Approval.

"So what does the W stand for?" Dean asked.

It took me a minute. "Oh, that W. It stands for Willow."

"Willow," he repeated. "Zöe Willow Martin. Beautiful."

"Thanks." I could feel myself blush again. "I'm a little self-conscious about it. It's such a hippie name."

"Absolutely not," Dean said.

"No?"

"No. First of all, the willow is a tree that predates hippies and all the rest of American culture by thousands of years. It figures prominently in classical literature. Nothing to be self-conscious about. Second, the term 'hippie' is an obsolete pejorative. It refers to the youth counterculture of a generation that's no longer young."

"Were you a hippie?" I asked, then wondered if that was rude. Was that too long ago? How old was he, anyway?

Dean laughed. "There were probably people who thought of me that way. I suppose it's a matter of perspective." I met his gaze, and his eyes were really amazingly blue. Bluer than the sky.

"So... Dean..." I fumbled. "I'm, I'm curious... how did you know who I was?"

"Your name's in the records," he said, looking mildly surprised. "Incoming freshmen. I always look over the new crop, you know, try to get acquainted with everyone. It makes it easier for people to approach me later, if they have a problem with something. Or just want someone to talk to."

6

"I notice you said 'people', not 'kids'."

"That's right. You're very perceptive, Zöe." Again, I had a flip-flop sensation inside, like something turning over quickly. My heart was beating a little faster, and the blush that had just gone away was back in my cheeks. Wow. Pheromones.

"How, um, how long have you been a counselor? Um, here?" The words came out wobblier than I was expecting.

"Oh, I've been here a while," Dean said. "Longer than I'd like to say." His smile was radiant. "I've been all around the world, but this is the place I call home. The people who live here... they're my people."

"So, about how many, um, people do you counsel?" I asked.

He looked up, knitting his eyebrows. "Mm. All of them."

I started to laugh. "All of them? You mean everybody at this school?"

"Everybody in Ferngrove, too."

I stopped laughing. "You're exaggerating, right?"

"No, I'm not. I counsel every single person on campus, and every single person in town."

"But that's, like, hundreds and hundreds of people. How could you possibly have time for everyone?"

Dean mused for a moment. Then he shrugged. "I'm very efficient," he said, and he glanced at me again. With a smile crooking the corners of his mouth. And his eyes... his eyes were calm, deep canyons.

"W-wow," I stammered. "You must be. What do you do?"

"I listen and I offer suggestions."

"You make it sound so simple," I said.

Dean smiled. "It is."

"Does it work?"

"Every time."

"So what makes you so good at this?" I asked. My heart was racing now, blood rushing through my veins, circulating madly through my body.

Dean didn't answer at first. He just looked at me out of his still, fathomless blue eyes, that little crook of a smile on his lips. Then he said: "You look lovely, Zöe Willow Martin."

I thought I was going to swallow my tongue.

"Your name is beautiful, but it barely does you justice. It has been a while since I've spoken with a student as attractive as you."

A wave of gooseflesh prickled across my body with a sudden, delicious shiver. I struggled not to move; I knew I'd start shaking if I tried. I had to remain perfectly still. "Thank you," I gulped, "Dean."

"In answer to your question," he said, "I simply provide another perspective." I loved the way his mouth moved when he said *perspective*, but I couldn't remember what my question had been. What was this? What was happening to me?

"I like talking to people, helping them to understand," he went on. "Most people who are having some kind of emotional discomfort just need to consider things from a different point of view. I provide that point of view."

I wanted to talk. I wanted to be witty and charming, but I didn't think I could be any longer. I was terrified that if I opened my mouth I might say something really dumb, something I didn't want to say. Something inappropriate.

"I can show you what I mean, if you're interested," he said. I nodded my head and smiled. I was interested. I wanted to know more about Dean. He was such a fascinating man. Oddly fascinating and oddly handsome; more attractive, in fact, every time I looked at him. I tried not to look.

"Stay here," he said, getting up. "I'll be right back." He walked out onto the grass, heading across the quad.

I sat there and didn't move, just watched his back recede. Then I averted my eyes. I looked down the mountainside to the river, a little silver curve down in the depths of all the shifting trees.

It was so strange, this sudden surge of feelings inside me. I mean, I wasn't naïve. I had a healthy resistance to pick-up lines, of which I'd heard plenty. Most 19-year-old girls — women — have. But somehow this was different. Dean was different — although that wasn't his real name, was it? He had told me his real name, but I couldn't remember it now. Something like Ken, or Calvin. It didn't really matter. He looked like a Dean. It fit him. Everything about him fit like a glove. His voice was so calm and assured. And somehow, when he looked at me...

When he said *You look lovely, Zöe Willow Martin...*

"Zöe," Dean said.

I looked up. He was standing in front of the bench with a girl I'd seen before but hadn't met. She was noticeable everywhere because of her hair, which was white-blond, long and perfectly straight. Now that she was close, I could see her roots just beginning to show. But it didn't matter. She had perfect breasts, perfect thighs, a perfect ass. I could only imagine how many creeps she'd had to deal with in her life.

"I want you to meet Jill," Dean said. "She's in her second year."

"You must be Zöe," she said, shaking hands with me. "I'm really glad to meet you. I love your name."

"Thanks," I said. "I'm getting a lot of that today."

"Jill, I was just telling Zöe about what I do here," Dean said, sitting down next to me on the bench. "She was asking how I'm able to counsel so many people."

"Well, you answered that," I said. "You said you're efficient."

"Yes, then you wanted to know what makes me so efficient. What makes me so good at this, you wanted to know."

"Okay," I said, not sure what he was getting at. We looked directly at each other for a moment, and I saw his brilliant blue eyes again. The color was almost too intense to believe. My heart accelerated, my cheeks flushed.

"I mentioned that resolving emotional discomfort is usually just a matter of perspective," Dean said. "Then I saw Jill sitting over by those trees, and I thought it was a perfect opportunity to show you what I mean. Jill here has been seeing things from a new point of view since we got to know each other last year."

I looked at Jill. She smiled.

"Jill," Dean said. "I wonder if you'd consider a suggestion."

"Sure, Dean," she said cheerfully. She seemed just as fascinated as I was with him. "What do you have in mind?"

"You probably should consider taking off your shirt and your bra right now," Dean said, "and handing them to me."

"Really?" Jill said. "Huh. Okay," and then without further ado she reached down and pulled her shirt up over her head. Unhooked her bra. Peeled it off her chest, folded it into her shirt, and stepped forward, bare-breasted, to hand it to him.

Chapter 2
A Matter of Perspective

Zöe

I couldn't look away. I couldn't believe what I was seeing. Jill's nipples were dark pink, distinct and erect at the tips of her breasts. For a moment I couldn't use my voice. Then I said: "What is this?"

"It's a matter of perspective," Dean said, looking at me. "Does it bother you?"

"Well, it's... you... she's naked."

"Half-naked."

"Half-naked, yes, and Jill, I think you should put your shirt back on before you get in trouble."

"I'd have to disagree with you, there," Dean said. "That's one way of looking at it, I suppose, but there are other ways that I think we should explore. The way I see it, Jill, this is a good thing. You might even want to take off the rest of your clothes."

"I've got to agree with Dean, Zöe," Jill said, shaking her head, looking at me with her eyebrows raised in shy apology. "I understand what you're saying, I think, but this still seems like a good idea." She slipped out of her clogs and began undoing the buttons of her jeans. "I've been here for a year already, and I'm telling you, Dean just has the best take on things. I swear. Whenever I'm feeling bad or confused or whatever, I just talk to him and it's like it all clears up, you know? Like those eyes, oh my God."

"Yeah, I know," I said. "Dean, did anyone ever tell you that you look like Paul Newman?"

"Or Gabriel Byrne," Jill said.

Dean smiled and put up his hands in a gesture of modesty. I couldn't believe what I had just said. I couldn't believe I wasn't screaming at the top of my lungs and running for help. But that would have been... I don't know, disruptive. Rude. Jill didn't seem upset. Jill was taking off her underwear now, right out in the middle of the quadrangle in the afternoon sun; Jill was entirely naked now, and she didn't seem upset about it.

"I don't understand," I said to Dean. "How are you doing this?"

"What don't you understand?" he said. "I made a suggestion to Jill, and she followed up on it. That's all."

"Yeah, it's really no big deal," Jill said.

"But don't you care?" I said to her. "You just took off all your clothes. Everyone can see you. Don't you think that's dangerous?"

"It doesn't seem dangerous to me," Dean said. "Jill doesn't appear to be in any danger right now. Do you?" He turned to her for confirmation.

"No, I sure don't." Jill said, smiling. "I feel pretty safe."

"Isn't it nice to be standing out here in the sun, with no clothes on?" he asked.

"Oh yeah, totally. I wish I'd thought of this sooner. It's really warm and comfortable like this. You ought to try it, Zöe, come on. You'll like it."

"Um, I don't know," I said. "You're not embarrassed by this?"

"No, I'm not embarrassed," Jill said. "Should I be?"

"I don't see how that would be helpful," Dean said.

"Yeah, neither do I," Jill said. "It feels so good, anyway."

"I don't understand," I said again.

"Jill," Dean said, "how would you feel about having my cock in your mouth?"

"I think that would be nice," Jill said. "You know, kind of a change of pace. I talk too much, anyway."

"That's true, you do," Dean said.

"I sure do. I should stop talking so much. It would be a good idea to put your cock in my mouth and suck on it, because then I wouldn't be able to talk at all."

"That's an interesting perspective, Jill," Dean said. "I think you're on to something. Maybe you should unzip my pants."

"You're right, that would be a good first step," Jill said, with no trace of irony. She knelt on the pavement in front of Dean.

"She's following every suggestion you make," I said, finding my voice again. "She's agreeing to everything you say."

"Very perceptive of you."

"And I'm not leaving. I'm staying here watching this happen."

"That is also true."

"I don't understand why, you know?" I said to Dean. I was smiling, because... well, I guess because it was funny. "It's strange. I don't know why I'm watching this. It's sort of offensive, the way she's naked, right out here in the open. And I don't—"

I had been looking away, avoiding the sight of her down on her knees like that, but now I turned and saw that she was just parting her lips over the head of Dean's exposed cock. Inside I flip-flopped, flip-flopped, then began to thump. I was thumping, and it wasn't my heart, it was my whole body. My whole body was throbbing hard. I rubbed my thighs together around the center of the pulse. My face felt hot.

"Uh, I mean, what if someone sees you? What if the police see you?"

Her mouth slipped farther down the trunk of his cock. It seemed so thick. How could she get her lips around it? How could she breathe? It filled her mouth completely. Her lips were stretched taut around its girth, the smooth circumcised head of it buried somewhere very near the opening of her throat. It was obscene. Wasn't it?

"Someone could call the police," I said. "I could call the police."

"I don't think the police would mind if they found out," Dean said. His hands were in Jill's long blond hair, holding her head as she began to suck in long, slow, deep strokes. "I know the sheriff very well. In fact, I know the entire police force. I'm pretty sure they wouldn't mind that this is happening. And if anyone else should mind, the police will be able to detain them until I have a chance to sit down with them and listen, and offer suggestions." He paused for a moment as Jill circled the head of his cock with her tongue, swirling around and around before plunging back down its length.

"I feel so strange," I said.

12

"In what way?"

"It's hard to describe," I said to his eyes, his blue, blue eyes. "I know something wrong is happening here, and I feel like I want to call someone I trust. Like my mom and dad. Maybe they could help me."

"But you aren't doing that, are you?" Dean asked.

"No. No, I'm not."

"Why do you think that is?"

"I really don't know."

"My guess is that it's because you're new."

"I'm new?"

"New to this school. And to me. Keep in mind that we've only just met, Zöe."

"Oh, that's right. We just met today." How stupid of me. Of course. That was obvious. Of course I was new.

"I find that the longer someone's known me, the less upset they are by my point of view. Any point of view takes time to fully comprehend, and the longer people know me, the more they are able to understand how I see things. That seems reasonable, doesn't it, Zöe?"

I nodded. It made so much sense, what he was saying. The more I got to know Dean, the more I would understand him.

"So just give yourself time. And if you're ever feeling worried or confused about something, just come see me. By the way, you mentioned talking to your mom and dad. You didn't want to do that now, did you?"

"Oh God, no," I said and laughed, "Not now. Jesus. Some other time."

"Right, that's what I thought. But when you do decide to call them, why don't you come see me first? It's not a good idea to use the dorm phones for long-distance calls. The phone in my office is a lot easier to use, and while you're there maybe you and I can get together and talk. You know, no pressure, no agendas, just hanging out."

"Sure, that would be fun," I said, beaming. He wanted to hang out with me. Why me? I talked too much.

I was watching Dean rise a little off the bench so that he could thrust his hips forward. I watched him take Jill by the back of her head and pull her toward him firmly, all the way to the root, and I heard a "glk" sound as he entered her throat and cut off her air entirely.

"Jill, you're absolutely right," he said, looking at me. "You can't talk at all like this, can you?" Then he reared back and in again.

glk.

ulkg.

glgk.

He came, holding her head firmly to him, his hips jerking and bucking as he emptied himself down her throat. His eyes on me the whole time.

"Aaah," I breathed. My whole body was pulsing, my thighs slid past each other, and I felt a damp trickle ooze down my leg. I was very wet, much wetter than I'd ever been. I was dripping.

I didn't know what I was going to do. I felt like I could hardly think, I wanted him so much. I hoped he didn't think I was stupid. I hoped he liked my body.

Dean sat back on the bench as Jill came off him, gasping for air. She panted for a moment, then said, "Oh Dean, oh wow, that was really exciting." Her voice was husky. "That was really intense. I couldn't breathe. It turned me on so much, not being able to breathe at all. You could have killed me. I was in your hands."

"You didn't come, though, did you?" Dean asked.

"No, I really wanted to, but I couldn't, somehow. I guess I wasn't supposed to come."

"I think you're probably right," Dean said. "When it's a good time for you to come, I'll let you know, okay?"

Jill blushed. "Oh, thank you, Dean. Wow, that is really sweet of you. You're so thoughtful. That would help a lot."

"Quite all right, Jill," he said. "Why don't you sit over there on the grass for a while? You can watch Zöe and I while we get to know each other better."

"That sounds like a good idea," Jill said enthusiastically, buoyantly, and she went over to the other side of the path and sat down resting on one arm, her legs tucked back under her.

Dean turned fully to me. I'm sure he saw me trembling. I must have smelled like sex. My cunt was dripping with sex, and I'd never thought of it as a cunt before, never really used the word before, but it was pretty clearly a cunt now. There didn't seem to be any other word for it. In fact, there didn't seem to be any other word for me. I was a slick hole waiting to be filled with something; that was all, nothing else. Nothing else of any importance.

"Zöe Willow Martin," Dean intoned. "Such a beautiful name."

"Thank you, Dean," I said, shuddering. But I was smiling.

"I think if you consider the alternatives, you'll find you want to take off your panties, but leave everything else on, your skirt and your socks and shoes."

"That's probably the best course of action," I agreed. I reached under my skirt and got my underwear off and down around my ankles. I had to kick it a little to get it over my shoes, and it ripped, but that wasn't important. I'd been planning to get rid of most of my underwear anyway.

"I have something I'd like to try with you," Dean said. "It might help you to get more in touch with how you're feeling."

"Whatever you think would help," I said anxiously.

"Well, to start with, I'll need you to come here and sit on my knee, facing me. I'd like to get a good, close look at your eyes. They say the eyes are the windows to the soul." I nodded, coming over to him, lifting my skirt out of the way as I sat down. My cunt lips glistened, and I heard them squish as I came to rest with the skirt falling all around, his kneecap bone-hard against me.

"I'm afraid I'm not good enough," I heard myself say to him. "I don't really deserve to have you as my counselor. I'm so weak. I ask so many questions."

"There's nothing wrong with asking questions," Dean said. "Just be sure to listen for the answers. Listening is the most important thing you can do, Zöe." He was looking straight at me with his crystalline, endless eyes. "That's the wonderful thing about college life. It's a time for inquiry, and it's a time to learn. The best thing you can do is to open yourself to new experiences, new points of view. Try to be receptive to what people tell you."

I was weeping. "I'll try," I said, rocking on his knee, pressing my cunt hard against his leg, mashing my little pleasure-button against his tight skin. I could see his cock, softened but full, lying against his thigh. "I'm so grateful to you," I sobbed, grinding my cunt, slipping down his leg a fraction. "I'll be open-minded. I want to know how you see things, Dean. Please. Tell me what you think."

His cock was stirring. I could see it begin to stiffen.

"Well, if you're asking my opinion, I think you're a slut," he said gently.

I exhaled. "That's just how I feel."

"Mm-hmm. Tell me about it."

"I feel like all I want to do, all I can think about, is being fucked. That's the way a slut thinks, isn't it? I don't know what I was doing before, but it isn't important. I don't care about anything except the way my cunt feels now, pressed up against you like this and sliding on your thigh, and the only thing I want is to feel your cock inside me, filling my cunt the way you filled Jill's mouth. I want to feel you come inside me. I... I guess I'm a slut. A thing for you to fuck. But it's okay. I'm supposed to be a slut. That's all I want to be."

"What you're saying makes a lot of sense, Zöe," Dean said. "I'm really pleased with your self-investigation. You're making remarkable progress."

"Thank you, Dean," I groaned, tears running down my face.

"I'm sure you'll understand that it's not really a good idea to have my cock inside your cunt," he said. "Not yet. Before that can happen, you'll need to go to the school clinic and be checked for venereal diseases. Are you taking birth control pills, Zöe?"

"Yes, Dean," I said.

"That's good. You'll go to the clinic soon, won't you?"

"Oh, absolutely," I said, rocking. "Tomorrow morning."

"Wonderful. You'll like the nurse, I think."

"I'm sure... she'll be nice," I said, a pulse passing through me.

"You really seem to enjoy doing what I say," Dean said. He lifted his hand and touched my cunt. It was like a jolt of electricity, strong and shocking. He began to stroke the lips, brushing against my clit with his fingers.

"Y-yes, oh yes," I moaned. "I like to obey you. I want to be commanded. I want you to decide what I'm going to do next. I don't need to know why. Just use me. Please. Uh. Gh, gah, aah, oh Dean, oh God..."

With his other hand, it must have been, he reached behind and followed the curve of my ass to the cleft, then down to the hole. He put a finger on the hole suddenly. I spasmed, grinding my cunt against

16

the fingers of his other hand. There I was, caught between his hands, trapped fore and aft, and I couldn't stop moving, rocking back and forth, and every time I moved back I felt his finger dip into my nether hole. It was as if he'd tapped into my inner will, what some might call a soul, and every time his finger dipped just inside the rim I felt him tapping, tapping as if my soul was an egg. An egg that he could crack into a thousand pieces with one touch. I made incoherent sounds, gasping, rolling my head. I think I was drooling.

"This would be an appropriate time to come, Jill," I heard Dean say. I couldn't see her, but I could hear her. I heard her cry out sharply, climbing octaves: "Oh. Oh. Oh. Oh. Oh. OH, GOD!"

"Zöe, I'm using you," Dean said. "I'm using your mind and your body and you can't stop it. You are helpless. You are mine. You could come just from the pleasure of knowing you are being used by me."

"Come," I repeated mindlessly. "For you."

"Yes," he said. "Come now."

I came. I cannot describe it. I came apart, flailing, my still-captive body pistoning on his fingers. I made guttural sounds, spasming again and again and again, coming exquisitely like a flood of honey over his hands.

When it had subsided, I got up and sat down next to Dean. I watched him pull himself up a little, lift on his pants, and zip up. Come trickled coolly down my thighs.

"Listen, I'm afraid I can't stay," he said, getting up from the bench. "I've got several other people to see today, but I want you to know I appreciate having had this little chat with you."

"So do I," I said. "It was really nice to meet you, finally."

"Let's keep in touch," he said, smiling, extending a hand.

"I'd like that," I said. "That would be great." I shook it.

"Jill, are you going my way?" he asked.

"Yeah, I'm headed in the same direction," Jill said, coming up behind him. She was wearing her clothes again.

"Great. Well, we'll see you later," he said, and Jill said, "Bye, Zöe, I'll see you around." We waved, and they set off down the path. I could see his hand resting on her ass, cupping one buttock casually as they walked.

I looked back down at the river, so far below. It was in shadow now, no longer silver. The light was golden through the trees, all the way down the side of the mountain to small, invisible Ferngrove. Dusk had begun to fall.

This university was set high above the world, and the world it overlooked was nothing but trees. Seen from here, the world was a new place, and I was new in it.

I had a new point of view, now.

Chapter 3
Bloody Thursday

Dean

The truth is a slippery thing. Some people—a lot of people, actually—believe they know the truth. It's in the Bible. It's in the Q'ran. It's in the movement of the planets, or the rigorous application of the scientific method. Whatever. It is always beyond the scope of human argument, or it wouldn't be the truth.

I believe in fiction. The truth, as far as I am concerned, is whatever fiction one finds most convincing at a particular moment. People have a need to believe in stories, because stories create order out of chaos, and there is nothing as frightening as chaos. People seek out truth because they want the world to make sense.

The chasm of disbelief is endless. A good story will suspend you over that bottomless pit, hold you charmed, balanced on a wire that exists only because you believe it does. If you're lucky, if the story is good enough, you can stay balanced for the rest of your life.

Then you die, and who the fuck knows?

This is my story. You might not believe it; most people wouldn't. But it's my story, nonetheless.

In 1969 I was an undergraduate at UC Berkeley. As a young man between the ages of eighteen and twenty-five, I was predictably caught up in the anti-Establishment fervor of the time and engaged in a number of demonstrations against what I and my compatriots believed to be the human manifestations of evil. Principal among those was the Vietnam War.

We liked to think of ourselves as peaceful people, but there was

19

an unmistakable eagerness to the way that we pushed back against The Man. We were spoiling for a fight, the good fight of freedom versus oppression. It was an especially exhilarating experience because it was a civil war, an internal struggle against the authorities of our own society. There is no conflict as righteous as the battle against your father.

I was a recovering dweeb at the time. I had arrived from the flatlands two years before, with my hair too short and my clothes too square, just in time for the Summer of Love. I didn't drink or do drugs, and I had never skipped a class in my life. All I was missing was a pair of horn-rimmed glasses.

My major was journalism, and as a photographer for the school paper, I had plenty of opportunities to observe social interaction up close. I came along to interviews and events, I started making friends, and bit by bit, I began to learn how to act like a native. I picked up the local slang. I grew my hair out. I started learning the guitar. I smoked a little grass. And I became an activist.

The principal source of inspiration for my metamorphosis had a name, and it was Gloria. G-L-O-R-I-A, like the song. Gloria in excelsis Daymore. Ms. Daymore was a sumptuous blond co-ed (as female students were known back then) possessed of a rapier wit and a body so sublimely creamy and curvaceous that I could hardly bear to consider it. But consider it I did, just like everyone else, male and female. You couldn't fail to notice Gloria. Wherever she went there were men, all of them entranced like I was, drawn irresistibly to her beauty. We swung in orbit around her star.

Gloria was polite to all of us, more polite than she had to be given her position, but it was obvious that some men were favored more than others. The men to whom Gloria displayed the deepest affection were, like her, deeply committed to social change. They rallied for women's rights and workers' rights, they protested racism and elitism and poverty and hunger, and most of all they marched for an end to the war. And though there was plenty of competition—though I was skinny and shy and knew I probably didn't stand a chance—I joined the rallies, I chanted slogans and waved signs, and little by little I circled closer to her.

Now, I wasn't pretending to hate the war, but my deeper motives

and fell to my knees, choking; and with a dull thunk on the back of my skull, I lost consciousness.

At first, they put me in a holding cell with a bunch of other protesters. I sat hunched against the wall, remembering the sight of Gloria's face, and wanted to ask if anyone knew what had become of her. I recognized a few faces, but I kept my mouth shut when I saw the way they were looking at me.

The lump on the back of my head was large and so tender I couldn't lie down, and I couldn't move the fingers of my left hand. I felt sick at heart, and my thoughts whirled through me in an incoherent babble of guilt and fear. I suffered then, but it was nothing compared to what was to come.

The riot made national headlines. Hundreds of injuries, more than fifty people treated for shotgun pellets; a policeman was knifed in the chest, and a student was blinded. There was only one casualty that mattered to me, though. As soon as I learned that Gloria was dead, I stopped listening.

I barely remember the arraignment. A few of my friends were there, and my mother, who cried the entire time; I know I spoke to them, but what I said was automatic and lifeless. A shell of silence had hardened around me, and my sense of hearing had faded until almost every sound was a dull buzz in the middle distance. When it was over, I was charged with involuntary manslaughter and sent to Vacaville State Prison for three to five years.

Days went by. Weeks. I opened my mouth only to eat. I learned to avoid trouble, and eye contact, and other people as much as possible. Of course, in prison, it's not always possible. Twice a gang of men held me down and raped me, and I took it in silence, feeling the pain as a sensation both vivid and faraway. It was no more than I deserved, and none of it—the agony, the loneliness, the bars of my cell—would ever be enough punishment for what I had done.

There were other inmates, kinder ones, who tried to talk to me at first, but they gave up when I made no response. There was nothing worth saying. I stared past them at the wall, or down at the food

I chewed and swallowed with mechanical necessity. There were no stories I believed in anymore, nothing to check my freefall into the abyss.

Then the spooks came.

Chapter 4

Hindsight

Dean

There are gaps in my memory here, black walls and cubes of shadow. Pieces of me are missing. The narrative breaks down.

What I can remember is so painful that I must consider it a blessing to have forgotten the rest.

Three men in suits, sitting in chairs. The suits are all the same. The men have tried to be all the same, but I can see that one of them has red hair. Pale eyebrows and eyelashes. He's saying something to me; he doesn't know about my shell of silence.

I watch his face for cues. I nod at all the right moments. I see him laugh. It's meant to be a kind laugh, but without the sound it's scary. His eyes don't move at all. I'm sitting on a bed in a new room, one with quilted walls. Everything is cream white. A nurse gave me a small, cream-white pill half an hour ago, and I think it was acid or something like acid because nothing stays, it just keeps going and turning in on itself like an impossible snake. Far fucking out. Star fucking out. Stars. Glitterlight.

Go to jail. Go directly to jail. Do not pass Go. Do not graduate with honors. Do drop acid. Dew drop inn. Shatterstar.

There are no windows. The light bulb is way up high in the ceiling where I can't reach it. So I can't smash it. So I can't slash my wrists. Like I slashed her throat. They don't want any blood. They'll be so angry when they see the blood. Blood under my fingernails. Parallel lines of blood across my chest like the tines of a rake. I try to wipe it away so they won't see, but I'm only spreading it around. A big mess.

A big sound. Comic-book sound. It hurts to hear it.

What's making that noise?

Oh. It's me.

A needle in my arm. Sleep slams down like an iron door.

Jerk awake into bright light. I can't move very well; I'm wide awake, but my body feels like stone. When I crane my neck to look down at myself, I see little blue and red wires all across my arms and chest, attached through suction cups. Through a window, I can see a corner of the yard, a basketball hoop. Armed guards in the tower. I realize there is something in my mouth.

Leather.

It is useless to try to prepare yourself for an electric shock. You don't need to. Your body responds automatically. Teeth clench. Breath vanishes. Everything stops and you hold on, riding the snake. Time cannot be measured. Not until the current clicks off.

Then the fluids flow. I'm weeping, vomiting, and pissing myself, all at once.

"Why?" I scream. "Why are you doing this?"

There is no answer.

The prison food was disgusting, but at least it was solid. Now everything can be eaten with a spoon: applesauce, beef broth, pudding. If necessary, it can be delivered via tube directly into the esophagus. The spoon is metal. I've been drugged, but I'm not so wiggy that I fail to notice the camera in the corner of the ceiling. I know better than to try anything like making a weapon.

My testicles are hugely swollen, injected the day before with pale green fluid from a syringe. The hurt goes directly to my brain and lives there, camped out near the front, swinging a stick. I try not to move much. When I move, the stick swings in a wide arc and the glowing end hisses against the walls of my skull.

I'm being tested. I can remember someone telling me that; just a series of tests, he said. Didn't say what for. His smile was kind, but he wouldn't answer any questions. Couldn't. Part of the test.

But he said I was doing fine.

The voice in my head is like dripping tallow, slow and smooth and unctuous.

Goodboy. Feelsgood. Believgood. Goflow. Flowgood.

Allsafe. Faithgood. Fearless. Flowing.

It comes and goes without warning, but I always hear it when I'm doing my exercises. I work out all the time now: sit-ups, chin-ups, push-ups, free weights.

Sillypain. Whocares. Ignorit. Paincum paingo.

Stronger. Strongestyet. Allstrong.

Didn't used to be such a jock. Now I like it. The juice they give me at the start of each workout has a pineapple flavor, but smooth, not so tart. Ice cream juice. I knock that back and I'm ready to go.

Ignorpain goodfeel. Strongfeelbetter.

Workdobest. Feelbest. Bestovall. Killit. Fuckit. Stabit. Shootit. Bestfeel. Goodbeast. Goodboy.

A long time is all I know it's been because there is no daylight, no windows, only rooms. Not the same room. They keep moving me. One room had gouges in the walls. In a corridor I heard screams that sounded like a voice box smashing itself against the wet sponge of a brain.

I know it's been a long time because what I can remember of myself is far in the distance like a child away down the years when everything was more real. I don't know what real is.

I know what they want me to believe.

I know it will be easier if I believe it.

I like watching movies.

This is a special theater. One chair just for me. No popcorn. Lights go down slow. (Big pink pill. I swallowed with cocoa.)

I can tell I'm going to like this one. This one has a naked girl in it. She's looking at me. Happy to see me.

I like a big strong man.

Long blond hair. Like her. Like the one I

Someone not afraid

murdered.

to kill. I like a big strong. Man. I feel weak. I like to feel weak.

Womanslaughtered. I made her bleed.

That's okay. I like blood.

If a man will kill, I'll do anything.

I'll fuck.

I'll spread. Open. Like this.

If only. If only you do it first. If only you kill.

If a goodboy kills. I like a goodboy. I like to fuck.

Fuck me, goodboy.

Fuck me hard.

I don't know this man. He's not one of them, I know, because he looks terrified. Hasn't shaved in a while. Stinks of piss and fear.

When he sees me, his eyes bug out and he backs against a wall.

"No, Jesus Christ, no," he babbles. "Listen, you gotta listen, I didn't do anything. I wanna cooperate. God, fuck, please don't fucking hurt me. Fuck. Fuck." Tears are running down his face.

Easykill.

He's shaking. Breathing hard. I can see his teeth. Abruptly he changes tack.

"All right, you fucker," he screams. "All right, come on! You want me? Let's do this! Fucking DO IT!" His voice breaks into sobs. He's still backing away, moving unsteadily, but his fists are up and he'll do what he can. Even if it isn't much. I've never seen anyone so afraid.

I don't want to do this. I don't even know the man. I want to tell him it's nothing personal, nothing I'd choose to do if I had a choice, but I know I'm not supposed to talk.

I want to tell him this is just a test. But he wouldn't understand.

Easykill goodboy.

So I do it quickly.

And perhaps I would have continued to do it again and again, for as long as they wanted, if only they had stopped there.

I was well-programmed. Pain was something I had learned to ignore, for the most part. What I couldn't ignore, I could usually avoid through correct behavior. When I did especially well, I was rewarded: I got good drugs, and sometimes the naked girl on the movie screen. She wasn't real, but she was close enough. I was no glutton for punishment, nor any kind of hero. I was already a prisoner; my life was fucked anyway. So I gave in, and I did my best to follow orders.

But I wasn't really what they wanted. I wasn't a warrior at heart, however square I might have been at first. Instead I was a lab rat, an expendable test subject. Once they determined what worked and what didn't, they could repeat the successful tests on real soldiers. In the meantime... well, I wasn't going anywhere, and they had enough experiments to keep me occupied for quite a while.

Then something went wrong.

"Hold still," said the man in the goggles. "This will only take a minute."

I hadn't realized it, but I was fidgeting in the chair. I couldn't help it; when I'd been shown into the room — square, fluorescent-lit, with a large pane of black glass set into one wall—I had seen the cart with the tray of gleaming metal instruments, and now I couldn't stop thinking about them. Now that I was in the chair and my head was locked into place with my face up against the apparatus, my eyes looking out through the square frame, I was nervous. This was a new test. I didn't know what kind of pain I would have to ignore, but I had a bad feeling.

"I haven't had anything today," I said. "Any medicine, I mean."

"Hold on," the man said. He lowered his head out of the frame and I could hear the clink of metal on metal. "Just hang tight and try to keep still."

"Will you give me some?" I asked, ashamed of the need in my voice. "Before you get started?"

"It'll be over before you know it," the man said. "It's nothing to worry about. Just try to relax."

I tried to relax and I tried not to imagine what was coming. I tried hard to think about the naked girl, but I kept seeing the tray of instruments, shining metal instruments like in a dentist's office.

"Open your mouth, please," the man said. "A little wider. Good. Now bite down on this."

Leather again. On a strap. Cinched tight around the back of my head.

"Good. Now just relax, and I want you to look directly forward, right at that black circle on the far wall. A little more toward the center. That's good. Now try to focus on that mark, and don't let your eyes wander. Try not to blink so much."

But I couldn't stop blinking, and the more I tried, the harder it was to stop. He was going to do something to my eyes. I had 20/20 vision, and I would have said so, only I couldn't talk now. And it wouldn't have mattered, anyway.

"He won't stop blinking," the man said, out of my field of vision. I thought about the one-way glass and wondered how many people were watching the two of us. "Right," he said.

A moment later I saw his hand coming at my eyes. "Easy now," he said to me. "I'm not going to hurt you." His thumb pressed gently into the skin of my right eyelid and lifted it, while with his other hand he applied a piece of tape. He repeated the procedure with the other eye. Now I couldn't blink. My eyes burned and watered, but I couldn't close them.

I tried again to think about the naked girl, but I couldn't do it. I couldn't let my mind retreat into the gauze of drugs because there weren't any. There were no distractions. I couldn't look away.

"Once more, look at that black circle. Try to keep your eyes on it no matter what happens. We'll make this quick, okay?"

I couldn't say *Quick would be good*, only think it. I focused on the black circle ferociously.

"Here we go," I heard him say, and my body tensed as something approached my right eye. I couldn't help it. I saw what it was.

A needle.

I clenched, bit down hard on the leather, and screamed from the pit of my soul as the needle slipped into my eye. I felt a tiny prick, then a cool rush of liquid inside, a gray whirlpool swirling up to cover the right half of my vision. It didn't really hurt, not in hindsight, not considering all the other things they did to me. But at the time, there was no hindsight to make things clearer. All I knew was that a needle was inside my eye, and the terror I felt was unparalleled.

I was still screaming when the needle slipped out, still screaming when it entered my left eye and I felt the liquid squirting into me again. My whole being was in that scream. There was nothing else.

Gradually the gray field started to dissipate. My eyes were still in agony, mostly from being held open, but I began to see again. The black circle on the bare white wall. The square frame just in front of me. Goggles peering in.

Get me out of this, I screamed inside my mind. *Get me out get me out get me out please please.*

"Absolutely," the man said. "Have you out in a jiffy. Just give me a second here..."

He reached forward and whipped off the two pieces of tape. I squeezed my eyes shut like hands clasping in fervent prayer: *oh sweet blindness,* I thought, a line from a song I'd heard once. The darkness was cool and soothing, like water at the bottom of a well. Damned if I was ever going to come up again.

But eventually, of course, I did. I felt the strap loosen around my head. The leather wad fell out of my mouth, gluey with saliva, and my head came away from the apparatus and I fell back against the chair, and my eyes opened again. Bleary. Stinging. I saw the goggles looking down at me.

"Are you okay?" Concern in the voice.

Static crackling in the background. "What the hell, Frank."

"He's in pain," the goggles said. "Jesus Christ. It's not like he's going to go anywhere."

"Ah ga," I said. I meant it.

"Steady there, champ. Let's get those restraints." The buckles around my wrists and ankles loosened and I slumped in my seat, but he was right: I wasn't going anywhere.

Through the intercom, the voice again, mildly exasperated. "All right, that's enough. Proceed as planned."

Frank wheeled the cart over and parked it in front of me, the tray of instruments at elbow level. "Go ahead and put your left hand on there for me, buddy," he said. "Palm facing up."

I did as I was told.

"Now look at me for a sec. Look me in the eyes. Good. I'm going to ask you to do me a favor now. You see that little thing on the tray there, looks kind of like a steak knife?"

I did. It was a short, narrow blade, about four inches long, serrated, bright silver.

"Pick that up with your right hand."

I picked it up.

"Okay, look at me again. That's it." He peered at me intently, watching for a reaction. "I want you to cut off your little finger."

I became very still. After all this time, all this torture, I still wasn't beyond surprise. I stayed deadpan, but inside, my mind was scrambling to find an alternate meaning for what he had said. I couldn't. It was too clear to be mistaken.

Why? I thought desperately, looking at Frank from behind my poker face. *Why?* The old question. The inevitable question that every suffering person asks — to God, to the torturer, to the pain itself. *Why?* The question is a reflex, like tears. There is never an answer.

Only this time, there was.

"Because we need to determine the effectiveness of the compound we introduced into your aqueous humor," Frank said.

It's amazing how quickly the brain can process information. No doubt it helped that I was already trying frantically to think of a way out of my predicament. I had not spoken, and yet Frank had responded to my question. Instantly I understood this.

What is the compound supposed to do? I asked without speaking.

"It's supposed to make you obey any direct order given to you, without hesitation," Frank said. "Of course, it's still in the experimental stages, so we're not sure if —"

The intercom crackled, and I heard angry voices overlapping. "Hold it," said the man nearest to the mike. "You're violating procedure, you dumb shit. Restrain him and get in here, now."

Do it, I thought to Frank.

"Be right there," he said, and leaned over to reattach the restraints.

Keep them loose, I thought. My mind was clear for the first time in... in I didn't know how long. I wasn't high on anything except adrenaline. *Get everyone who's watching us to come into this room,* I told him. *Tell them... tell them there's something happening in here that they have to see to believe.*

Chapter 5
The Confidence Man

Trevor

It was getting so bad I honestly couldn't sleep. I'd lie awake at night listening to my roommate snore, looking at the ceiling tiles while the same serrated thoughts cut a circular pattern through my mind, over and over and over. The tears would dry on my face, then I would cry again until my body was limp, and I'd lie there feeling the new tears dry over the old ones. Like layers of plaster. Like a mask I was building.

During the day I walked around with this mask on, exhausted from grief and lack of sleep, yet feeling a strange, zombified clarity that kept me from walking into telephone poles or falling down stairs. I guess I must have looked pretty bad, because people didn't even try to talk to me.

But the mask wasn't working. It broke open every night, and I couldn't sleep or concentrate on any of the books I was supposed to be reading, and I wasn't healing. I wasn't getting better. I was falling apart.

So I went to the campus clinic to see if I could get something to help me sleep, some knockout pills to beat the ache. Even a temporary respite would be something, I thought.

But it wasn't that easy. The nurse wanted to know why I was having trouble sleeping. At first I said I didn't know. A mystery.

Then she asked: "Are you feeling any emotional distress?"

I just started laughing. It was so clinical, the way she said it. "Yeah, I guess you could say that," I said. "I recently had my heart torn out of

34

my chest." Then I was crying again.

"I see," said the nurse. "Well, in that case, I think we'd better make you an appointment with the school counselor."

Under other circumstances I probably would have made an attempt at protest, but I was past the point of denial. I just nodded, miserably, while the tears ran down my cheeks.

It was autumn. The forest that stretched for miles around campus had gone from green to red and gold in the few months I'd been here, and now the leaves were falling in a hurry, leaving skeletal trees behind to wait for the cold snap and the first flurries of snow. I wasn't used to weather like this. Back in San Diego my mom and dad (five years divorced and living across the city from each other) were probably still in short sleeves. And here I was, far away from everything familiar, under all my layers.

I shivered as I stepped into the building and shut the door behind me. It was warm inside. On the other side of the room, a girl my own age sat at a desk talking into a telephone. As I approached the desk she set the receiver back in its cradle and looked up at me.

"Hi," she said. "Can I help you?"

Her hair was dark brown, her face clear and smooth. She was startlingly beautiful. I don't know how else to say it. She was beautiful enough that for a moment, just a moment, I wasn't thinking of anything but the way she looked. Then with a heart-wrenching twist I remembered Sarah, and the pain slammed back into me.

"I have an appointment," I said. "Four-thirty."

She looked down at the book on her desk. "Trevor?"

"That's me."

She smiled. "Go right on in, he's expecting you." Her voice was low and intimate, with a slight lisp. Her name tag said ZÖE.

I opened the door she had indicated and went in, closing it behind me.

The counselor's office was larger than the foyer, but just as warm. Even the light was warm; it came from two tall Japanese paper lanterns that glowed at the back of the room. There were no windows. In the middle of the room was a low table made of a large slab of dark, polished wood, and around it some comfortable-looking chairs and a black leather sofa. I smelled cedar and something else I couldn't identify.

"Trevor, is it?"

At a desk in the far corner of the room, a man was turning around in his chair to face me. I hadn't noticed him sitting there. "Yes," I said.

"Trevor Ethan Bailey. Welcome, Trevor," he said. "Can I ask you to take off your shoes at the door? You can put them on that shelf there."

I noticed his feet, in brown argyle socks. "Okay, sure," I said, and bent down to undo my laces.

"Thank you," he said. "It's an Asian custom that I've always rather liked. It helps people to relax, and it's good for the carpet."

I put my sneakers on the low shelf next to two other pairs of shoes. When I stood up, he had left the desk and was walking over to me.

"Hi," he said, shaking my hand. "I'm Kevin Carlson, but everybody calls me Dean."

"It's nice to meet you," I said dully. Dean looked about my father's age, maybe a little older, with gray at the temples. His face was weathered and creased, and his eyes were sky blue.

"You were at that big assembly last month, right?" I said. "Dr. Thornhill introduced you."

"I'm surprised you remember that," Dean said, chuckling. "It wasn't a very memorable event." He was right; it wasn't, actually. "Why don't you come have a seat?" he said, crossing out into the room.

"Where should I sit?" I asked. The carpet was deep pile, very soft under my feet as I padded after him.

"Anywhere. Wherever you feel comfortable. Would you like a cup of tea?"

"No, thanks," I said, sinking into one of the large chairs and closing my eyes. I was exhausted. I had slept a total of five hours in the last three days.

A moment later I opened my eyes again and Dean was sitting in a chair near to mine, looking at me with a kind smile on his face. "You look like you could use some sleep," he said.

"That's kind of why I'm here," I said. I unwound the scarf from around my neck and began unzipping my windbreaker.

"Mm-hmm," he said, nodding his head sympathetically. "Well, why don't you tell me what's been happening in your life since the last time you got a good night's sleep."

I took a breath. "It's probably going to sound really lame."

"I doubt that," Dean said mildly. "It can't be too lame if it's keeping you up nights."

"Yeah. Well." I put the windbreaker on the floor, next to my chair. "Basically, a girl broke up with me this summer."

"Ah. I had a feeling it was love, not death."

I gave him a bleak smile. "It feels like death."

"Tell me about it, Trevor," he said, leaning on one arm of the chair and looking at me steadily with his bright blue eyes. I had his undivided attention and it felt good. I found that I was able to talk.

"Her name is Sarah. We... we would have been together a year this December. We were both involved in drama in high school. That's how we met, working on the play. Sarah was acting and I was doing light and sound."

"What play was it?"

"*Guys and Dolls.*"

Dean nodded. "One of my favorites. Go on."

"I didn't really have a... a girlfriend before that. I hate that word. Girlfriend, I mean."

"Don't use it, then."

"I don't know what else to use. I mean, I'd gone out with people before I met her, but it was always a social kind of thing. Having fun, you know? Not serious."

"Being with her was serious?"

I hesitated. I thought for a moment. "Yeah, it was."

"Not fun."

"It's not that it wasn't... I mean, it changed my life. I'd never felt that way before."

"Were you sexually active?"

I blushed and looked away. "Uh, yeah."

"First time?"

"For me. Not for her. But it wasn't all about that. I mean, I was in love with her, you know? Just her. Nothing else was important to me."

"Did she feel the same way?"

"I thought so," I said. "At first, anyway. I think she did to begin with. But I guess I was more serious about it than she was."

And I had been from the start. I remembered our first moment well, having replayed it in my mind a thousand times. In the A/V eyrie, as Greg called it—the sound booth at the back of the room, up a narrow corridor staircase off the balcony level, looking down at the auditorium. Greg was the alpha techie, a bossy, overweight, pretentious but unquestionably skilled senior who knew everything about machines and was openly contemptuous of those who didn't. He was under the motherboard checking connections and barking commands to me while I flipped switches. The door opened and two girls came in, Sarah with Denise Kleinfeld behind her. They were singing together, loudly:

"And I shall meet him when the time is right... I'll know... when my love comes along..."

And our eyes met. Too corny, right? But it happened that way, with perfect timing, and it was so obviously perfect timing at the time that there wasn't any way to pretend it wasn't happening. A fleeting glance might have been ignored, but it wasn't that; I realized with a shock that I was continuing to look at her, and she at me.

That was the thing about Sarah, her superpower. She could make you feel like there was nothing else in the room but you and her, nothing else that mattered, and she could do it without saying a word. Between the end of the singing and Denise saying "Yeah, awkward! So anyway!" was a small moment when it didn't matter what Denise or anyone else noticed, didn't matter that we didn't know each other and were suddenly in this moment together. Sarah could turn that on like a light switch.

And off.

And she did, when Denise spoke, and the moment was broken, and the momentum of everyday life resumed. Greg came out from under the board, and banter ensued. Some question about the sound cues. I remembered Greg being friendlier than usual because they were girls, but also not quite being able to mask his contempt for their ignorance. I remembered taking part in the conversation, trying not to project anything of the intensity I was feeling, trying to give Sarah neither more nor less attention than anyone else, trying to be cool.

I remembered a glance from Sarah, as they were leaving, a sudden, quick glance out of the corner of her eye that went into me like an arrow. A confirmation.

"And that was it," I told Dean. "I was never the same. It was scary to feel that much attraction, but it didn't matter. I was in over my head and I didn't care and I went for it, I went for her, and we..." I broke off. I put a hand over my face, rubbed my eyes. "And we were together. And I can't even tell you how good it was. Until. Um." I bit my lip.

"How did you react when she broke up with you?" Dean asked, shifting in his seat.

"Not very well," I admitted. "She said she wanted to stay friends. I tried to do that. I thought I could do that."

I started crying again. My eyes ached, but the tears kept coming out of them. I covered them with my hand. "Shit, I'm sorry. This keeps happening. I can't seem to stop."

"Trevor, look at me. Look at me."

Something in Dean's voice made me drop my hand. He was looking straight at me, and his eyes were really intensely blue, a deep summer blue, like tropical waters. His smile was kind and reassuring. Fatherly.

"I'd like to make a suggestion," he said. "Would you like to hear it?"

"Sure," I said.

"You don't have to cry anymore."

"I don't?" I said, puzzled.

"No. You've been crying for a while now, haven't you?"

"Six days. Since I got the letter."

"That's long enough. You can stop crying now, if you want."

"Oh. I can?" And I could. I just stopped, the way you might stop tapping a pencil. It was so easy. Why hadn't I thought of that before?

"Tell me about this letter," Dean said, leaning back in his chair. Still looking at me.

"She wrote to tell me that she didn't want me to write or call her ever again," I said. "She wrote 'You. Me. Over.' in big letters at the bottom of the page." The ache rose again, and I tasted gall at the back of my throat. But I didn't cry.

"So you had been in touch with her, then. After she broke it off with you."

"Oh yeah," I said. "I was writing her a letter every day when I first got here. She wrote back, not as often, but she did write. Her letters were all about how great her college was, and all the clubs she was joining, and there was never anything about me. Never. Just 'hope everything's good with you, love, Sarah.' "

"You wanted her to miss you," Dean suggested.

"Yeah, I did. Of course I did. I wanted her to regret leaving me. I wanted her heart to be breaking instead of mine."

Dean raised his eyebrows.

It was true. Not nice, but true. I couldn't believe it had been so easy to say.

"Rejection's a bitch," Dean said matter-of-factly. I laughed. It felt surprisingly good to get all of this off my chest. Dean was listening so attentively. He really seemed to understand.

I realized I'd been looking him straight in the eyes ever since I stopped crying. His eyes were very blue, cool and incandescent. He had a weathered movie-star look about him. A trustworthy, no-bullshit sort, this Dean. What was his last name again?

"I remember rejection." He said it quietly, his eyes drifting from mine and unfocusing for a second, as if to look at a memory. For a moment he was silent. Then he looked at me again and said: "It feels like the end of everything good, I know. But eventually it'll pass. Another girl will catch your eye, and you'll be in pursuit again, and then you'll be in love and it'll feel like the end of everything bad."

"Then I'll get dumped again," I said. "And I'll feel like shit."

"Do you want to feel like shit?" Dean asked, leaning forward suddenly.

"No."

"You'd rather feel good about yourself, wouldn't you?"

"Of course."

"These feelings of guilt and inadequacy you've been carrying around aren't doing you any good. They're not leading to any positive changes. They're useless, aren't they?"

"Yeah."

"So let's consider, just for a moment, the possibility that you can let go of your guilt. Let go of your fear of failure. All your fears, in fact.

Just lay them down and walk away." His eyes stared into mine. I felt myself relaxing, as if a giant fist was slowly unclenching around my body. The chair was soft and so was the carpet. The room was warm, pleasantly fragrant. My eyes no longer ached.

"Your ex-girlfriend has made it clear that she doesn't want to continue a relationship with you. Perhaps, if you once loved each other, the best way to honor that love is to give her what she asks for now. Let go of her. Put her down. You're carrying too much as it is. Go ahead. Everything you're feeling about her, put it down. Everything you know about her, let it go. You don't need to keep track of that anymore. It's not your problem. Is it?"

I had been relaxing more and more as Dean talked, but strangely, I wasn't falling asleep. Instead I felt a steady clarity, a sense of wakefulness like a high plateau.

"No, it's not," I said. "It's not my problem. You're right."

"Just a suggestion," Dean said. "And you might also consider the possibility that—I'm sorry, what was her name?"

"Who?"

"The name of this girl you were with. Was it Sharon? Susan?"

"Something with an S, I think," I said. "I'm not sure."

"Well, anyway, consider the possibility that the end of that episode in your life, coinciding with your recent arrival in this new place, in the new role of college student, means that you have a perfect opportunity to reinvent your identity. You can change your self-image, and that will change how people perceive you."

I nodded. Dean was making perfect sense.

"So the question is, how do you want to be perceived? What do you want people to see when they see you?"

"I'm not sure," I said.

"How about confidence? You could come across as a man who's in control of his emotions. Not too bothered by what other people expect of him. Wouldn't that be nice?"

"Definitely."

"You seem intelligent to me," Dean said. "Don't need any help there. What about with women?"

"What do you mean?"

"Well, you're single again, aren't you? How would you like to be perceived by a beautiful girl?"

I thought about it. "Good-looking," I said sheepishly. "Strong."

"Powerful," Dean suggested.

"Yeah, I guess," I said.

"Sure. When you're powerful, you don't need to pursue. They seek you out. They need your approval."

"Right," I said. "It's much better that way."

"You bet it is. Now, all I'm saying is that you ought to be open to possibilities. Allow the possibility that you can have what you want. Open yourself to feelings of confidence."

"You seem pretty confident," I said.

Dean nodded, not smiling. "I am. Confidence is crucial to what I do here. I'll show you what I mean." He got up and went over to his desk. He picked up the phone. "Zöe? Would you come into the office for a moment, please?"

Chapter 6
Depth Perception

Trevor

I sat up straighter in my chair. The door opened and the girl from the lobby came in. I swiveled to face her.

Again, the sight of her was startling. Some girls are like that, so beautiful they catch you by surprise. Zöe had on a skirt of dark brown velvet and an oatmeal-colored, scoop-necked top that fit her closely, offering a subtle glimpse of cleavage. Her feet, like ours, were in socks. She smiled at me.

"Hello," she said.

"Hi," I said.

"My shift is over in a few minutes," she said to Dean. "I have a paper to write for Poli Sci tomorrow."

"You wouldn't mind staying a bit late, would you?" Dean asked, sitting back in his chair.

"No, I don't mind," Zöe said with a slight shake of her head.

"I'm sure that you'll have time to finish the paper tonight," Dean said. "I wanted to introduce you to Trevor Bailey."

"We met at the front desk," Zöe said, smiling at me again.

"Trevor, would you stand up for a minute?"

"Sure," I said. I got to my feet.

"You remember what we were just talking about, don't you?" Dean asked me. "About perception, and how it can change?"

"Yes."

"Good. Would you like to touch her breasts?"

"What?" I said, turning to look at him. Was he joking? He didn't

43

look like he was joking.

"I said, would you like to touch Zöe's breasts?"

I glanced at Zöe. She was listening quite calmly.

I wasn't going to lie; I couldn't say no. I swallowed and nodded.

"You can, you know." Out of the corner of my eye I could see Dean sitting in his chair, two points of blue watching me as I looked at Zöe. "Go ahead, try it," he said. "Remember, the way you perceive yourself affects how others see you."

Powerful, I thought. Confident. I walked over to where she was standing. "Hello," I said.

"Hi," she said. Shyly. Zöe was a few inches shorter than me, so that her eyes looked up at mine. She smelled nice, faintly of roses. When she breathed in, her breasts swelled out slightly against the cotton cloth of her shirt. I had spoken less than ten words to her, and now I was looking openly at her body. It didn't seem to be a problem.

"If you want to touch her breasts, she won't stop you," Dean said. "Will you, Zöe?"

"No," she said, looking at me. Her eyes were hazel green, flecked with brown spots.

My heart was pounding and my cock began thickening, lengthening in my pants. I reached out and put my hand on a swell of oatmeal-colored cloth, feeling the firm shape of her breast beneath. When I stroked the soft cotton, I felt the hard nub of a nipple pass under two of my fingers. Zöe never took her eyes off me, but I saw a tiny shiver run through her.

Like a horse in a field, I thought. *Like a trembling mare.*

"She's a very intelligent girl," I heard Dean say. "Valedictorian of her class, in fact. Still, she's powerless to stop you, and she won't resist, no matter what you do. Why is that, Zöe?"

Zöe bit her lower lip. I was cupping her breasts, which were just the size of my hands, and moving my thumbs back and forth over her nipples. Her words came out in a shaky whisper. "Be-cause I'm... v-very attracted to him."

My cock was rigid, thick, straining against the elastic band of my briefs. It felt solid, like a baseball bat or a length of pipe. Something to be reckoned with.

"Zöe has developed a new point of view since she came to college," Dean said. "Haven't you, Zöe?"

"Yes, Dean," she breathed.

"Trevor, would you like to take off her shirt while she tells us about it?" Dean asked.

"All right," I said. My hands moved out to the sides of her chest. She raised her arms above her head, and kept them raised as I moved down to her waist.

"Go ahead, Zöe," Dean said.

"I... I think about sex almost all the time," she said. "Even when I'm writing a paper or taking a test." I put my hands under her shirt — her skin was smooth and very warm — and lifted it up over her head. Zöe was wearing a light cream-colored bra. The top of her chest, just above her breasts, had flushed fever-pink. So had her cheeks. She was blushing.

"Last week I had a calculus test," she continued, still looking at me. "I couldn't stop touching myself, even though I was right in the middle of class. I was stroking myself with my left hand while I wrote down answers with my right hand. I... I tried to be discreet about it, but I'm sure the people next to me could see what I was doing. As soon as I finished writing down the last answer, I started to have an orgasm. I bit my lip and held onto the desk, but I couldn't keep from making noise. When I looked around I noticed that everyone in the room was watching me, but it was too late. I just couldn't hold back. I came right there, in f-front of the whole class." She stopped. I saw another shiver pass over her, though the room was quite warm.

"I'm surprised I didn't hear about this," I said.

"It wasn't really a big deal," Dean said. "Almost everyone forgot about it a few minutes later. There was one student who was upset by it, but I had a chance to talk with her and now she's doing fine." He crossed his legs. "Tell us, Zöe, what makes you sexually attracted to someone else."

"When I know that someone is attracted to me, I become attracted to them," she said.

"That seems like a natural response," Dean said.

"Yeah, I think so," Zöe said, nodding slightly.

"So if you knew that a man wanted to have sex with you, how would you feel?"

"Excited," Zöe said. "Aroused. My nipples would get hard, like they are now." The tip of her tongue darted out to moisten her lips. "When I'm attracted to a man, I become completely submissive. Whatever he tells me to do, I'll do."

She stopped, her eyes still fixed on me. I thought I saw a flicker of fear in them, somewhere beneath the desire. Wondering what I would do now, after what she had said.

"So this is Zöe's new point of view," Dean said to me. "It's up to you, Trevor, but it seems to me that the best way to deal with a girl like her is... firmly."

My hands were steady. My mind felt calm and clear. "I think you're right, Dean," I said. "I think you're right."

Zöe looked up at me, beautiful, helpless.

"Take that off," I said sharply, motioning to the bra.

"Yes, Trevor," Zöe said. She reached behind her back.

"Don't use that name when you speak to me," I said. "Call me Master."

"Yes, Master," Zöe said, her eyes downcast. She unhooked the clasp and the bra came away in her hands. Her naked breasts were a shade paler than the rest of her. They swelled into tips where dark nipples rose erect from tight circles of dark flesh.

I reached forward and hefted one breast in my palm, as if weighing a melon. Zöe gave a small gasp. I bent down and put the hard nipple between my lips. I heard her breath catch. I ran my tongue around her areola and sucked more of the breast into my mouth, pulling her toward me. I rolled her nipple between my teeth, gently.

But I didn't have to be gentle, did I?

I rolled harder, biting into the firm, springy flesh. Bit down. Zöe cried out and I stopped myself before I drew blood. I held her breast still in one hand, the nipple still between my teeth and my tongue lapping at it, stroking it as if to coax out a drop of milk. Then I pulled away. The nipple popped from my mouth and Zöe gasped again.

"Delicious," I said.

"Thank you, Master," Zöe said.

"Spread your legs. Wider. That's it." I began to walk around her slowly, touching her lightly across the tops of her breasts, her shoulder, her cheek, the nape of her neck. When I stood behind her I reached down and took a firm, plump buttock into my hand. All the while, Zöe stood as I had instructed her, legs apart, trembling at my touch.

The skirt slid easily over her skin when I stroked her, and I could feel that she had no underwear on. But there was something under the skirt, sort of like a seam. I followed it down the cleft of her ass to the shape of something hard and flat.

"Get up on that table," I said. "On your hands and knees."

"Yes, Master," Zöe whispered. She moved to the big coffee table and without hesitation stepped up on it, knelt, and bent over facing away from me. I came up behind her and raised the skirt up over her ass.

The flat shape was a rounded triangular plate made of hard plastic, held in place and connected to a belt around her waist by three flat straps: one going straight up the back, and two others that went between her thighs and up the front of her pelvis on the other side. Below the plate, within a fringe of dark, curly hair, I could see the naked pink of her cunt.

"That's a little luxury item I mail-ordered for Zöe," Dean said. "It holds a dildo in place inside her ass. She's had it inside her for the last four hours, ever since she started her shift."

She'd been wearing it when she greeted me at the front desk. I never would have guessed.

"This is the fifth week," Dean said. "I started her on something very slender, not much bigger around than a finger. You like a finger in there, don't you, Zöe?"

"Yes, Dean."

"We've gone to a slightly larger size each week, and by now, hopefully, she'll be able to accommodate a cock. You're welcome to try her, if you like."

"I just might," I said. Dean chuckled, and I broke into a grin. This was confidence. This was power. I liked it.

I began to walk around the table. Zöe's breasts hung suspended over the gleaming surface of the wooden slab, and I reached under to caress one and watch it sway. Her eyes stared forward at the nearest wall. Her lips were parted. I stopped in front of her.

"You've known me for less than fifteen minutes," I said, "and already you're on your knees, on a table, with your breasts out and your skirt hiked up." I held her face in my hand, as I had her breast, and lifted her chin so that her eyes met mine. "Just because I told you to." I stroked her lower lip with my thumb. "Isn't that right?"

"Y-yes, Master."

I lifted my hand and slapped her cheek. She gasped. "You're a slut, aren't you?"

"Yes, Master."

I slapped the other cheek. Harder. Her cheeks blazed red and her chin wobbled, as if tears were about to come. I unbuttoned and unzipped my pants, and pulled out my cock. It was dark red, with a line of clear fluid gleaming at the opening.

"Say it."

"I am a slut," Zöe said, lowering her eyes.

"You must be, if you'll take your clothes off for someone you've just met." I caressed her lips, again, with my thumb. "Being slapped in the face turned you on, didn't it?"

"Yes, Master." A tear broke loose from her left eye and ran down over my hand.

"You like being treated this way, don't you, slut?"

She shuddered. "Yes. Yes. Master."

"Beg for it."

Another tear rolled down. "Please... please hit me again."

I slapped her cheek hard. It sounded like a pistol shot. She gave a choked cry—of pain or pleasure, I couldn't tell.

"You've got a dildo in your ass, Zöe," I said. "Tell me how it got there."

"Dean. He wanted it inside me. He's training me for anal sex."

"Training you. Like a dog in obedience school."

"Yes, Master."

"Have you learned how to suck cock yet?"

Zöe opened her lips into an oval. Her tongue moved out and around her lips, moistening them, then settled over the lower lip, extended as if waiting for a vitamin pill.

"You'd like that, wouldn't you?" I said. I held the shaft of my cock and stroked her lips with its smooth, plum-colored head. Her tongue snaked out and ran down the underside of the shaft.

I pulled it away and slapped her again. She whimpered. "Not this time," I said coldly. "This time it's going somewhere else. Can you guess where?"

Zöe looked up at me, tears in her eyes, and nodded.

"Have you ever taken a man's cock in your ass?"

"No, Master."

"Are you ready for a cock there?"

"I—I don't know. I've nev—never had anything so big."

"But you'll take it whether you're ready or not. Won't you?"

"Yes, Master. I'll do anything you say."

I walked around the table until I was behind her. I unhooked the three straps, took the triangular plate in my hand and began to pull, slowly.

"Oh. Ohhh." Zöe's breath caught again and broke into a sigh as I pulled, and the shaft of the dildo began to appear, black and gleaming like new vinyl. It came out smoothly, neither as long nor as thick as me, but close. The tight brown iris of her asshole lay pulsating before me.

I put a hand on the top of Zöe's ass and moved in closer to her. I slipped the dildo into the glistening folds of her cunt, and in the same moment stroked the moist aperture of her asshole with a thumb. She spasmed, her ass moving in a tight circle.

"Ngh. Ah. Oh, Master—ye—"

I brought my cock into position where my thumb had been. "I'm going to fuck you in the ass now, Zöe," I said. "And you're going to take it. You feel that, slut?"

"Yes, Master."

"Take it in. Open up and take it in your ass. Open up. That's it. That's it. Take this cock up your ass, you slut. Take it."

The head of my cock slipped in and Zöe groaned. I could feel the shaft of the dildo just below me. I began to work it in and out of her cunt. Slowly, her sphincter relaxed further around me and I slipped deeper in. I put a hand on the small of her back and sank into her.

"Oh God," she sang. "Oh God. Ma—Master. Master."

She thrust back onto the pole of my cock, and I was inside her to the hilt. "And now you're going to come," I said.

"Oh. Oh God. Oh God, I'm coming. Master, oh God, fuck me, use me, I—oh! OH! AaaaAAAH!"

I thrust in and out, alternating strokes with the dildo in her cunt, and I felt myself start to come, rising steeply as I heard her cries; then I was pumping fiercely into her, loosing a flood of come, the trunk of my cock greased with semen and slipping in and out, popping out of the hole and shooting semen in erratic white spurts over the globes of her ass.

I staggered back and fell into a chair. Zöe collapsed on the table. For a long while no one said anything, and the only sound was the sound of our breathing.

"That will be all, Zöe," Dean said. I looked over and saw him sitting across the table from me. Zöe raised herself on one arm and slowly rolled over to a sitting position.

"Thank you for staying past the end of your shift. You should still have plenty of time to write that paper for Poli Sci."

"Oh yeah, that'll be easy," she said, sliding off the edge of the table and bending down to pick up her bra and shirt. "I can stay up later if I need to. Did you want me to put this back in the front desk drawer before I go?" She was holding up the dildo.

"If you would, please. Thanks again for your help."

"No problem. It was really nice to meet you," she said to me.

"Same here," I said. We both smiled.

"Yeah. Would you maybe like to have lunch tomorrow?"

"Sure," I said. "What's your number?"

"5402."

"I'll give you a call," I said.

"Okay. Well, it was nice to meet you. I already said that. Bye." She blushed, waved at Dean, who waved back, and walked out of the room, shutting the door behind her.

"That's what confidence can do for you," Dean said. I turned to face him. His brilliant blue eyes looked back at me.

"I can't thank you enough, Dean," I said. "I've never felt anything like that before."

"I'm glad to help," he said. "Listen, I think you'll find that the problems you were having earlier are pretty much out of your system. But if for some reason you start to feel anxious again, or you have trouble sleeping, I want you to make another appointment, okay?"

"Okay," I said.

Dean got to his feet and so did I. I carefully lifted my pants on, zipped and buttoned them, and leaned forward to shake his hand. "It's been a pleasure to meet you, sir," I said.

"The pleasure was all mine," Dean said, smiling kindly.

That night I slept soundly, and I had no dreams.

Chapter 7
Looking Out for Number One

Dean

They saw it, and they believed it. Every one of them.

Somehow, the scientists had made a mistake. Somehow the compound did the inverse of what they expected. Instead of making me a puppet, it made me a puppeteer. When I made eye contact with another person, they became completely susceptible to any command I might give.

I learned as much of the truth as I wanted to know, but it arrived haphazardly at first. I was strung out on a variety of drugs, exhausted, confused and terrified. I didn't know what I was doing; I didn't know what I was capable of. Only gradually, randomly, piece by piece, did I assemble the mosaic of a story that made sense to me — that I could allow myself to believe, given what I had experienced.

I was one of a group of fifty Vacaville inmates selected for testing by a clandestine program of the CIA, code-named MK-ULTRA. The purpose of the testing was to create torture-proof couriers and programmed assassins. To this end, the doctors and scientists of MK-ULTRA concocted a rainbow of mind-altering substances ranging from mutations of LSD-25, steroids and amphetamines to other, more exotic pharmaceuticals that have never seen the light of day. In addition to the drugs, they used radiation, electrode implants, ultrasound and microwaves on their human guinea pigs. Quite a few of them died — some as a direct result of the tests, and others who went so crazy that they became useless and had to be terminated.

No one missed them. People die all the time in prison.

I learned that I was the first test subject to receive the new compound, which was, as Frank had said, still in the experimental stages. Nobody really knew yet what they'd created, and there wasn't much documentation on the stuff. That was a stroke of luck for me; it made it easier to destroy the evidence of its existence.

Erasing the evidence: that was the first priority. The truth had to be contained, or any escape I might make would be all too temporary. So I was methodical and thorough, just as I knew the CIA would be.

In the beginning, when I still didn't know much, my methods were crude; effective, but crude. I thought I had to give commands like a drill sergeant. Over the years, I've learned that suggestion usually works better, particularly on people who are naturally inclined to question authority. Of course, my initial receptors were CIA spooks, so they took orders like dogs take hamburger.

One thing I was fortunate to learn almost from the start was the importance of names. Full names are best, including the middle name, but any part of a person's name has power in it. In all honesty, I don't have any idea why. I've done research, and there's plenty of mythological precedent—look at Rumpelstiltskin for just one example—but as for reasons, your story is as good as mine.

When I don't use a person's name, my influence is effective only with direct eye contact. After about half an hour, the conditioning begins to break down. The person might not notice the difference—if I've been subtle in my application, they'll continue to believe that my suggestions were their own ideas—but without renewed eye contact, their natural capacity for independent thought will reassert itself. If I use their name, however, they'll retain conditioning for as long as necessary.

My initial impulse was to destroy MK-ULTRA: burn all the documents and free all the lab rats and make the evil mindfuckers forget they'd ever started this program. But I quickly realized that I had no idea how far the subterranean tendrils of MK-ULTRA extended. I had this amazing power, true, but I was still only one person, and I'd be going up against a vast, well-established terrorist organization. Revenge would be nice, but I preferred escape. So I discarded that notion.

I wanted to disappear without a trace, but I had to figure my name was in a lot of file cabinets by this time. Tracking everything down would take years, and how could I ever be certain I'd finished the task?

So I kept it simple. I established my death.

"You have no idea who I am," I told the men in charge of the prison testing. "You will not speak of me to anyone. The test subject known as"—here I gave them my original birth name, which is not Dean, nor Kevin Carlson—"died by his own hand during testing." I gave them a date and a time of day. I told them the circumstances surrounding the subject's suicide were sensitive in nature, and that anyone who might ask after him should be told as little as possible.

The wardens of Vacaville also heard this spiel and swallowed it whole. To them I gave a canister of ashes that once had been another test subject, a man who really did kill himself shortly before I received the compound. This man, who was up for a string of armed robberies, had no family; no one would ever question or investigate his death, I felt certain. His ashes became mine, and they were sent to my mother in the Midwest.

After I'd handled that, I erased all evidence of the compound: records, memories, and the stuff itself. There was about a pint of it, all told; clear, harmless-looking, like water. I flushed it down the toilet. (I also took a small sample with me, thinking I might someday need to use it again, but I never did; my power remained constant, and the risk that the compound might somehow fall into other hands was serious enough that I destroyed the sample, about five years later, by sprinkling it one drop at a time over a ten-mile stretch of Nevada desert.)

I left Vacaville State Prison one night, a few hours after sunset, in the back of a metallic blue sedan with tinted windows. My driver was an MK-ULTRA operative named Stan. It was all much more cloak-and-dagger than it needed to be, really, but I was still getting the feel of my power and I didn't want to take any chances. We passed through the gates without a hitch, and soon we were headed southwest down I-80, following a sparse line of red taillights, anonymous in the dark.

It was still hard to believe that I was free. Stan turned the radio to a rock and roll station, and we listened to the Stones while I smoked cigarettes and tried to figure out what I was feeling, what I was going to do next.

Pleased to meet you. Hope you've guessed my name.

My life was over; my life had begun again.

The shell of silence was gone, but a new kind of distance had arisen in its place. I was not like other people. There was nothing arrogant about this realization; I didn't think I was better or smarter; but I knew I could do something that was impossible for anyone else, something powerful and dangerous, and it set me apart from the rest of my species. My ability was something any government in the world (not to mention any corporation, or even most private citizens) would kill to acquire, and that meant I had to keep it scrupulously secret.

I anticipated the loneliness I would feel. But I won't deny that I also felt a great thrill, a literally unspeakable excitement at the knowledge of my power. When I got out of the sedan that first night, after I sent Stan on his way back to headquarters with no memory of me, I stood on a street corner of the City with a cold wind flapping my new trenchcoat—a present from one of the spooks—and didn't move for several minutes, just stood there facing out into the intersection, letting the waves of exhilaration pass through me.

I was exhausted. A week before, I had been a brainwashed rhesus monkey. Now I was a free man, free in ways that I was only beginning to understand. Before I did anything else, though, I had to crash for a while. So I walked until I found a hotel, paid for a room with money I'd taken from the spooks, and fell onto the bed like wreckage.

I slept for eighteen hours. When I woke up, it was Christmas.

My new life had no structure. Aside from keeping my secret, there was nothing I had to do. A career would be superfluous; if I wanted to work, I could, but it wasn't necessary for survival. When I needed something, all I had to do was ask. I preferred to pay for goods and services whenever possible, since I had no desire to complicate the finances of honest grocers, haberdashers and cashiers. Besides, it was more discreet that way. The money itself came from wealthy men I encountered in the financial district, men with thousand-dollar suits, gold watches, and leather briefcases.

I collected during the morning rush hour, falling into step beside a mark as he strutted down the crowded avenue. On my first attempt, I dressed in Salvation Army issue and posed as a beggar asking for spare change. The problem with that approach was that most of these well-heeled gentlemen wouldn't look me in the eye, and I couldn't force eye contact without making a scene. So the next day I switched into nice clothes, blending in as a young junior executive. That worked like a charm.

"Hey!" I'd say, clapping my mark on the back as if we were officemates. They'd look at me, startled, and I'd hold them with my eyes while I continued with the spiel: didn't they recognize me? Joe from Allied Mutual? That conference last October? At the same time, in my mind, I'd think at them: *You'd really like to give me some money. The more money you can give me, the better you'll feel about yourself. Isn't it satisfying to give me a fifty dollar bill? How about another one? Doesn't that feel great?*

After an hour's work I'd have a few thousand dollars in my pocket, more than enough to get me through the day. I went sightseeing, floating through all the tourist traps, browsing in bookstores, grazing at cafés and bistros. I thought about buying a car, but I didn't need one. Cabs and buses were everywhere, and besides, if I saw some wheels I liked, I had only to charm the owner into giving me a ride. Public transportation took on a whole new meaning.

Housing was a similarly nonchalant affair. The hotel where I crashed the first night was low-rent, and adequate for the purpose of sleep. After that, however, I chose my lodgings with greater care. If I wanted a hotel room, I had my pick of the City's finest suites; most of the time, though, I preferred to stay in private residences. Places where people actually lived made me feel less ghostly. I could drift off to sleep listening to the slow tick of a grandfather clock down the hall, and pretend that I belonged there, that I was one of the family.

I had very few belongings. I kept a few sets of clothes on hand for days when I didn't feel like prowling the garment district, but that was about it. Plenty of things caught my eye, but I hardly ever felt the need to take them with me. Why should I, when I could visit them whenever I pleased? Nowhere was off-limits to me. The entire City was my home.

I kept my distance from the university across the bay. There was no need to rub salt in old wounds, and besides, I might be recognized. After the riot, my face had been in all the newspapers. Even though months had passed, even though no one was looking for me, even though I had grown a mustache and dyed my hair, I still felt it would be smarter to stay west of the bridge. Besides, I liked the City.

It was the beginning of a new decade, the Seventies, and the purposeful anger of the previous years was beginning to mellow into something more nebulous, less urgent. People wanted to forget about the ugliness all around them and just have fun. The fun had a kind of desperation to it, a willful blindness, but it was energetic all the same. It felt like the last party before the end of the world, like a disco dance on the grave of Western civilization.

I observed the contortions of denial with bland amusement. Aside from cigarettes, coffee, and the occasional joint, I stayed away from drugs; coming down from the stuff I'd been fed in prison had been hard enough, and I wasn't anxious to get hooked again. I wanted to keep my mind sharp in case of danger.

I was twenty-one. I had a nice set of muscles, thanks to the MK-ULTRA exercise regimen. When I looked in the mirror, I liked what I saw. I dressed sharp. My eyes had always been blue, but now they were piercing, unnaturally bright. I think I would have been charming enough without the power—except that without the power, I would still be a zombie in a cage.

I could have done things differently, I suppose. I could have made the world a better place. I could have gone back to Vacaville and rehabilitated all the rapists, thieves and killers; I could have bankrupted the prison system. I could have made environmentalists out of all the captains of industry. I could have kept Ronald Reagan out of Washington.

Why didn't I? Three decades later, it's still hard to say. I told myself I had to keep a low profile, but that was just an excuse—a story to help me do what I wanted to do. The truth of it was, I had changed in prison. I wasn't a nice person anymore. I had killed people, and that isn't something you just apologize for doing. There was no point in atoning for my sins. I had already suffered enough for a lifetime, and it hadn't made a difference. I guess it comes down to this: now that I had finally broken free from responsibility, I wasn't about to take it on.

Something else had changed, and it didn't take long for me to notice it. My sex drive was through the roof. Granted, I was a young guy, and sex had been on my mind often enough before any of this started; the thought of Gloria Daymore had brought me to more than a few shuddering, hand-held explosions in the dorm lavatory. Still, I'd had my limits.

Now my appetite seemed boundless. I dimly recalled having a pale green liquid injected into my testicles, back in prison, and I figured that probably had something to do with it. It seemed entirely possible that the spooks had pumped up my libido as another tool to encourage compliance—a carrot for the donkey, as it were.

At any rate, I found myself inspired almost constantly by thoughts of sex. It would have been terribly frustrating if that had been all.

But it wasn't, of course. I had my blue, blue eyes.

Chapter 8
The Smell of Apricots

Dean

Her name was Nadine Oh. She was the first, and one of my favorites. When I think of those early years, I always think of her.

Nadine was Korean-American, with long, jet-black hair that fell to halfway down her breasts, although I didn't know that at first. When we met, her hair was wound on top of her head and held in place with an engraved ivory hairpin that looked like a chopstick.

It was a dark midwinter afternoon, chilly and overcast. For the last few days, it had been raining sporadically. After sleeping in, I'd spent the morning browsing North Beach, drinking coffee, smoking cigarettes and watching people. I'd picked up a copy of *Tropic of Cancer* in a bookstore and leafed through some of the more explicit passages, which had started me thinking about the possibilities of sex within the parameters of my new life. Now I was across town at the Tea Gardens, which were almost deserted. All the trees had been stripped bare by the rains, and a few shiny red leaves from the Japanese maples lay plastered to the wet pavement of the footpaths. I walked carefully up a high curved bridge over a koi pond, holding onto the railing, and paused at the top to light another cigarette.

That was when I saw her. She was standing with her back to me, up at the gold-painted shrine on the hill across the pond. I could tell by her hair that she was a woman, and although I couldn't see much else, it was enough. I got down off the bridge and walked around the pond, then up the stone staircase that led to the shrine. She hadn't moved.

"Hi," I said as I approached. She turned to look at me, and I saw that she was young and beautiful, with clear, dark eyes and pale skin. "You look familiar," I said. "What's your name?"

It was so easy, and it was all I ever had to do. Originality was not required. I just looked a woman in the eyes and asked for her name. She always told me, and once I knew it, I had her.

"Nadine Oh," she said. She told me her middle name, too, but I have since forgotten it.

"That's a beautiful name," I said. "It fits you well."

"Thank you," she said, smiling shyly. "What's your name?"

"Jake," I said. It was the pseudonym I was using then. "It's nice to meet you. What brings you here on such a blustery day?"

"I like this weather," she said. "Bright sunlight hurts my eyes. It's nicer here when there are not so many people." Her accent was very faint.

"I think so, too," I said. "Do you come here often?"

"Every week," she said. "This is my favorite Buddha." She indicated the large stone figure in front of her. "I like his face. It makes me feel peaceful to look at him."

I smiled and took a deep breath, and for a moment we both looked at the Buddha in silence.

Then I said: "May I buy you a cup of tea, Nadine Oh?"

We sat at a small wooden table, our knees almost touching, with a pot of jasmine tea and a plate of almond cookies between us. The café in the Gardens had a plastic roof and no walls, and we were the only ones there. We sipped our tea and she told me about her life; I listened, smiled, and watched her talk.

Nadine was charming and funny, and very beautiful; I wanted to fall in love with her. I would have, if things had been different. But then, if things had been different, she wouldn't be drinking tea with me. She wouldn't have given her full name to a strange man just because he asked for it. Things don't really work that way; most beautiful women know better than to be so trusting of strangers. What I had with Nadine was not honest, and I knew it. I could feel a yearning for honesty, but it just wasn't possible. I was too powerful. This wasn't love.

"It's starting to rain," she said, interrupting herself in the middle of telling me about a cat she had when she was a little girl. She pointed out at the pond, where a few faint drops were falling on the surface of the water.

"Did you have any plans for today?" I asked her.

"Not until this evening," she said. She pronounced "evening" with three syllables. "My boyfriend is taking me out to dinner."

Boyfriend. It should have occurred to me, but it hadn't. "What's his name?" I asked.

"Ray." A flicker of concern passed over her face. She hadn't been worried, because I hadn't been worried; now it occurred to her that maybe it was a little bit strange, talking to me like this, telling me all about herself when we'd only just met. I couldn't actually read her mind—the power only allowed me to send thoughts, not receive them—but her face made it plain enough.

I thought at her: *There's nothing to worry about. Ray doesn't have to know. I'm more attractive than he is. You like me. It's exciting to be with me. Risky and exciting.*

"Well, perhaps I should say goodbye, then," I said out loud. "You probably need some time to prepare for dinner. It was a pleasure to meet you, Nadine Oh. Perhaps our paths will cross again." I rose and held out my hand.

She stood up and took it. Her hand was warm from the teacup, and soft. "Jake," she said. There was a catch in her voice. "I don't want to impose, but... would you walk me home?"

My cock stirred and began to swell. Just the way she said it. A feeling of warmth spread through me, and I felt a peculiar twisting in the pit of my stomach, a kind of frightful pleasure. I was going to fuck this beautiful woman. It wasn't a desperate wish. It was as certain as my desire. If I wanted her now, right here, I could have her; I could back her up against the wall and rip her clothes and fuck her in the cold open air of the Tea Gardens, a quick and brutal fuck that wouldn't be rape because she'd want it, she'd love it, I'd make sure of that. Then I'd make her forget, her and the old man who gave us the tea and cookies; I'd make them both forget all about me, and Nadine would find enough cash in her purse to cover the loss of any clothing I tore.

I could have that if I wanted it. But I didn't want it that way. Not this time.

"I would be honored to walk you home," I said. "Here, let me open my umbrella. I'll hold it over your head."

"But what about you?" Nadine asked as we stepped out of the pavilion onto the wet garden path.

"I don't mind a little rain," I said, smiling. I didn't, either. The rain was light, and I was warm inside my overcoat. I felt an amazing mixture of cruelty and tenderness. This wasn't love, but it was as near as I could get. Nadine walked close beside me, shivering, looking up at my eyes every few moments with something like awe. She was smitten, and she didn't know what to do about it. Drops of rain fell on her head and shoulders. I didn't have an umbrella.

I was shivering, too, by the time we reached the vestibule of her apartment building off 19th Street. I followed Nadine up the staircase and through the door of 3B. Nadine tossed her coat over the arm of a couch.

"My place, it's, uh—"

She gestured into the air, passed into another room and came back a moment later to light a gas burner on her stove and set a teakettle on top.

"It's not very, I don't keep it clean, I'm, uh, I'm not often here," she stammered. "I work, you know, and—I don't, I don't have many, I don't entertain, you know, very often. It's kind of a mess."

"I like it," I said, hanging my overcoat on a hook on the back of the door. I wasn't lying. It was warm, for one thing, and I could tell Nadine had good taste. Nothing here was gaudy or cute; everything had been chosen with care, and if it looked somewhat askew, what of it? I'd seen much worse.

"That's my mother," she said, coming back into the main room, where I was looking at a faded photograph on the wall. Below it was a small altar, and on the altar was an orange and three sticks of incense. "She died when I was six years old."

"I'm sorry," I said. "Your father raised you?"

"Me and my sister. She lives in Fresno." Nadine stood beside me. "I don't remember her very well—my mother, I mean. But I still pray for her every day."

We stood without talking for a moment, the way we had stood in the Gardens, watching the Buddha. Meeting the silence of the past on its own terms. There was so much behind me that I could never speak of, never share with anyone. I thought about my own mother, who had raised me alone, who now believed I was dead. Did she pray for me?

Abruptly, I turned away from the photograph. I hadn't come here to think about mothers. The past was dead and that was that. It was time to get on with things.

"Jake?"

Across the room, a door stood partly open. Through it, I could see the edge of a bed.

"Are you all right?"

"What's in there?" I asked, pointing at the door.

"That's my bedroom," Nadine said. She looked nervous. "Would you like to see it?"

"Yes," I said. I followed Nadine across the room, watching the ovals of her buttocks shift under the sleeve of her skirt as she walked. She had nice legs, long and tapering in pantyhose.

The room we entered was small, as most apartment bedrooms are; the four-poster bed took up most of the space, with just enough room for an end table on either side. Dim rain-light filtered through the curtains over the small window. Near the foot of the bed, just beside the door, was a bureau covered with a disarray of scarves, stockings, candles, and dishes of jewelry, and on the wall behind it, a mirror.

"Not much to see, really," Nadine said. "It's just where I sleep and get dressed in the—"

I was standing behind her, and I reached out and put my hand on the curve of her ass. She stopped in mid-sentence, as if time had been frozen. Slowly, I moved my hand. Stroked her.

"Morning," she finished in a rush of breath.

"Nadine Oh," I said.

She shuddered. "Yes, Jake?"

"Take off your clothes."

She turned to face me, her lips quivering.

I am, by far, the most desirable man you have ever seen. I make you feel nervous and excited and pliant. You are a little afraid of how much you want to please me.

Nadine undressed, never taking her eyes off me except when she lifted her blouse over her head. Her hair came down, long and midnight black, falling to the tips of her dark brown nipples. Her breasts were small and taut. I touched one lightly with the tips of two fingers, and she shivered. Her skin was still cold from walking in the rain.

"Now undress me."

"Yes, Jake," she said.

How wonderful it was to have her remove my clothes, so gently, so tentatively. My cock slid free of the elastic band of my briefs to jut at a high angle, hard and blood-warm. I heard the intake of Nadine's breath. She had brushed it with the back of her hand.

We were both naked now.

I kissed her. (It was my first kiss in a long time. There had been a few girls when I was growing up, back in the flatlands, including the girl with whom I lost my virginity, who threw me over for a guy with a car. College was a dry spell as far as women were concerned; I was all hung up on the unattainable Ms. Daymore. After that was prison. The men who raped me didn't kiss first. The blond girl on the screen did sometimes, but she wasn't real.)

She was real. Our mouths were parted. Her lips were soft and moist. I slid my tongue across one of them and felt her tongue rise like a minnow to touch mine, and dart away. I followed it. I caressed it. I could feel her moan.

Acquiesce.

That's always been one of my favorite words.

I stroked her tongue with mine, and the stroking became a thrusting, and Nadine acquiesced, sucking my tongue, licking it underneath, and when I withdrew she was moaning and her eyes were closed. I licked her lips, took them into my mouth one at a time to pull on and gently bite, then kissed her chin and across her cheek and pushed her head back to run my tongue and lips over the downy skin at the side of her neck, then down to her throat. I licked it. It shone.

"Jake... I feel so..." she whispered. "I don't know what's happening to me. I hardly know you, but I... please, I want... I want you inside me, Jake. Please."

I didn't feel like talking anymore. I sent a few thoughts.

"I'll show you." Nadine crawled up on the bed and got on her hands and knees. The face she turned to me was like an orchid, suffused with exquisite, painful beauty. "Like this," she whispered, looking straight into my eyes. "I am your slave."

I stroked her hair. Then between her shoulders with the back of my hand, and down her spine to the shallow dip at the small of her back, and up again onto the high curve of her up-thrust ass. Nadine's lips were parted and she was breathing audibly, a quiet moaning whimper of need. I got up on the bed behind her and reached between her spread legs to cup the thatch of silken black hair. She choked back a cry. Her pussy fit neatly into my hand, warm and moist, smelling of apricots.

With my other hand I held my cock and slid it down the cleft of her ass to the long slot of her cunt, where it parted the lips and slid between, slid in, and Nadine said, "Oh, oh, oh," her last name over and over without voice, just an opening and closing at the back of her throat, a broken fluttering sound. When I looked up, I could see her in the mirror across the room: her face, eyes closed and mouth open, and her small firm breasts hanging down between her arms. I took her hips in my hands and pulled her back against me, back onto me, and began fucking her in slow, deep strokes, watching us in the mirror.

You have never felt so penetrated, so filled. This is the most incredible sexual experience of your life, and it's going to keep feeling better and better, and you won't come until you hear me say "Now."

Slowly I increased the tempo of my thrusts, lifting Nadine by the hips so that her knees left the bed when I was deep inside her. Her sounds had voice now, helpless, uncontrolled vowels of pleasure. Her face was transformed, flushed. I felt myself approaching the edge, and although I didn't want release—although I wanted to prolong this—I knew I couldn't hold back much longer.

Neither of us had heard the front door open. It must not have been closed all the way when we first came in. The first thing I heard was a "Hello?" from out in the living room, and then, a second later, I saw a man standing in the doorway. Asian features. About my age. Carrying a bouquet of long-stemmed roses.

In the mirror, I saw Nadine's eyes open. "Ray?" she whispered.

His eyes met mine. I thought: *Don't move or speak.*

I lifted Nadine's hips and filled her. "Now," I said out loud.

I watched her face in the mirror, full of lust and shame, her eyes open, staring at her motionless boyfriend, suddenly overcome with the tremendous orgasm that surged through her.

"Ray — no! N — oh! Oh! God! OH! GOD!"

She screamed, she sobbed, and I felt her cunt contract around my cock as I thrust into her, and then I was coming with a roar, both of us coming, savagely, pitching forward as her arms gave way, the bedspread suddenly muffling her cries, jets of ecstasy coursing terribly/wonderfully through my brain as I emptied myself into the silken heart of her sex.

The sweet smell of apricots filled the room.

We knelt there panting, still joined, and I heard the sound of the kettle screaming in the kitchen. We had forgotten all about tea. I raised my head. Ray, who hadn't moved or spoken per my instructions, was looking at us with an expression of such baffled anguish that I immediately felt sorry for him. The poor guy had brought flowers. He didn't deserve this.

Go into the kitchen and turn off the stove, I thought at him. *Then come back here.*

I waited while he did that, my hands still on Nadine's hips. The shrill whistling stopped and a moment later Ray reappeared in the doorway, looking despondent.

What you've seen here isn't important, I told him. *It's really nothing to be upset about. In fact, the best thing to do is to forget all about it. It's too early to be here, anyway. You should go for a walk and come back in about an hour; Nadine will be ready to go to dinner then. By the time you get to the bottom of the stairs, you won't remember any of this. You'll be thinking about how much you love Nadine, and how lucky you are that she loves you.*

Ray's expression changed. I could see his emotions uncomplicating themselves, the shock and anger fading away.

Go now. Close the door on your way out.

Ray left without saying a word, and I heard his feet descending the stairs. I knew he'd be smiling by the time he stepped out onto the pavement.

For a few moments I did nothing. Neither of us moved. I could feel Nadine breathing below me, her face still buried in the bedspread, her slowly pulsing cunt still stroking the length of my cock. Our thighs were slick where come had overflowed.

I began to harden again inside her. Instead of feeling depleted in the wake of the receding orgasm, I felt more powerful than ever. I felt as if I could fuck for days without stopping.

I took one of Nadine's small plump buttocks in each hand and squeezed as I slid part of the way out of her, then in again. I felt her cunt clench around me in answer. It felt like a muscular sleeve, a fist pumping me — and it crossed my mind that what I was really doing was masturbating, just jacking myself off using the body of a woman. That's all she was to me. Just a fist.

I felt myself begin to shrivel. I fought it. *That's all you are*, I thought in Nadine's direction. *Just a toy.* That was all she could be. That was all I could allow her to be. *You'll do anything*, I thought fiercely. *You'll spread. Open. Like this.*

"Jake—" Nadine moaned. "Ohgodoh, unh, g-g-aah. Fuck. Fuck me. Fuck me, ohgodfuckme, ohgod. Ohgod. Nngh. Ng. Gonna. Come. Oh. OH GOD!"

I felt her come around me again, spasming, and I smelled ozone, tasted leather for a few seconds. Being fucked. I'd been fucked plenty. Now I was in charge. I was in charge.

I pulled out abruptly, and Nadine sprawled on the bed, mewling, curling up, uncurling, shuddering. I squelched the urge to curl up behind her and hold her and rock her to sleep. That would be nice, but she had plans. Ray was coming back. I couldn't stay.

I stood up beside the bed. My clothes were scattered across the floor. I gathered them and headed into the living room, where I began putting them on. When I took my overcoat from the back of the door, I heard a sound behind me. I turned around. Nadine was standing there, naked, her thighs glistening, her hair tousled.

"Jake—" she said.

"Don't worry," I said. "Don't worry about anything."

"I don't understand," she said. "I'm not like this. I've never felt anything like—like what you did to me. I want you to do it again. I don't want it to stop. Ever. But I—I don't want to hurt Ray. I've already hurt him. I didn't mean to, I just couldn't stop. I don't know what's wrong with me. I just want to be fucked by you." She was weeping silently. "Please, Jake. Help me."

I felt a deep stab of guilt, even as I felt my cock begin to swell. I knew that I could have her again if I wanted her, and I did want her. I could banish Ray from her life; I could make her my sex slave. I could erase her conscience.

"You could use a shower," I said.

She blushed. "Yes, I suppose I could."

"Why don't you go take a shower now?" I suggested. "A long, hot shower. I'm sure you'll feel better afterwards. In fact, by the time you finish your shower, you'll have forgotten all about me. You won't remember meeting me or walking home with me or having sex with me. You'll feel clean and happy. You'll be ready to spend the evening with Ray, the man who loves you."

"Sure," she said. "That sounds like a good idea. I'm going to take a shower now, if you don't mind."

"I don't mind."

"Well, thank you." Nadine smiled shyly, the way she'd done when I first met her and told her she was beautiful. "It was very nice to meet you, Jake."

"Likewise, Nadine Oh," I said. I was tempted to kiss her goodbye, powerfully tempted, but I knew once I did that I would be inside her again. So I stood, put on my overcoat, and bowed to her. She inclined her head. I walked out of her apartment and down the stairs, quickly, before I could change my mind.

Out on the sidewalk, I lit a cigarette. The rain had stopped. I walked away down the slope of the wet street with my hands in my pockets, inhaling the bitter, narcotic smoke. I never saw Nadine again.

Chapter 9

Wirewalker

Dean

One could say that my new life began when Frank slipped the needle into my eyes. Or one could say it began the night Stan drove me through the gates of Vacaville, or perhaps the next evening, when I woke up in a hotel room and realized that I no longer had any responsibilities. But in a very real way, my tryst with Nadine Oh was also the beginning.

Being a full-time tourist with a bottomless wallet and no itinerary was enjoyable, but lonely. Of course I was free to strike up a conversation with anyone, and I often did, although I still felt like an outsider. I found it fiendishly difficult to look people in the eyes without controlling them, so I took to keeping a pair of sunglasses in my pocket for occasions when I wanted a moment of sincerity. Those moments were like glasses of water, cleansing my palate between manipulations. They never lasted long.

The truth was, I enjoyed fucking with people. The opportunity was too luscious to resist. I was not the only man who had such impulses in the '70s, nor the only one who acted upon them; but unlike such sloppy celebrities as Jim Jones and Charlie Manson, I had the ability to direct my will with laser-like specificity, thereby avoiding loose ends before they began to unravel. Also, I wasn't psychotic. I had no desire to damage anyone. Debase them, sure. Make them dance a funny monkey dance, absolutely. I could do these things without regret because I knew I could undo them just as easily. What I did and who I was remained invisible: theater for an audience of one.

And so I accepted my predilection on the grounds that I was doing no real harm, only amusing myself. Like the idle rich, of whom I was now an unrecognized peer, I had a powerful need to be entertained. And the most entertaining game of all was sex.

With Nadine I had found my theme, my motif. I was armed with a ravenous libido and a pair of undeniable eyes, and with these I became a prolific and invariably successful cocksman. Since I had no interest whatsoever in fatherhood, I got my tubes cut at a clinic in Marin one fog-cold day in January. One less thing to worry about.

Wherever I went, I sized up the women I saw, considering their potential as sexual playthings. I could afford to be choosy. When I found an especially toothsome candidate, I could either pounce immediately (if the surroundings were suitably discreet) or determine contact information—full name, phone number, address—and follow up at a later time. My little black book was not so little.

After I'd explored the City thusly for several months, I decided it was time to travel. Despite my precautions, I knew that the longer I stayed in one place, the more conspicuous I would become. Besides, I wanted to see the world.

My first destination was the Caribbean. I flew first class, of course, and was entertained by two comely stewardesses (as flight attendants used to be called, back in the days when one could still smoke on airplanes). Sex at thirty thousand feet is worth trying for the novelty of the experience, but space in an airplane is limited, particularly in the restrooms. I was more amused than aroused.

I spent a few weeks after that sunbathing on white sand, drinking mai tais, swimming in warm blue waters, and sampling the bodies of delicious women. One evening I had six of them in my hotel suite, all selected from the beach that day. We held a beauty pageant of sorts; I lined them up and evaluated their appearance, the firmness and color of their breasts and so on, then the relative moisture and tightness of their cunts as I entered each one in turn. Those with the three highest scores joined me on the bed, while the other three had to watch from chairs across the room, stroking themselves but unable to come.

After I'd had my fill of island fare, I flew to Sweden and spent two wonderful months wandering across Scandinavia before zigzagging down through Europe to the Riviera. I ate in the finest three-star restaurants and picturesque holes-in-the-wall, took in concerts and museums and the cinema, hiked and bicycled through the Alps, and brought a wide array of European women to stunning, occasionally earsplitting, orgasms.

(Naturally, many of these women did not comprehend English. The words I spoke aloud had no effect on them, but the silent mental imperatives I sent their way were obeyed without hesitation. I am left to assume that such nonverbal messages are conveyed as matters of intent, not language.)

I had planned to skip over to the Pacific Rim next, but I hit a snag in the south of France. Considering the frequency and variety of my sexual interactions, I'm astonished that it took as long as it did to happen. The snag was a hellacious dose of the clap, aka gonorrhea, which I'm fairly sure I picked up from a dirty-blond, strawberry-lipped woman I met on a crowded bus in La Teste. For several weeks I holed up in a beachside resort with penicillin on the nightstand, unable not only to screw but even to urinate without agonizing pain.

By the time I recuperated fully, I'd learned all I could about STDs. Needless to say, my painfully acquired knowledge put a rein on my sex life. I found it frustrating to resort to masturbation, even when it was administered by a nubile Italian girl who climaxed when I came on her face. Deeply frustrating.

I continued my travels, looping the Mediterranean, but it wasn't as enjoyable as before. Every beautiful woman I seduced seemed a potential petri dish of disease, and no matter how much I craved the primal satisfaction of entering their sweet, willing bodies, I couldn't quite forget the sting of La Teste.

I found ways to compromise. Hand jobs were always safe, as were the remote-control orgasms I distributed when I was feeling generous. I could fuck a woman's breasts without risk. Oral sex, alas, was just as dangerous as vaginal or anal when it came to things like the clap. Then, reluctantly, I took to wearing condoms, which allowed me to resume penetrative scenarios; but it wasn't the same, wasn't at all the same, felt like fucking a plastic bag. I longed for the warm wet slide of skin on skin, tongue on cock, cock in cunt with no barriers.

After a while I just couldn't stand it. I began asking women up front if they had any sexually transmitted diseases. If the answer was yes, I bade them a hasty good night; if it was no, I carried on, condom-lessly. The women were always perfectly honest, but alas, not all of them knew the truth. I found that out the hard way on a small island in the Philippines, where I wound up with chlamydia after spending the evening with a quartet of buxom, coffee-colored ladies.

The nearest hospital was in Manila, and while the doctors there were probably just as professional as anywhere else, I decided I'd had enough of globetrotting for a while. I took a long, painful flight back to the States, got a prescription for some antibiotics, and spent another couple of weeks sulking in a hotel room and watching TV. After that, it was back to condoms again.

To tell the full, unexpurgated story of my life would take more pa-tience than I possess. In my time I have visited almost every country in the world, and wherever I've gone I have sought and found the intimate company of women. Small plump punk rock chicks, elfin blondes, brassy redheads, lanky cowgirls with and without the blues; ink-black and caramel and porcelain skin; experienced and virginal, freckled, tattooed; mothers, daughters, orphans; women of every con-ceivable shape and shade and style caught my eye, and while I didn't find all of them sufficiently desirable for my purposes — the elderly and the preadolescent, for example, were exempt — I did savor a wide range of feminine flavors. My sexual partners number well into the thousands, I am sure, though I never bothered to keep count. The ex-periences themselves were far from dull, but a narrative tally would be exhausting to write or to read.

Suffice it to say that years passed as I wandered, homeless, job-less, without friends or family, a wealthy itinerant man growing slow-ly older, as all men do. I quit smoking cigarettes, with some difficulty. I learned to speak French, Spanish and Japanese. I read Dostoyevsky and Proust. I took up photography as a hobby. Out of habit, I remained circumspect in my manipulations of the human will, although I no longer had any real fear that the CIA would come looking for me.

In the early Eighties, I had a sudden flash of inspiration. It was late at night in Pittsburgh, and I'd just finished an unsatisfying bout of coitus with a young woman named, if memory serves, Deirdre.

My heart just wasn't in it that night. It wasn't that it was too easy; I'd learned how to make it more interesting, long ago, by modulating the level of a woman's anxiety. And Deirdre was nothing if not beautiful as she wavered between apprehension and desire. I came in her mouth, then allowed her to come three times — my standard ratio — while I took off the condom and dropped it in a wastebasket. After she put her clothes back on, she thanked me very prettily before I erased her memory of the night's events and sent her on her way.

Then I was alone again. It was late, but I wasn't tired. I turned on the TV, then turned it off. I lay on the bed and stared at the insipid landscape painting on the wall. I was restless. Unsatisfied. I examined this feeling. What did I want that I couldn't have? I wanted to do away with the damned condoms, but that was nothing new.

I lit a joint and tried to look deeper. Why had Deirdre's departure left me feeling so empty? It wasn't her in particular, I knew that. Tonight's restlessness was a symptom of a deeper malaise. There was something unsatisfying about the pattern my carefree life had taken.

I reminded myself that I was quintessentially free, freer than anyone else on the planet. If there was a problem with my routine, I was free to change it, as long as it didn't violate my two rules. Rule One: My ability to influence the minds of others must always remain a secret, known to no one but myself. Rule Two: I must do nothing with my power that cannot be safely undone, especially where the mental and physical well-being of others is concerned.

Sex was not my only interest in life, but it was my favorite activity. Clearly I had ample opportunities to indulge that interest, as indicated by my recent rendezvous with Deirdre, whom I'd known for less than two hours. But now she was gone.

Why was she gone? Because I had dismissed her. Why had I dismissed her? Because of Rule Two. I didn't want to fuck up her life. A few hours wouldn't be missed, but that was about all I could justify. If I wanted to have sex again, I didn't need her. I could find somebody else.

There was nothing permanent about my life. That was the problem. I went from one place to the next, one woman to the next, and when I was gone it was as if I'd never been. Rule One.

If only I could find a place to stay where I wouldn't be conspicuous. But how could I do that? I'd have to isolate myself, reduce the variables. I'd need a fortress. An area that could be controlled. Somewhere safe, where I could gather beautiful women to me. Keep them there, away from the rest of the world, for as long as I wanted. Weeks. Months. Years? A rotating harem. A bevy of concubines.

And how to create such a fortress? How to acquire these women without arousing the suspicion of their friends and families?

Inspiration struck then, as I lay on the bed in a cloud of marijuana smoke; it struck in a flash of neural lightning and altered the course of my life.

A university. That was it. I'd go back to college. Not the same place where I'd been a student before all this began, of course not; somewhere new. A private college. Small and exclusive. Rural. Miles away from any major city. I would get to know the faculty and the local police force; I'd make friends, establish security. I'd meet and greet every student admitted, and I'd see to it that plenty of them were attractive females.

That was it! Here was my harem, an endless supply of young pussy constantly in flux; new girls arriving every fall, remaining safely within my power for four years, then departing to make room for others. I could make sure they were disease-free. I'd have time to get to know them well. I wouldn't feel like such a ghost anymore. I'd have a place of my own, somewhere I belonged. And work to do, at last; for I knew the creation and maintenance of such an environment would require my full attention.

I was terribly excited. I jumped out of bed, put on my coat, and left the hotel. That night I didn't sleep. I walked the chilly streets of Pittsburgh, going over the details of my new plan.

I spent the next eighteen months scouting locations, taking my time going from state to state, methodically checking out every accredited private university on the map. I thought I'd start by seeing all there was to see, then revisit the most promising locations a second time, then a third time, and keep winnowing the list bit by bit until I was down to one perfect spot.

As it turned out, that wasn't necessary. I knew I'd found the place almost from the moment I first saw it, when my taxi came up through the wrought-iron entrance gates at the top of the mountain. It was a warm day, I remember, with a slight breeze. I liked the old brick of the buildings and the rolling green lawns, though they weren't anything I hadn't seen before. Nothing about the campus was, really, and yet... yet there was something different about it. It felt safe. Everything was clean and peaceful. No distractions. A place where people came to learn.

I stepped out of the cab. All around me was blue sky. The closest city was 85 miles away, and the nearest outpost of commercial civilization was the small town of Ferngrove down at the foot of the mountain. The campus sat on a high plateau, surrounded by an ocean of trees in every direction. I turned in a circle, listening, inhaling the smell of the newly mown grass. It was so quiet. It felt like heaven in that moment as I circled slowly with my eyes closed, feeling the warm sun and the cool breeze on my face. I was home.

And because I felt so sure, because I wanted it so much, it didn't matter that I had to work hard to make it happen. I welcomed the challenge. I set up one-on-one meetings with everyone of consequence; then, with their help, I set up larger meetings, until I had met with everyone else. Everyone: the faculty, the students, the local police, the citizens of Ferngrove. All of them. I looked each one of them in the eye. I made sure we understood each other.

Things were pretty bumpy in the first few years, when I was still getting organized; I had a number of close calls with people who'd somehow slipped through the net, hadn't been processed, and got freaked out by the things they saw. Once I had to deal with a private investigator who'd been called in on the sly by, of all people, a janitor; another time I was obliged to have the police chase down a fugitive payroll assistant who fled in her car. Problems like these took time to resolve, but the support system worked. Most people who felt suspicious or anxious about the changes on campus sought out the administration or the police on their own; those who didn't were referred there. Eventually, they found their way to me, and I took care of everything.

I made myself at home. Soon I had a spacious office on the ground floor of a campus building, with my living quarters directly above it. I became Kevin Carlson, the new school counselor. Although I'd never received formal training in the science (or is it art?) of therapy, I had by this time acquired a pretty decent layman's grasp of human behavior—as well as a dark talent, unmatchable by any therapist, for solving problems. Thus it was that students with suicidal ideation left my office wanting to live; overweight kids who wanted to slim down found the willpower to do so; people addicted to hard drugs could quit them cold turkey; and anyone coping with the loss of a loved one found the process much easier after talking to me. I made friends out of enemies, enthusiastic students out of listless ones.

The world beyond Ferngrove was as screwed up as ever, and so it would remain as long as people made it that way. I wasn't going to fix it. I wasn't God. That was too big a job for one person, anyway. All I could do—all I wanted to do—was make my little corner of the world as pleasant as possible.

So I made the people around me happy. I took away their anxieties and fears, and gave them new perspectives on life. And the changes I wrought, however cruel or unusual they might have appeared to the untrained eye, were never unwelcome. I was beloved by everyone I knew, because I made them feel good.

That is my job, and I've been doing it for more than fifteen years now.

I have had unusual luck, but I am not a bad man. I do not believe that what I do is wrong, and even if it is, I have the power to put it all right. Graduates of this university leave without a trace of physical or psychological damage. When I die, if all goes as I hope it does, it will be as though I never existed.

In the meantime, I walk on a wire suspended over an abyss. The wire exists only because I believe it does. I tell myself that I am not a bad man, and I believe that, too.

I keep my balance. It's a good story. It's better than falling.

Chapter 10

Intervention

Dean

Mrs. Crawford was quite upset. I could hear her from all the way down the hall when I stepped out of the elevator.

"You must be out of your minds, both of you. This is not a misunderstanding. This is not just going to go away. Our daughter goes to this school, do you understand that?"

Officer O'Brien was standing outside the door to the conference room. We nodded to each other as I opened it and went in.

At one end of a long table sat Alvin Barlow, the university provost, and Jim Hardesty, chief of police for the town of Ferngrove. They looked grim. Across from them were the Crawfords: Mr., scowling in his seat with arms folded, and Mrs., vivid in powder blue and mascara, looking as if she were about to leap down Alvin's throat and tear him a set of gills.

"Hi, everyone," I said as I shut the door behind me. "I'm sorry to keep you waiting. I was just finishing up with a client."

"And who are you?" asked Mrs. Crawford.

"Kevin Carlson," I said. "I'm the school counselor."

"Lilian Crawford," she said, ignoring my outstretched hand. "My husband, David. I don't mean to be rude, Mr. Carlson —"

"Please, call me Dean."

"Dean. All right, fine. Dean, I don't quite understand what you're doing here. You're a counselor? Like a psychiatrist or something?"

"Not exactly, but I think you have the right idea," I said. "I came because I heard there had been a problem."

"Yes, you could say that," Mrs. Crawford said. "There has definitely been a problem."

"I'm still having a problem," Mr. Crawford muttered.

"Well, that's why I'm here," I said, hanging up my overcoat and taking the seat at the head of the table. Jim slid the report over to me. "Problem resolution is my job."

"Oh really?" Mrs. Crawford said. "That's nice. Maybe you can give a few pointers to these gentlemen, who as far as I can tell don't seem the least bit interested in dealing with the situation."

"Now that's not fair, Mrs. Crawford," Jim said. "I told you, I've got two officers out there right now looking for witnesses, trying to find out what happened. It's going to take some time to sort this thing out."

"We're witnesses," Mrs. Crawford said. "We told you what happened. I want to know what you're going to do about it!"

"Perhaps I can help," I said. "I came straight from my office, so I haven't heard the details yet. Would you mind going over it one more time for me?"

"Unbelievable," she said, shaking her head. "Unbelievable."

"Thirty-eight thousand dollars a year," Mr. Crawford grunted.

"I can see that you're both very upset," I said. "I want you to know that I don't intend to leave this room until we've resolved the matter to your satisfaction. Please, if you wouldn't mind, I'd like to hear exactly what happened. In your own words."

Mrs. Crawford turned to face me squarely and took a deep breath, as if to summon the last reserves of her patience.

"My husband and I flew in from Rhode Island this morning," she began in cadenced tones. "We came here to surprise our daughter and wish her a happy birthday. We had just parked the rental car and we were walking over to her building, and — we saw —" She closed her mouth and looked away. "I can't even stand to say it. We saw this... young lady," she continued carefully. "Well, first we saw the young man. He was coming down the path toward us, and he was holding onto a leash, and about five steps behind him, on the other end of the leash, was the young lady. She was wearing —"

Mr. Crawford snorted and shook his head. His wife paused, searching for the right words.

"Well, very high heels, for one thing, and this—I don't even know what to call it, a catsuit? Made out of very shiny black material, very tight-fitting. The top part of it was like a corset, laced up in the back, and it stopped just under her, her... breasts, and she wasn't wearing anything above that. Except for the collar." Mrs. Crawford glared at me; she was embarrassed and trying not to show it. "I mean, not even a brassiere. Nothing."

"Thirty degrees out there," Mr. Crawford muttered.

"Just strolling along like everything was perfectly normal," Mrs. Crawford went on. "Though I don't know how anyone could stroll in heels like those. Well, naturally, my husband and I were somewhat taken aback by this."

Mr. Crawford snorted in what I assumed to be agreement.

"So I said to them, I said, 'Excuse me. *Excuse* me. What do you think you're doing?' And the young man—they stopped, and he said 'We're on our way to class,' like he was surprised by the question. And I said, 'Well, do you realize this young lady doesn't have her shirt on?' "

I suppressed a smile.

"And he said to me, 'Oh, she doesn't mind.' Just like that. 'She doesn't mind.' And the girl just looked at me, and I said, 'Well! Maybe you don't mind, missy, but other people do! Now get yourself into some decent clothes before I call the police!'"

Mrs. Crawford's face was red. She drew another deep breath.

"I said, 'You ought to be ashamed of yourself,' and all of a sudden—it was like I flipped a switch or something. She started crying and said, 'I am, I'm so ashamed.' And the young man, he—" Mrs. Crawford shut her eyes for a second, wincing at the memory. "He yanked on the leash, pulled her toward him, and slapped her right across the face. I couldn't believe my eyes. Then he looked at my husband and said 'Your turn.'"

She stopped and looked away, embarrassed into silence. I had a feeling the story was coming to a conclusion.

I turned toward Mr. Crawford. "How did you respond?"

He scowled at me, cocking an eyebrow. "I told that little punk we were going to call the cops, and he said, and I quote, 'Whatever, dude.'"

"That's right," Mrs. Crawford cut in, "then he pulled on the leash, and the two of them just walked away."

"And you called the police?"

"That's right," Mrs. Crawford said again, nodding. "We couldn't find a pay phone, so we went to the student center and had the young man at the desk dial the number for us. Then the police came, and Chief Hardesty brought us up here, and we met Mr. Barlow, and we filled out a form and explained the whole thing five or six times, and apparently this incident isn't the least bit upsetting to anyone but us. Frankly, we are outraged at this point. And we would like to see our daughter now."

I glanced at Jim.

"Already on it," he murmured to me. To Mrs. Crawford, he said, "The minute we find her, we'll bring her in."

I decided it was time to establish a better rapport. I glanced down at the top of the report, where Jim had written their full names. "Lilian Marie Crawford," I said. "David Allen Crawford."

They looked back at me, and this time, for the first time, they really noticed my eyes. How interesting they were; how very blue.

"I can understand why you might be upset by what you saw," I said. "That's a natural response. I have to admit, some of the things young people wear these days... well, girls didn't dress that way when I was in college." I smiled ruefully. "Madison Avenue has come a long way, hasn't it?"

"You got that right," Mr. Crawford said, smirking.

"Sure," I said. "I mean, let's face it, these kids who pierce their eyebrows and dye their hair green and purple and whatnot, they're doing it to shock their parents. That's the main reason. They're trying to push our buttons. It's what young people do."

"Natalie," Mrs. Crawford said, "told us she wanted to pierce her tongue, of all things. I said, what, you're not satisfied with ears now? It's got to be the tongue? No one can see it if it's in your mouth, and you're rude if you stick it out, so what's the point?"

We all smiled: Jim, Alvin, the Crawfords, and I. "Rude is the point," I said. "I'm sure your daughter loves you, but she's also trying to offend you. She's in transition, you know. She's testing the boundaries of her new freedom, trying to figure out where she fits in."

I could see Mrs. Crawford softening; still upset, still concerned, but mollified by my words. And my blue, blue eyes.

There was a knock at the door, and O'Brien poked his head into the room. "Chief? We've picked the girl up. They're on the way over."

Jim nodded. "Thanks, Mike. You see now," he said as the door closed. "Your daughter will be here in just a few minutes."

"As I was saying," I continued, "most young people, when they come to college, are getting their first real taste of independence. It's perfectly normal for them to experiment with new appearances and lifestyles. By the time they graduate, they've outgrown most of their, ah, youthful exuberance, and they're ready to get serious about a career. But you've got to allow them some time to be foolish and impulsive first. I mean, better here than out in the real world, right?"

"Can't expect them to get it right on the first try," Mr. Crawford said. He didn't sound angry; disapproving, maybe, but not unsympathetic. I wondered how upset he had actually been, to begin with.

"No, I suppose not," Mrs. Crawford said. "Still... there should be limits."

"Of course," I said. "That's exactly the point. What you saw out there were two young people exploring the limits." I leaned forward. "What was it, exactly, that bothered you?"

"Well, her—her breasts were... out," Mrs. Crawford blurted, frowning, as if uncertain of what she was saying.

"And why was that a problem?" Mrs. Crawford wasn't sure how to answer. She looked to her husband, but he had nothing to say. "Don't all women have breasts?" I asked. Gently. As if speaking to a child.

"Well..."

"You have breasts, don't you?"

Mrs. Crawford blushed. "Yes... of course I do, but—"

"Of course you do. And when Natalie was a baby, you nursed her, didn't you?"

"Yes. Yes I did."

"Well then. There's nothing inherently shameful about breasts, is there?"

"Oh, certainly not," Mrs. Crawford said. "I didn't mean... no."

"Men have been going shirtless in public for years," I said calmly.

"Why should it be a problem for women to do the same thing?"

Mrs. Crawford looked confused. "But it's so cold," she said. "It was snowing when we left the airport."

I had to think about how to reply—I was a bit worried about that, myself. "Kids," I said, shrugging. "They can live on pizza and four hours of sleep, and they can walk around in the freezing cold with nothing on. I don't know what to tell you. They're young and plastic."

Mrs. Crawford smiled uneasily.

"Personally, I wouldn't recommend going topless in weather like this," I said, "but that's just me. The young woman you saw, did she seem uncomfortable?"

"N-no," Mrs. Crawford said, shaking her head, her forehead furrowed. "But... she said she was ashamed."

"Ah, yes. That was your suggestion, wasn't it?"

Mrs. Crawford didn't answer. She was trying to regain her sense of outrage, but she had run out of ammunition. She couldn't remember the slap.

"From what you told us," I said, "it sounds like she was doing just fine until you spoke to her the way you did."

Now there was silence. Everyone was looking at Mrs. Crawford, who was looking baffled. I had a feeling that she wasn't often at a loss for words.

The silence was broken by a knock on the door. It swung open, and there was Natalie Crawford.

Chapter 11

Revision

Dean

"Mom! Dad! What's going on?"

Natalie and I hadn't seen much of each other since her individual session earlier in the year. Her major was electrical engineering; she was an attentive student, but not especially interesting in person. Not to me, anyway. She had her share of friends.

"Oh, Natalie," her mother said, rising to hug her, then hold her at arms' length. "Let me look at you. What have you done to your hair?"

"Happy birthday, sweetheart," Mr. Crawford said.

"How does it feel to be eighteen?" Mrs. Crawford asked.

"It's... fine," Natalie said. "You flew out here? Why didn't you tell me you were coming?"

"We wanted to surprise you," Mrs. Crawford said.

"We brought you something," Mr. Crawford said. "It's down in the car."

"I don't understand," Natalie said, pulling away from her mother. "Why are the police here?"

"Natalie Barbara Crawford," I said, and she noticed me for the first time. "There was a misunderstanding, that's all."

"Hey, Dean. What was it? What happened?"

"Have a seat, Natalie," I said. "Apparently your mother was upset about something. Perhaps she can explain it best."

Once again, all eyes were on Mrs. Crawford.

"I—well, I—I saw a young lady who was dressed, uh, provocatively," she stammered. "I felt it was in bad taste, so I insulted her and—and called the police." Her voice trailed away as she finished the sentence. She hadn't planned to say that.

"Mom!" Natalie shouted. "My God, what did you do that for?"

Mrs. Crawford's face grew redder. "David," she said. "David, say something, please."

"Your mother overreacted," Mr. Crawford said to Natalie. "She was upset. She spoke without thinking clearly." He glared at his wife in disapproval.

"Has this sort of thing happened before?" I asked him.

"Oh yes," he said. "Lilian can be very judgmental of people who are different from her."

"David," Mrs. Crawford whispered.

"It's true," Natalie burst out. "She's always talking about how tacky other people are. It's like her hobby. It's so embarrassing. Mom, I can't believe you would do this to me! Is this your idea of a birthday present?"

Mrs. Crawford crumpled under the onslaught, hunching inward with arms folded defensively. "I just don't understand," she mumbled to the table. "I—I thought..."

I waited, but she didn't finish her sentence. "Lilian," I said. She raised her head. "May I call you Lilian, Mrs. Crawford?"

"Oh,—yes, certainly," she said. Looking into my eyes.

"As I said before, I can understand why you were upset by what you saw. I don't imagine you get much of that back in Rhode Island. It can be difficult to keep pace with the cutting edge of fashion, especially when you're—forgive me—no longer young. I think we all understand that." Mrs. Crawford made a shaky little smile, her eyes still fixed on me.

"But, Lilian," I said in a deeper voice, "it is a serious thing to involve the police. A very serious thing."

She flinched. The smile vanished.

"Chief Hardesty is a busy man, and so is Mr. Barlow. For that matter, so am I. We've all taken the time to meet with you and your husband, at your insistence, and we've listened patiently to what you have to say. The chief here has pulled four officers off the beat—"

"Five," Jim said.

"Five officers. To deal with a situation that involves no crime, only your personal discomfort."

Again we waited. Again, Mrs. Crawford seemed bereft of words.

"I'd like to apologize on behalf of my wife," said Mr. Crawford, after a moment of silence. "Like I said, she can be a real hard case about things like this."

"And you indulge her?" I asked, turning my gaze to him.

He withered slightly. "Well, I—I don't—"

"You don't say much when Lilian's on the warpath, do you?"

Now it was his turn to stammer. "Well—you have to understand, my wife—my wife has very strong opinions, uh, Dean, and there's no sense—it, it doesn't work very well to, uh, to argue with her when she's, when she's in the midst of—"

"Mr. Crawford," I interrupted. "David. I understand what you're trying to say. It is difficult to challenge someone who has a dominant personality—believe me, I know. Still, it seems to me that you bear some responsibility for this situation. For allowing it to progress this far."

"I do, yes," Mr. Crawford said. "I apologize."

"And you, Lilian?" I said, turning back to her. She'd been looking down at the table again, and she jerked her head up guiltily when I said her name.

"I'm sorry," she said in a whisper.

"What was that?"

"I'm sorry," she repeated, her chin trembling. She looked around the room. "I'm terribly sorry. To all of you gentlemen. I don't know what came over me, I'm—I'm so sorry. I talk too much." A tear ran down her face, suddenly. "I feel so ashamed." Another tear broke loose, trailing a black line of mascara.

"Do you think it's fair, Lilian, for you to belittle people because they're different?" I asked. She shook her head mutely.

"Did you know that your daughter is a lesbian?"

The faces of the Crawford family froze in surprise. It was a moment to savor.

"Natalie?" I said, glancing at her.

"It's true," she said, looking worried now. "I am." Her parents stared at her, astonished. "I didn't know if I should tell you," she said

85

to them.

Mr. Crawford found his tongue. "You mean you... you..." Or perhaps he hadn't found it yet.

"I like girls, dad," Natalie said.

"But, how do you know?"

Natalie snorted. It was such a stupid question that she forgot to be worried. She wasn't going to remember, either.

"H-how long?" Mr. Crawford asked. "How long have you been—"

"A lesbian, dad." Natalie leaned forward, gripping the arms of the chair. "Say it. Lesbian. I've known since I was eleven, and I never said anything because I knew you and mom would throw a fucking fit."

"Easy, Natalie," I said. "Nobody here is going to throw a fit. Certainly not your parents. I think there have been enough hysterics for one day. Isn't that right, Lilian?"

"Yes, Dean," Mrs. Crawford said meekly.

"There's nothing wrong with homosexuality," I said. "It's not to everyone's taste, but neither is chopped liver. Or a vinyl bodysuit."

"I like that bodysuit," Alvin said dryly. It was the first time he'd spoken since I came into the room. Alvin and I had known each other for years, and he was familiar with my *modus operandi* by now; he knew how to keep quiet and wait.

"So does Trevor," I said. "Apparently."

"I wonder how she'd look," Alvin said, indicating Mrs. Crawford.

"Ridiculous," said Jim. He smirked. "If you could get it onto her in the first place."

"Oh, I could get it on," Alvin said.

"Well, it's a moot point, gentlemen," I said. "It's not going to happen. I mentioned it only as an example of how preferences can differ." I turned to the Crawfords. "I'm sure I don't need to belabor the point. From now on, I think you would do well to keep an open mind. No matter how unusual a stranger may seem, they deserve no less respect than your own daughter. Is that understood?"

I wasn't usually so emphatic, but the Crawfords were bigots of the first order, and I didn't want any loose ends. They nodded together.

"Then if there's nothing else—" I put my hands on the table and stood up.

"Actually, Dean," Alvin interrupted. "If it's not too much trouble, I'd like Mrs. Crawford to suck me off."

Jim snorted. I raised my eyebrows.

"You should have heard the things this woman called me. Her self-righteousness."

"Her apology wasn't enough for you?"

"Not the kind of lip service I prefer," Alvin said with a quick smile. "I have been very patient."

"So you have," I said. "Well, then. Mrs. Crawford — Lilian — are you familiar with the concept of fellatio?"

She blushed. Didn't say anything. Nodded.

"Have you performed fellatio on a man before?"

She couldn't meet my eyes, but by now she didn't need to. She nodded again.

"Your husband?"

Nod.

"Lilian, I know you're sorry for what you've done. If I might make a suggestion, I think that fellating Mr. Barlow would be an excellent way to make amends for wasting his time. Not to mention harassing our students. You won't press charges, will you, Mr. Barlow?"

"No, not this time," Alvin said gravely. "As long as it doesn't happen again."

"Oh, thank you," Mrs. Crawford said, looking up at him. Fans of moistened mascara ringed her eyes. She looked like an alcoholic clown.

"Think of it as a tangible expression of your gratitude," I said to her. "Naturally, the more Mr. Barlow enjoys it, the more convinced he will be of your sincerity."

Mrs. Crawford's face was a battlefield of emotions: shame, relief, penitence, fear. She looked at her husband. "David?"

"I think he's right," Mr. Crawford said, putting a hand on her knee. "It's for the best, darling. You go ahead, and I'll take Natalie down to the car. When you're finished, you can meet us there and we'll give her the present. Then maybe we can all go out for dinner."

"Right on, I'm hungry," Natalie said.

"You'll probably want to head back home after that," I suggested.

"Of course," Mr. Crawford said, nodding. "We've got work to-morrow. But we couldn't miss our baby's eighteenth birthday."

"Dad," Natalie said, pretending to be exasperated.

"Go on, you two," I said good-naturedly. "Get out of here. Happy birthday, Natalie."

"Thanks, Dean," she said as they got up to leave. "Bye, you guys."

"Dean," Mr. Crawford said, shaking my hand. "Pleasure meeting you. Mr. Hardesty. Mr. Barlow, take as long as you need with her. My apologies, again. Thank you for your time."

The door closed behind them with a soft click. I was still standing.

"Well, Lilian," I said. "Perhaps now would be a good time to be-gin. What do you think?"

"O-okay," she said.

"Alvin, would you like her as she is, or — "

"Unbutton your blouse," he said to her. "Take off your bra, but leave the jacket on. I want to see your tits."

"Yes, Mr. Barlow," she said.

"Jim? You want some?"

"Oh, hell, why not," Jim said affably. "Long as I'm here. You stay-ing, Dean?"

"No, I've got some other business to attend to," I said. "You boys go ahead and have fun. Just don't keep her too long, okay?"

"You got it," Jim said.

Mrs. Crawford was undoing the buttons of her white blouse. I reached out and touched her face, stroking her tearstained cheek with my thumb.

"Lilian," I said, "you just do as you're told and everything will be fine. After you leave here, you won't need to mention what happened, not to your husband, not to anyone. It'll be just for you to think about. Does that sound like a good idea?"

"Oh, yes, yes it does," Mrs. Crawford said.

"All right, then. Jim, Alvin, I'll see you around." I nodded at them, they nodded at me, and I left the conference room.

I turned up the collar of my overcoat as I stepped outside. The air was bracingly cold after the warmth of the administration building. While I'd been in conference with the Crawfords, dusk had fallen.

The lamps were switched on, casting aureoles of pale light along the pathways. I walked with my hands in my pockets, hearing only the faint crunch of snow under my feet. I thought about my plans for the winter break, which was only a couple of weeks away.

Evening classes were still in session; the windows of Hanover Hall were a checkerboard of light and dark. I entered through a side door and went down the hallway to Room 119. Quietly, I opened the door and slipped inside.

Dr. Edwin Graham stood at the lectern, using one of his ever-present laser pointers to indicate the movement of tectonic plates on an overhead projection. Freshman geology. For most of the students, it was a required gen ed course that had nothing to do with their field of study; that, and Dr. Graham's monotonous manner of speech, left me unsurprised by all the blank stares and slumped heads I saw in the audience. But I also saw Brad Oberholt, who was sitting behind Nancy Clark and reaching down her scoop-necked shirt to fondle her breasts; they were paying attention, and Nancy was even taking notes. Claire Pollard was sucking on a seven-inch dildo, practicing her deep-throating technique while she drew horses on her folder. I noticed Teresa Avila moving rhythmically up and down in her seat, and remembered what program she was on. And at the back of the room, in the last row, were Trevor Bailey and Zöe Martin, the two I had come to see.

"Everyone," I said. Dr. Graham stopped in midsentence. All heads turned in my direction, seeing me for the first time. Around here, people generally don't notice me until I call them by name or use a key word.

"Oh, hello, Dean," Graham said, clicking off the laser. "What brings you here?"

"I'm sorry to interrupt," I said. "I just wanted to borrow Trevor and Zöe for a minute, if that's all right."

"Absolutely," he said. "No problem at all."

They got up from their seats. Trevor attached the leash to Zöe's collar and gave her ass a gentle swat, like a carriage driver might flick a whip lightly over the rump of his horse. She started walking and Trevor followed behind, holding the leash.

We stepped out into the hall and I closed the door behind us.

"Hey, Dean, what's happening?" Trevor said, grinning. Happy to see me, as always. Zöe, still dressed in the black vinyl bodysuit that exposed her breasts and shoulders, said nothing, but she smiled warmly at me.

"What's happening is that I just came from a meeting with the parents of Natalie Crawford," I said. "Do you know her?"

"Unh-uh," Trevor said. "Oh, wait. She's that lesbian chick, right? Gearhead type?"

"That's her," I said. "Today's her birthday. Her parents came here unannounced—I guess they didn't read the letter we sent out about surprise visits. Anyway, they saw the two of you on your way to class, and they got very upset."

"You mean those two old farts that got on our case?" Trevor said scornfully. "Yeah, they were all like, 'Oh my word, she doesn't have a shirt on, we can't deal with this, we're calling the puh-leece, waah waah waah.' We were totally polite to them, too."

"Well, they did call the police," I said, "and we all had to sit down and have a long talk about it. They were about ready to sue the school."

"Jesus," Trevor said. "What the hell is their problem?"

"Fortunately, they don't have a problem anymore," I said. "It was just a misunderstanding, and it's been cleared up. But I'm still concerned about one aspect of it. Zöe, you've been wearing this outfit quite a lot lately, haven't you?"

"Yes, Dean," she said. "It's my Master's favorite."

"Well, I'm a little worried about your health," I said. "It's very becoming, don't get me wrong—I'm glad we ordered it for you. It's just that—well, I guess I assumed you'd be wearing it indoors. Frankly, I was surprised to hear that you'd been walking around outside dressed like this. You may have noticed the snow on the ground. That means it's freezing."

"She doesn't mind," Trevor said. "It makes her nipples hard." He reached over and twisted the nearest one between his thumb and forefinger. "Like that." The nipple stiffened. I thought of holly berries in the snow.

"Even so," I said, "you could catch a cold. Or worse."

"I like how my skin kind of burns and tingles when I come back inside," Zöe said. I shook my head. Trevor pinched the other nipple, and she squealed.

They weren't listening to me, and I couldn't really blame them. They were young, and far more interested in each other than in anything I had to say, especially since I'd been keeping a light touch on the controls. But it was getting late, and I was ready to call it a day.

"Look," I said, snapping my fingers. Their heads lifted like marionettes; their eyes fixed on mine. "I just don't think it's a good idea, okay? It's not worth the risk. We don't want any permanent damage, do we?"

"No," they chorused.

"Trevor, this isn't San Diego. Winter doesn't fuck around up here on the mountain. People can die of hypothermia. Do you understand?"

"Yes, Dean," he said. "Hypothermia is dangerous. That's why I always make sure Zöe and I dress warmly when we go outside."

"Always?"

He nodded, smiling brightly. "Always."

"Good," I said. "Thank you for humoring an old fart like me. Now get back to class."

They smiled, and Trevor gave Zöe's ass another mild slap as he opened the door to 119. "See you later, Dean," he called over his shoulder.

"Not if I see you first," I said softly as the door closed; an old wiseass comeback from when I was growing up, so many years ago.

I didn't mean it, of course. We'd see plenty of each other, Trevor and Zöe and I. They made a great couple, and I was fond of them. Even if they did do stupid things sometimes.

But, hey, you know. Kids these days.

Chapter 12
The Gift of Clear Sight

Zöe

The table had been cleared and we'd all moved to the floor of the living room, where we sat on pillows with our mugs of tea and hot chocolate. Olivia went first because she was the youngest, and to no one's surprise she chose the biggest box under the tree.

"Livvy, honey, why don't you save that one till tomorrow," mom said. That was our tradition: one present the night before Christmas, and the rest in the morning.

"Aw, man," my sister moaned. "I bet I know what it is, too."

"Well, keep it to yourself," dad said. "Go on, pick again."

Olivia pouted theatrically, then picked out a small square box. She ripped off the paper. "Oh, cool, body glitter," she said, unscrewing the lid of the little jar. "I'm gonna try it on."

"It's almost bedtime, Liv," dad said. "Why don't you put it on in the morning?"

"No, I want to wake up all glittery." Olivia dabbed some of the gel onto her face. "How do I look?" she asked me. "Simply ravishing?"

"You look like a pixie," I said, smiling and brushing her hair back over her shoulder.

"Okay, your turn. Which one do you want?" Olivia asked, turning back toward the pile of presents.

"Hold on," mom said. "Wait a minute. This year I want to choose Zöe's first present for her, if that's okay. I've got something special to give this year."

"That sounds promising," I said.

"It's a family heirloom, kind of," mom said, reaching into one of her pockets and bringing out a small bag made of black velvet. "At least for the last four generations. Before that, I'm not sure." She shifted forward on her pillow. "My mother gave this to me when I was about your age, just like she was when her mother gave it to her. I've had it for the last twenty years or so. Now it's time to pass it on to you."

I took the bag from her and turned it gently upside-down. Something slid into my palm.

"Oh wow," I said, lifting it up on its necklace of blue beads.

"It's a chamsa," my mother said. "This one's carved out of lapis lazuli. Your great-grandmother made the necklace, but the chamsa itself is very, very old."

"A what? A hamster?" Olivia craned her neck to get a better look at the thing. It was smooth and dark blue, shaped like an open hand. Carved into the center of the hand was an eye.

"Chamsa," mom repeated. "That's Arabic for 'five', like the five fingers of the hand. It's a protection against the Evil Eye."

"What's that?" Olivia asked.

"An old superstition," mom said. "A lot of different ancient cultures had the idea that certain people could jinx you, or cause you harm, just by looking at you. The chamsa was supposed to keep you safe from their influence. This symbol of the eye in the hand shows up in artwork going back thousands of years, all over the Old World."

The chamsa turned a slow circle in the air as we watched it.

"Anyway, it seemed like this was the right time to give it to you, now that you're living away from home," mom continued. "After you left for school in September, I realized how much I miss having you here. I know I have to let you go, but I'm still your mother. I can't help it."

"I know," I said, pretending to roll my eyes.

"Okay, so what this means, this present, it means I recognize that you're old enough to be on your own," mom said. "You don't need me and your father to protect you from the dangers of the world. I'm very proud of you and I know you'll do fine, as long as you're careful. There are a lot of con men out there."

"What's a con man?" Olivia wanted to know.

"It's short for confidence man," dad said. "It's someone who tricks you."

"So this is the gift of clear sight," mom went on. "That's what Grammy Rachel called it when she gave it to me, back when I was your age. It's a very rare, very precious gift, not just a piece of jewelry. I know I don't usually make such a big deal over presents, but this is different. I want you to put it on and keep it on for a couple of weeks, at least. Wear it all the time—in bed, in the shower, everywhere."

"Why?"

"You'll see after you wear it for a while," she said. "It makes you feel more centered, like..." She hesitated, looking for the right words. "Like, you don't get distracted as easily. You pay closer attention to what's going on."

"So it's a magic necklace," I said.

Mom read the look on my face, and the corner of her mouth smiled. "I wouldn't choose those words to describe it, no," she said. "That makes it sound hokey. I think it's very powerful, but I don't expect you to believe that yet—in fact, it's good that you have a skeptical mind. You don't have to believe anything to wear it. Just try it out for a while, see how it feels. Go ahead, put it on."

I slipped the necklace over my head. The chain of beads was long, and the chamsa fell just between my breasts. I looked up at my mother and smiled. "Thank you," I said. "It's beautiful."

"You're what's beautiful," she said, "come here," and we held each other close. "I love you, Zo," she whispered into my ear. "Don't let anyone pull the wool over your eyes, okay?"

"I won't, mom," I said.

I used to have nightmares all the time when I was little. Most of them involved the bogeyman, whose face looked like it had been turned inside out. He'd see me and chase me, and I'd run as fast as I could but he'd still be gaining, so I'd have to hide somewhere. I'd move like lightning and find the best hiding places, but it never worked. He could smell my fear, I think. Eventually the cabinet door or shower curtain would be flung open, and I'd see the bogeyman's wet, inside-out face leering in at me. Then I'd lurch awake, screaming.

But I hadn't had a nightmare for years, now. And I'd never had one like this.

A man was slapping my face. My head jerked to the side from the force of his blow, and a second later I felt the hard, stinging impact against my cheek. I turned back to him and he slapped the other cheek, and again I heard the smack of his palm an instant before I felt it. A whipcrack of pain, softening out to a rosy glow. The blush of shame or excitement.

I turned to face him again. My mouth was open and I was breathing hard. On my hands and knees. This was what I wanted. Wasn't it?

The man was unzipping his pants, his cock was coming out, and it was a beautiful cock, so beautiful I couldn't look away. Another whipcrack, sudden stunning pain across the side of my face that left me warmer than before; then another slap, this time across my ass; then a rain of slaps everywhere, invisibly, all over my body. My face, my ass, my... my sex. Spread open and slapped. Pain everywhere, softening to pleasure.

I couldn't see the cock any longer; I had to feel for it blindly with my hands while the beating continued.

"Please, hit me," I heard myself say. "Harder, I'm begging you. Hurt me."

As I said this, I felt my consciousness divide. It was like looking through two different lenses. I was horrified and not horrified by what was going on, and I could feel both versions at once, separately. I didn't want to be slapped in the face or anywhere else. These were hard slaps; they really hurt. At the same time, I liked the intensity of the pain, the ringing aftermath, the spreading warmth. It made me feel sexy. I did want to be slapped around. Or: I felt sick. This was wrong and I wanted it to stop. But: I enjoyed this. It felt too good to stop. I was meant to serve. And: it wasn't right. I was going to scream.

I found the unseen cock and took it in both hands, guiding it to my lips, feeling my mouth open around it. So large. It hurt my jaw to be open this wide, but it felt so satisfying to have a mouth full of cock. I took it deeper, breathing through my nose. I was going to choke if it went any deeper. I wanted to bite it off and spit it out. My tongue cradled the cock from underneath, sliding. I tried to scream but I couldn't, now, with my mouth so full; I couldn't move away from the approaching cock, no matter how hard I tried, and all I wanted was more of it. I felt it at my throat. I was going to choke. My throat fluttered, then surrendered, opening to receive more cock, and it kept coming, and I kept taking it in. I was salivating around the thick smooth pole of flesh that thrust into me, impossibly long; and I screamed around it, a faint humming sound, screamed at the top of my lungs as I began to choke, then — then I was sitting up in bed in the dark, my heart racing.

The light flicked on.

"Zöe?" It was my dad. "Was that you? What's going on?"

I was bathed in cold sweat. "Jesus Christ. Did I scream?"

"Uh huh," he said, coming into the room. "Bad dream?"

"Oh, God," I said, putting my hands over my eyes. "God. I haven't had a nightmare like that... ever."

"You want to tell me about it?" he asked.

"No, no," I insisted. "I... sorry I woke you up." I put a hand against my chest and felt the chamsa resting there, just to the right of my heart.

"It's not your fault, honey," he said, smiling. "Can I get you anything? Glass of water?"

"No, I'm all right," I said. "Thanks. Go back to bed."

"Okay. Sleep well. I love you."

"I love you too," I said. The light turned off and I was alone again. I exhaled and lay back against the pillow.

I'd never dreamt anything so disturbing. My dreams were hardly ever sexual, and far from graphic when they were. This, on the other hand, was some intense S&M shit. I'd never been into that stuff before.

Was I now? I wasn't sure. In a way the dream had been arousing, a kinky little surprise from my subconscious; in another way it was a violent, sexist nightmare that freaked me out. I'd been turned on and off at the same time. I didn't know what to make of it. I couldn't sleep.

I was exhausted the next morning and not much in the mood for Christmas. All day I was troubled by the memory of my dream. I could recall exactly how the cock had felt against the back of my throat; I remembered how it felt to choke on it.

Remembered?

I smiled and thanked Livvy for the Tracy Chapman album, and dad for the Margaret Atwood novel, and all the while my thoughts circled the memory of the dream. Or was it the dream of a memory? Somehow it all felt very real, and connected to something larger. Although my eyes ached from lack of sleep, I also felt strangely awake, as if I was surfacing from a long walk on the bottom of the sea. I spent the day quietly, avoiding conversation.

That night I had another dream. This one began with a black cat sitting on a fencepost, staring impassively at me. I recognized it from an art nouveau poster that I'd had since high school, and then I realized that the cat wasn't real. I was looking at the poster, which hung now on the wall of my college dorm room. Right above the foot of my bed.

I was on my hands and knees on the mattress, staring at the black cat.

A man spoke suddenly, from behind me. "One finger."

My left hand moved between my spread legs. I was warm down there, slippery warm everywhere. I had been rubbed down with oil. The man liked the smell of extra virgin olive oil on my skin. I was glossy with it.

I slid my hand past a furrow of curled hair and up behind, then I touched a fingertip to the dark, shiny-smooth pit of my ass. I felt a galvanic shudder, as if I had just touched the inner core of my will.

It surrendered immediately. There was no resistance. My will was not my own. The finger slid slowly in, and shivers of heat and cold raced over me. The black cat watched.

Deeper in and deeper surrender.

All the way in.

"Now suck it," said the man. A wave of electric pleasure coursed through me at the sound of command in his voice. I felt my clit tingle. I removed the finger from the tight, moist grip of my ass and brought it up to my lips. Oily.

"Five-inch," he said, and my unquestioning hands found an object on the bed beside me, an object that felt like a cock; and without hesitation I put it between my legs and up behind me. Up inside. Up my ass. So wide, and myself so helpless. Impaled.

"Speak," said the voice.

"I am your slave," I heard myself saying, but again, as in the previous dream, I felt my perspective split when I spoke. I was saying it and listening to it, together and separately. "I am yours to use. Use my cunt for your pleasure, use my mouth." It was not me who said this, and yet it was. It was my mind and my body, operating without my will.

But my will had not been destroyed, only silenced. And now it stood apart and looked at the rest of me, the prisoner with the five-inch dildo up her ass. The slave. It listened to the words coming out of her mouth and did not like what it heard.

"I exist only to serve you," I said.

Then I screamed: "LIAR!"

I screamed it so loud I woke up.

Now I was really frightened. Two nights in a row of masochistic sex fantasies? Something very strange was happening to me, and I didn't know why. Yet it all seemed to make sense, in a way—as if it should be no surprise that I had these twisted thoughts in my mind.

I wanted help, but it seemed impossible to ask for it. How could I tell mom that I had dreamed about putting a dildo up my ass and calling myself a slave? It was absurd, but not in a funny way. It wasn't me. Was it? Why did it seem so familiar?

I was too embarrassed by the contents of my mind to face anyone, so I feigned illness and stayed in bed. It wasn't hard to do, given my lack of sleep and overall state of mind. Still, Mom gave me a sharp glance out of the corner of her eye, like a bird, when she brought me tea. I curled away, facing the wall.

Of course I thought of the chamsa. It didn't make sense, though—why would something designed for protection give me nightmares? If it was supposed to give me "clear sight", why did I feel so confused?

I didn't know, but I knew I felt awful. So I took off the necklace and hung it around a post on the headboard of my bed. I drifted into a midday nap, and when dad came in to wake me up for dinner I was disoriented, but refreshed — and I'd had no dreams at all.

Winter break lasted another ten days. There were no more nightmares, although I couldn't stop thinking about the two I'd already had. The chamsa remained on the bedpost.

Mom knew something was wrong, and I could tell she wanted me to talk about it. But I wasn't volunteering, so she kept her distance. We'd had a series of fights, before I left for college in the fall, about the extent of her control over my life (I wanted less) and the level of my privacy and freedom (I wanted more). Standard mother-daughter stuff. Now, so soon after giving me the chamsa and making that speech, she couldn't quite bring herself to butt in. Part of me wished she would, and another part was terrified of her or anybody finding out what was on my mind.

I wondered if I was going crazy.

The dreams kept replaying in my mind, becoming more and more vivid each time until they seemed like memories of something that had actually happened. I couldn't quite believe that, though. If it was real, why hadn't I remembered it until now? That kind of sex isn't something you just forget.

Besides, it really wasn't my style. Of the five serious boyfriends I'd had, only the last one ever got beyond heavy petting. That was my senior year at high school. The sex was a little awkward at first, but nice once we got used to it. In the end I broke up with him because of his constant self-loathing, which had seemed romantic at first but eventually drove me up the wall. He'd certainly never slapped me around.

Who, then?

Someone at college? Did I have a new boyfriend?

How ridiculous was it that I wasn't sure?

Chapter 13
SOTY

Zöe

At the airport, Olivia wrapped her eight-year-old arms around my legs and wouldn't let go. She put her head on my belly and said: "You're staying."

"Can't stay, you goofball."

"I don't care. Make an exception."

"Can't make an exception. You gotta go back to school, too." I ran my fingers through her hair.

"Come on, Liv," my dad said. "Finish your goodbye now so I can have my turn." Reluctantly, she let go of one leg. Dad leaned in to give me a hug. "Goodbye, sweetheart," he said into my hair. "Have fun and learn a lot. Your mom and I are so proud of you."

"I love you, Dad," I said. I started to cry. Proud of what? What had I been doing at school? Why didn't I know?

When I tried to think about the last four months, nothing came to mind. I'd been at college, sure, I knew that; I remembered my room and my building and the twisty steel sculpture outside the library. I knew what classes I had, because my schedule was written down in my pocket calendar. But I couldn't remember actually being in a class, although I knew I had been. I knew I'd been living at school, but I had no memory of that, either. I didn't know why. It just wasn't there.

Either I had amnesia, or I really was going crazy, or something terrible had happened to me at the university.

Mom was next, hugging me close, and after a minute we let go and she stepped back, studying my eyes. "You left this in your room," she said quietly, pressing the chamsa into my hand.

"It was giving me nightmares," I said.

"You'll get a few of those, sometimes," she said, looking not at all surprised. "It usually means you're in trouble. Are you?"

"I... I don't know," I said, shoving the chamsa into my pocket. "I'm still trying to figure out what the nightmares meant. Anyway, I don't want to have any more of them."

"Well," she said, "I can't make you wear it, and anyway, that's not the point, is it?" She brushed a strand of hair out of my face. "Just keep it, in case you change your mind. If you need protection, all you have to do is slip it on again. You know you can always call me, don't you? Any time, day or night."

"I know," I said. "Thank you."

"Take care of yourself, love," she said, and held me again.

I spent that morning on the plane, riding above the clouds in a desert of blue sky. When I got to O'Hare there was a two-hour lay-over—the second plane had been delayed because of a storm—so I passed the time on an airport bench, reading my new novel and listening to CDs.

I dozed on the second flight, and woke again in the early evening, just before the plane dipped a wing and began to angle down into the clouds. Suddenly the light was gone and we were flying through snow, down under dark skies again, landing with a bump on a runway of blurry blue lights.

From the airport I took a bus and rode an hour north to Stuartsville, where I caught another bus out to the boondocks. A few students were riding this bus, but nobody I knew. I chose a seat near the back and put a balled-up sweater between my head and the window. I pretended to be asleep, and almost was by the time we stopped in Ferngrove.

Snow was falling steadily. With the others, I huddled on the cold benches at the courier stop and waited until the headlights of the school van came cutting through the curtain of snow. There were eight of us, and we all piled into the back.

The heater was on, musty and rattling. The van leaned around switchbacks as it climbed the mountain. Although there were no windows in the back, I knew we'd reached the university when the road became flat again. At last the van stopped, and we all piled out into the snow and the light of the streetlamps. We were in front of the dining hall, and the drivers now herded us into a line that passed through the open doors.

I was exhausted and starving. I filled my plate and ate quickly, then pushed the tray aside and leaned forward on the table, my head in my folded arms. Maybe I'd go to bed early.

"Hey, it's Zöe! You guys, she's over here! Hello? Zöe?"

I raised my head. It was Jill, a girl I knew. Well, everybody knew her, I guess; she was a second-year student with long, straight, white-blond hair and the kind of figure most women torture themselves trying to mimic. We smiled when we met, but we didn't know each other well enough to be friends.

"Someone get this girl a cup of coffee," one of her posse said, and they laughed.

"Yeah, naptime is over," Jill said with mock sternness.

"Could we do this tomorrow morning?" I mumbled.

"I know, you got here late, didn't you? You must have been on the last van in. You better hurry up, sweetie, it's only like an hour till showtime."

I blinked. "Showtime?"

"Hello! The SOTY Awards? Biggest event of the year?"

"Oh, right." I feigned comprehension. "One hour, huh?"

"Yep. We got tickets this morning. You'd better get going if you want time to change. You're not wearing that, are you?"

"Oh," I said, glancing at my jeans. "It's a dress-up thing?"

"Well yeah," Jill said, frowning. "I mean, what if you get picked for first-years?"

"Huh?"

"Oh, come on, you know it could happen. You're totally popular, you and your *man*." She said the last word with sultry emphasis.

My man?

A thin stream of fear trickled through me.

"Yeah, well, I guess I better go," I said, standing up and grabbing my duffel bag. "Thanks. I'll see you there."

"Good luck, Zöe," she said. Was it my imagination, or was there a hint of condescension in her friendly smile?

"Good luck yourself," I said, and left.

I lived in Weldon Hall; I could remember that, and I could remember the way there over the snowy, lamplit paths. My room number was 29. I had a key; it fit into the lock and turned, and I was back in my old familiar room, with the lamp and the green couch and the low futon against one wall. Facing the poster of the black cat.

One bed. No roommate? No, I lived here alone, of course. Although people often came by to visit.

Friends.

I tossed my duffel bag and backpack on the sofa, and went into the bathroom. I looked at my travel-worn face in the mirror as I washed my hands, and figured that if I was planning to dress up tonight, I ought to take a shower first.

I emptied my pockets as I took off my clothes, and found the chamsa nestled in a coil of blue beads. I left it on the countertop with the ticket stubs and chapstick, and got under the spray of hot water.

It was nice to have a private bathroom and a showerhead with multiple settings on a long flexible metal stalk. Rather grand for a college freshman, although maybe not, considering the tuition. My dad complained about how expensive this place was, even with my scholarships, but he paid for a good reason. For the last twelve years, the university had turned out record numbers of successful alumni, waves of cum laude prodigies who promptly found good-paying jobs in their chosen fields.

The exclusivity of the school, so expensive and renowned and isolated on its plateau, along with its famous deep focus approach to academics, had intrigued me the first time I read about it. I didn't think I had a chance of being accepted, but I sent in the application anyway. I applied to Bryn Mawr and Sarah Lawrence, too, and Oberlin, and the local JC, just in case. But it didn't matter. When I got the acceptance letter I screamed "Yes!" at the top of my lungs, right there on the street by the mailbox.

Five months later, I was on my way here for the first time. My parents came with me and we went through orientation, then they left, and...

Then I... went to classes. Studied. Made friends.

Nothing too remarkable. Just college.

I stepped out of the shower, dried off, and walked across the bedroom to the closet. When I opened the sliding door, the first thing I saw was a black vinyl corset hanging by itself in the center of the rack. No, more than a corset, leggings too; a bodysuit. It looked really sexy, although it seemed a little too small for me.

Was it mine? It had to be. It was hanging in my closet. Maybe this was what I had planned to wear to the ball, or the awards show, or whatever it was. Too bad, though; there was no way I could put it on by myself.

I looked through the rest of the closet and settled on a chenille top the color of crushed raspberries, a black skirt and black suede pumps. There didn't seem to be any underwear, so I went with black hose. I was pleased to see that I hadn't lost my fashion sense, although I couldn't imagine where I'd come up with the money for all these clothes. Had I ordered them online? I must have. There were no clothing stores in Ferngrove, certainly not any that stocked four-inch spike heels. Those were kind of scary looking, actually. Had I really worn them before?

I got dressed in a hurry. By the bathroom sink I found a dark, blood-red lipstick that looked very dramatic against my pale skin. As I was rubbing my lips together, I glanced to the side and noticed the chamsa where I'd left it on the counter. I looked back at my face in the mirror. It told me nothing.

Suddenly I was angry. I was tired of being afraid. *If you're crazy,* I said to my reflection, *then go see a therapist. Talk to somebody and deal with this. And if you're not crazy, then you've got work to do. Because something is seriously wrong here, and you've got to find out what it is. No matter how much it scares you.*

I picked up the necklace and lifted it over my head. The chamsa lay cool on the flat space between my breasts, out of sight beneath my shirt. I smoothed back my hair and turned away from the mirror.

It was showtime.

Fensler Auditorium was a blaze of light, snow falling in endless descent past its golden windows. Just inside the front doors of the lobby, a man in a tuxedo was waiting.

"Good evening," he said as the doors swung closed behind me. "May I take your coat? They're just about to start. Do you have your ticket? No? Okay, right over there at the check-in. Have your ID ready."

Across the room was a row of box office windows, only one of which was open. I joined the short line of people waiting in front of it, and leaned against the wall to slip off one of my shoes and take out my student ID. No pockets.

There was my picture on the card, staring blankly at the camera with my mouth open. My first day here. God, I looked so clueless.

For a moment I felt prickly all over, as if a draft of night air had blown past me. But I wasn't cold. Just... tense. My antennae had risen.

A few stragglers joined the line behind me, and I recognized a girl who was in a few of my classes. She had on a thin white top that was very see-through and a couple of sizes too small for her — riding the line between sexy and slutty. And she wasn't the only one, I saw now that I looked around; all the girls in line were dressed to kill. Maybe I should have found someone to help me get into that catsuit, after all.

It was my turn. I stepped up to the window, holding out my ID, and got my first good look at the man who was stamping hands. I felt a sudden wrench of terror inside me, as if my heart had seized up.

I knew him.

"Well, there you are," he said affably. "Just in time. We couldn't start the party without you, Zöe Willow Martin."

His eyes were a weird, deep blue. Of course I knew him. Everyone did. He was the school counselor, a popular man on campus. Everyone liked him. I worked for him part-time as a receptionist, and we were good friends, me and...

Dean.

"Hi, Dean," I said automatically.

That was what everyone called him, but it wasn't his real name. And we weren't really friends. I'd been thinking that, but it wasn't true. Friendship had nothing to do with it.

Dean was a liar.

I knew this for certain without knowing how or why.

His stare was open, unblinking. Creepy. I fought down the shaking inside me. "Here you are," he said, handing me a ticket. His fingers stroked my palm as they withdrew. "You have a box seat. Up the stairs, last door on the right. Good luck." The look on his face was strange, a gentle smirk.

"Thanks," I said, managing a quick, plastic smile as I left.

At the top of the stairs, several ushers were waiting. One of them took my ticket and escorted me down a long hallway. We reached the last door on the right, and he held it open for me.

Heads turned as I entered the box. About ten people were here, mostly girls. The last empty seat was next to a girl named Fawn, who I knew from debate club. She smiled excitedly and waved me over. "Hey, Zo, good to see you. Wow, you just made it," she said as I sat.

"Yeah, I didn't realize I was cutting it so close," I said. "This place is packed."

She raised her eyebrows. "You kidding me?" she said. "It's the SOTY Awards, you can't miss this! I might get picked this year. I think I actually have a chance against that blond bitch."

"Jill?"

"That's her. She's not even really a blonde, you know."

"I know," I said. I'd seen Jill's roots before, though I couldn't think where.

"Everybody's saying you're in the running for first-years," Fawn said, giving me a quick once-over. "I'm surprised you didn't go with the bodysuit."

"You know about that?"

Fawn snorted. "Girl, who doesn't? You've been flaunting it ever since he got it for you." She gave an air-brained giggle.

I stared at her for a moment, then did my best to giggle too. "Well, you know, I don't want to be too predictable," I said, looking out at the stage. "I probably won't get picked, anyway."

I hoped I didn't get picked, whatever it was for. Everyone seemed to know what they were doing here except me. SOTY Awards? Some kind of beauty contest, it seemed like, and apparently I was a contender. Big emphasis on appearance. Very popular; the whole school was here, undergrads, faculty, everybody. Everybody here to see the girls in their sexy outfits.

Well? Put it together. Come on.

The lights began to dim. Low trumpets sounded from somewhere at the back of the theater, and the chatter of the crowd softened into silence. It was the theme from *2001: A Space Odyssey.*

"Ladies and gentlemen," a voice intoned. "The Student Body Association is proud to bring you, for the first time this millennium, the annual SOTY Awards show."

Dah... dahhh... daaahhh...

Pounding drums. A beam of light illuminated the curtains, on which four large letters, S O T Y, were sewn in blue sequins. The crowd burst into wild applause.

"And now, your host, SBA president... Nick Halloway!"

Dah-DAH!

The applause grew even louder. A spotlight stabbed the front of the stage as a guy strode out from the wings, and we all rose to our feet, clapping and cheering. Fawn was jumping up and down like a cheerleader. "Nick!" she screamed.

"Thank you, thank you," Nick said, beaming. "Thanks. It's great... great to see everyone here. Welcome back... thank you. Okay." He held up his hands. "Enough, you'll spoil me."

Not bad looking, but full of himself. That was obvious.

"Welcome back from winter break. You all glad to be back?"

"YES," roared the crowd.

"You ready for some action?"

"YES!"

"Take me, Nick!" a girl's voice screamed.

"Wait your turn, bitch," he barked. The crowd laughed and applauded, and Nick grinned widely. A curl of dread went snaking down my spine.

"All right, all right, it looks like some of you just can't contain yourselves, so-o... without any further ado, let us commence. Let's get it on... with... Slut of the Year Two Thousand and One!"

Spotlights swooped across the auditorium, the music blared, and as I joined in the screaming and clapping, my mind said calmly: *here's your answer.*

I wasn't crazy. I wasn't dreaming. This was real.

"Please, everybody, if we could —" Nick shouted over the roar of the crowd. "People, the sooner you're quiet, the sooner you get to see some pussy."

That brought laughter. I laughed, too, just like everyone else in the box. SOTY. Slut of the year. This was really happening.

"Ladies and gentlemen," he continued, "girls and boys, teachers and students, masters and slaves — as you know, we at the SBA review literally hundreds of applicants every December. Nice work if you can get it, right? Hey, I'm not complaining. But I'll tell you, it wasn't easy to narrow the field. We had some *stiff* competition this year."

A wave of laughter rippled through the crowd. It sounded canned, like the joke. And suddenly I knew that it was all fake, all of it, everything I was seeing and hearing.

Scripted. Orchestrated.

Mass hypnosis.

Masters and slaves.

You're totally popular. You and your *man.*

The dreams. The cock in my mouth. The dildo in my —

No, I couldn't bear it. I sat down quickly, covered my face with my hands, and bent toward my knees. I wanted to scream, but forced myself to breathe deeply instead, deep lungfuls of stale air that smelled of sweat and old popcorn and perfume. My anus tingled, clenched with memory. I couldn't bear it and I couldn't make it stop. It was all true. I was weeping.

Then, in the distance, I heard my name spoken aloud. A roar of noise. Fawn's hand on my shoulder. "Zöe?"

I lifted my head. The bodies around me had shifted, turned toward me amid an excited babble of voices, and Fawn was helping me to my feet. I rose into the blinding stare of the spotlight and heard Nick Halloway say: "There she is! Give her a big hand!"

And Fawn: "Congratulations! Go get 'em, girl!"

Applause. The whole school, clapping for me.

I had been chosen.

Chapter 14

Showtime

Zöe

How strange it all was, anyway, how like a movie. The door opened behind me, and the usher was there to take me down the last few feet of hallway and through the exit doors. I floated, high on dream-like fear, down and up two short flights of steps, then through another door that led backstage. The usher gave way to another usher who took my arm and led me through the wings, behind the curtains. Here, in the dark, there were four empty chairs in a line across the stage. I was led to the nearest one, and I sat obediently.

From the other side of the curtain I could feel the heat of the lights and hear the friendly cadences of Nick Halloway's voice. I took a deep breath and tried to slow the pace of my thoughts, to listen to what it was that I understood. It wasn't really that difficult to figure out, after all — only difficult to accept.

They're all hypnotized. That came first.

All of them, the whole school. Everyone but me.

Me and one other person: the one who made this happen.

And I knew, without question, who it was.

Dean the liar. The liar who calls himself Dean. The man with the blue eyes. This is his show.

He's put the Evil Eye on everyone.

He likes to fuck with people. Especially women.

He uses women for sex.

And I'm one of his favorites, I thought as a roar of applause rose from the other side of the curtain. My gorge rose with it and I tasted bile at the back of my mouth, remembering the feel of a penis there, so deep inside I couldn't breathe around it. And couldn't say no. And didn't want to say no, although I was choking to death. I remembered the taste of it bursting inside me, milky and bitter like dandelion sap, like bile, and I remembered the pleasure I felt swallowing it.

He made me want it.

I heard a noise behind me and turned around to see the usher leading another girl onto the darkened stage. It was Jill, her white-blond hair gleaming faintly in the dark. She walked by without turning to look at me, and sat in the nearest chair.

Gotta play dumb, I thought. *Play along. If anyone knows I'm not with the program, I'm done for.*

I had to go through with this, get through it, pretend. Pretend to be a hypnotized slut, just the way I used to be. I would play the part and make them all believe; then I'd find a phone, call the cops, and bring that blue-eyed liar down.

Except, I told myself sharply, *if it was that easy, someone else would have done it by now. Think. If he has the whole school hypnotized, he's probably got the cops, too. And the phones.*

But I've got the chamsa.

That was it: of course. The reason that I was not under Dean's control was hanging around my neck right now, on a strand of blue beads. I was carrying the gift of clear sight, given to me by mother and her mother before her.

I'd never believed much in fate, but what kind of coincidence would deliver the chamsa into the life of someone like me, who so desperately needed it? I hadn't believed in the power of hypnosis, either, but that had changed. I was learning to believe all kinds of unbelievable things about the world.

I looked around and saw a third girl on the chair beyond Jill. I couldn't make out who it was, but she was sitting backwards, facing away from the front of the stage. Striking a pose, I realized suddenly. Of course. It was show time.

It was time to get ready. I felt a moment of panic: afraid of what I had to do, afraid of not doing it well enough. Then I set that feeling aside—surprisingly easy to do, much easier now that I had the chamsa. I stood, closed my eyes, and took a deep breath.

I was an actress. I had been onstage before; I knew how to step out under the hot lights, with the invisible eyes of the audience upon me, and repeat what I had rehearsed. Acting always felt dangerous. That was why I liked it. I liked the rush of conquering my fear... and I loved the attention.

I was an actress, and I had a role to play. That was all. I just had to let myself remember what I had rehearsed, what I'd practiced over and over again with Master.

Master! I almost lost concentration, but kept my eyes closed. That's right, that's what I called him; he was a boy my age and Dean had introduced us. I was his personal slave. I had practiced for tonight a thousand times with him.

Remember?

The curtains parted, and a white roar of sound and heat washed over the stage.

"Our first contestant tonight is a pretty young thing from western Massachusetts," Halloway said. "Valedictorian at Grantham High School... National Merit Scholar... a very intelligent and if I may say so very *shapely* little girl who's going for a double major in English literature and political science. On top of that, she's active with the forensics team and our chapter of Amnesty International. Of course, many of you also know her as the property of Trevor Bailey, who was kind enough to unleash her for the evening. Ladies and gentlemen, a warm round of applause please for our freshman, or rather fresh-*woman* candidate, Miss! Zöe! Martin!"

The lights came up on my end of the stage, and I heard clapping, whistling from the darkness beyond. I put on my most dazzling smile and waved my hand, turning my wrist from side to side like a princess on a parade float. *Trevor,* I thought. *My Master's name is Trevor.* A moment later, the light turned blue and I heard the sound of synthesized chimes coming from the speakers behind me, spiraling down the scale. A beat set in, the flat bass beat of a drum machine.

One. Two. Three. Four.

I began to dance.

The movement came without conscious effort, smooth from many hours of practice. My shoulders rolled back; I arched my neck and lifted my hands high with the fingers spread, fluttering them as they came down. I didn't have to remember the steps. My body knew them by heart. It was like the split perspective of the dreams I'd had, the memory-dreams; I was both in my body and outside of it, being and observing at the same time.

Then I heard myself speaking.

"I have no control."

It took me a moment to realize that the words hadn't come from my mouth, but from the speakers. It was a recording.

"I think about sex all the time," my voice said. "It doesn't matter where I am. I have an obsession. I have an obsession."

The bass thumped in time to the words, and now there was a melody line as well. Synthesizers. House music.

"There's something about a man who wants me. *It just makes me feel so.* When I know he wants to have me. *It just makes me feel so.* Whatever he wants to do to me. *It just makes me feel so.* And all I want to do is please him. *Just makes me feel. So. So horny.*"

I'd been walking forward one step at a time, rolling my hips, and on the word *horny* my hands came up to cup my breasts through the soft chenille. The music slammed. The light turned red.

"*Oh.* I want to be fucked. *Oh Oh.* I want to be. Fucked."

That was my voice. I had said that. It was a remix of the recording from my audition back in December, I remembered now, when I told the SBA why I wanted to win the SOTY Award. Or, rather, why Master wanted me to win it. It was all about what he wanted.

"It's like flipping a switch. Something inside me just surrenders. I have to give in. I have to obey every order. Like flipping a switch. Like I'm a machine made for pleasure. I have to give in. I'm under your power. I have... no control."

Slam went the music; one hand clasped my throat and the other went between my legs.

"I have no control."

Something was wrong. The effortless movement of my body had halted. My fingers were plucking at the top of my shirt just below my neck, searching for something that wasn't there.

A zipper. I was supposed to pull a zipper now.

But there was no zipper to pull.

I was wearing the wrong clothes. Even as I felt the spike of panic, I knew I had to ignore it. There was no time for fear. *Improvise,* said the calm place inside me. My hands went to the bottom of my shirt and I began inching it up my belly, slowly, the way I thought a stripper might do. *Don't let them see the chamsa.*

"Do you like my body?" my voice asked from the speakers. "Do you want to take me? Do you want to make me? Make me come? *Oh!* Do you like my body?" It sounded like I really wanted to know the answer. My voice was husky with strange desire, strange and yet familiar. It was me and it was not me.

I lifted off my shirt and the chamsa with it, undulating to the rhythm of the music, and let the bundle fall from my upstretched hand. Then I swung down, reaching around behind to unhook the clasp of my bra. I should not have been wearing one. I was supposed to have on a sky-blue pleather top with a zipper down the front, and nothing underneath, but it was too late for that now. They wanted to see my breasts, and here—the bra fell away—here they were. I heard the crowd roaring, male voices shouting "Yeah!"

It was me and it was not me, up here on this stage, leaning forward with my hands on my knees so that my breasts hung down; me/not me miming a coy smile as I lowered into a squat with my legs spread open, sinking to my knees in the blue light.

"I want to be your plaything," said the voice that was mine and not mine. "I will come when you call. I want to be your sex toy. I want to be your fuck doll."

I brushed a hand lightly across my breasts and found my nipples hard. I realized, with an ugly shudder, that I was enjoying this performance. It wasn't real, of course, none of it was really about me, I would never have chosen to do this; it was grotesque, it was awful, it was rape.

And on some level, it was turning me on.

Go with it, said the clear center of my mind. *Use it. Play the part. Make them all believe.*

So I licked my fingers and strummed my nipples, thumbed them, made them shiny with saliva, rolled them and pinched them and gasped at the delicious pain. I cupped my hands under my breasts, offering them up to the audience. I felt the blush burning in my cheeks, my throat and the top of my chest: the flush of arousal and shame. I rode the shame, stayed with it. Exploited it.

"Your wish is my command. To hear is to obey. My life is in your hands. I will do anything you say."

"Take it off, bitch!" a voice shouted from the darkness.

But of course. I was already doing it, back in the flow of the dance, following the familiar steps. A twist to the left, to the right, and the suede pumps came off behind me. Swaying to the music, I rose slowly to my feet and turned. Bent from the waist. Reached behind to caress my ass and slipped my hands under my skirt. Hooked the waistband of my pantyhose and began to slink them down my legs.

I was looking upside down at white light and cheering darkness. Dizzy. Blood pounding in my face as I stepped out of the hose. A thumping in my gut, counterpoint to the rhythm; a scary hiccup throbbing all the way down, all the way up to my sex suspended above me. The rush of performance. Stage fever.

"I'm so wet. I'm dripping. The thought of you inside me makes me crazy, cra-crazy with desire. *Oh.* I want to serve you. I know I don't deserve you. And I don't want to disturb you but I think I'm catching fire."

Slowly, I lifted my skirt. It moved over bare skin. Up over my buttocks, slowly, and the roar of the audience rose through the light as they saw me, saw my sex inverted at the apex of my naked thighs, displayed for them. Splayed open for them.

And they wanted it. They wanted to fuck me, all of them, all of the men at least; and the women were dying of admiration and envy. A thousand of them, maybe more. They wanted me.

"Fuck my willing cunt," said Zöe. "Fuck me till I can't stand. Fill me with your seed. Slap me with your open hand."

Tears were running down my face. I felt humiliated and horribly aroused. My hands were moving shivery light over my ass, caressing my thighs. I lifted my head slowly, seeing spots, blood draining out of my face as I looked over my shoulder at them. As I touched the lips of my sex.

(No, not my sex. My cunt. And not mine. Master's cunt. Master wanted me to do this, and I wanted whatever he wanted, and we both wanted this—we all wanted it—because of Dean. Sick mindfucker Dean.)

Touched the lips of Master's cunt and parted them and felt the slick inside. The helpless response of Pavlov's dog.

"I have no control," the slave said again. "No control." Repeated it like a mantra. Stroked the tender flesh, circled the clitoris. So wet. Memories flowing back now, rubbed back to the surface. Dog collar and chain. Drinking milk from a bowl on the floor. Endless rehearsals. Sociology class, fingering myself while taking a test, uncontrollably rubbing until, the moment I finished, I came, came bucking against my hand while the whole class watched me. Walking through the snow with a dildo in my ass, strapped into place. On my hands and knees. My legs over Master's shoulders. His cock inside me. His thick, hard cock inside me and his finger in my ass and his tongue in my mouth and I acquiesced to all of it, I existed only to serve him, and I was going to come, I was blind and mindless and teetering on the pinnacle, and only one thing held me back —

Now.

His command rang through me like a gong and I screamed as I came, spasmed, fell crashing to my knees and writhed as the electric current of my orgasm arced through me.

Chapter 15

Puppet Play

Zöe

A while later there was sound: the ebbing tide of applause, Nick's voice saying something banal. An eruption of laughter.

I lifted my head. Nick stood in the spotlight at center stage, cracking jokes and grinning away. My side of the stage had gone dark. I sat up slowly, wincing at the pain in my knees, and rubbed my hands over my face. Coming back to my senses.

My skirt was bunched up around my waist. I smoothed it down over my legs and began searching around for the clothes I'd dropped.

"...spread 'em apart and put 'em together for Miss! Jill! Rrrrrandall!"

Lights came up on the section of stage next to mine. There was Jill, dressed in a tight white T-shirt and jean shorts that showed off her smooth, toned legs. An odd choice of attire for the middle of winter, but I had to admit she looked good. And it was certainly warm enough in the auditorium. The light on her was noon-bright, and the sound that came filtering in from the speakers was of waves crashing, seagulls. Then music: a bouncy keyboard, very summery, very Eighties.

"Hi, everybody!" Jill's voice chirped from the sound system.

"Hi, Jill," the crowd responded in unison.

"Wow, it's so exciting to be here," the voice said. Jill rose to her feet, smiling a big cheerleader smile. "I'm totally stoked. You guys are the best. Let's hear it for the SBA!" Applause.

I put the chamsa around my neck and slipped it under my shirt. It was a relief to have it on again, to feel the cool weight against my breastbone. I began to roll on my pantyhose.

"Is it hot in here, or is it just me?" Jill giggled. "I could sure use a cold shower." She turned around and bent over, slowly, to pick up a plastic water bottle from the floor by the chair. Men in the crowd started a grunting football chant—*Hu! Hu! Hu!*—at the sight of her denim-laminated ass. She turned around again with an ingenuous little-girl pout. "I'm all sticky."

Oh, please, I thought. *Pathetic.* But it was working. And now she was raising the bottle high above her head, tilting it, squeezing. A stream of water splashed onto her upturned face, down her neck and all over the front of her shirt. Her nipples stood out through the thin fabric, and the real Jill squealed along with the recording. The noise of the crowd was deafening. She wasn't even naked and she already had them.

I noticed myself starting to feel jealous, and took a mental step back. This wasn't a contest I wanted to win. There was no need to feel contemptuous of Jill for the way she was acting, I reminded myself; it wasn't her choice. It wasn't Nick's choice to be a glib emcee for a strip show, either. All of it was involuntary, including that Neanderthal chorus out there in the dark. Only one person deserved my contempt.

It was time to plan my next move. Now that I was out of the spotlight, I could think more clearly. The stage fright was gone, the orgasm only a shallow glow ebbing away between my hips. Jill lifted her shirt, revealing taut, perfect breasts—

...breasts I had seen before. The image flashed across my brain, suddenly: those same dark pink nipples appearing from behind a bra. Out on the lawn, on a fall afternoon. Jill undressing calmly for Dean— yes, Dean was there, sitting beside me on a bench. Getting acquainted. I was meeting them both for the first time. Dean was so handsome, like Paul Newman with those beautiful blue eyes. Jill was down on her knees, on the sidewalk, sucking Dean's cock, and I could see the dark roots of her hair as her head bobbed. And I didn't understand what was going on. I didn't know why none of the people around us were upset, or why I wasn't sure if I was upset or not. I could call the police, I said—more of a suggestion than a threat. Dean didn't mind. He didn't think the police would mind, either. He knew them. He knew everyone.

"You know what I really like?" Jill's voice asked. "I really like it when I'm, like, bent over a couch or something, like at a party, and I have my shirt off like this and there's two really hot guys in front of me, and they each take one of my tits and suck on the nipples. It feels soooo good. And I'll be moaning because it feels so good, so my mouth is open, and sometimes a third guy will slip in between the two other guys and just put his cock in my mouth. Oh my god, you guys, I love to suck cock. I swear, it's like my favorite thing, 'cause I talk too much anyway, and when a guy puts his cock in my mouth, I'm like, oh! Duh! I should just shut up and suck like the dumb cunt I am. Sometimes I forget, you know?"

Oh Jill, poor helpless Jill. This was so unfair. But what could I do? Dean knew everyone—cops, administration, the whole town of Ferngrove. I would have to get far away from this place to find help.

And when I did, what then? Who would I tell, and what would I say to them? Even if they believed my bizarre story, which wasn't likely, what would they do? Come to the university and check it out. Meet with the authorities. Dean would get wind of it somehow, and he'd turn his blue eyes on my parents or the FBI or whoever I brought in, and they'd be his.

No, I had to do this right. I had to outthink him. Conventional approaches wouldn't work against Dean, because he had a weapon that didn't fit the program. I couldn't bring him down until his power was neutralized. That had to happen first. So I'd seduce him. I'd get him alone in a room and—and hit him over the head with something heavy. Knock him out, blindfold him, tie him up, stuff him in the trunk of a car—

Ridiculous. There was no way I could lift him, let alone get him into a car without being seen. I wasn't even sure I could knock him out. A wave of despair washed over me, deepened by fatigue. I felt like I hadn't slept in days. The plane, the bus, the van, the hot shower; performance anxiety; orgasm. I shouldn't have to think any more. The only thing keeping me awake now was fear. Fear and anger.

And the chamsa.

It always came back to the chamsa, and suddenly it was so obvious: I couldn't do this alone. I needed an ally, someone to watch my back and help me think. The chamsa worked for me; why not for someone else? I had been brainwashed, and now I was free. All I had to do was put the necklace on. If I could persuade someone else to wear it...

I thought about this while Jill went through her contortions, eventually fingering herself to climax as I had. By the time she collapsed to the floor and the lights went down, I had the beginnings of a real plan.

The next contestant was Melody, a junior from Michigan who was double-majoring in Economics and Sociology. Not that it mattered. What mattered was her curly hair, brown streaked with gold, and her glossy lips, and her doe-eyed gaze, and her large breasts, and most of all her ass. That was Melody's specialty, her real major. She liked it in the ass. I suppose we all did, all of us acquiescent girls, but Melody really liked it. It was the only way she could come. And she came, of course, two fingers plunged deep inside, head thrown back, moaning in ecstatic defeat.

I didn't want to be turned on, but I was. It was like watching a train derail or a building explode. So horrible you can't look away. You're drawn to it, not for any good reason, not because you can help; your only motive is brute fascination. It's good theater. It'll make a hell of a story.

And this story was about sex. I didn't like it, but I couldn't deny its power. Watching Melody fingerfuck her ass summoned the memory of all the times I'd been touched there, penetrated by fingers and cocks and other foreign objects. It wasn't my choice, but I had been made to enjoy it. I couldn't separate the pleasure from the memory, no matter how involuntary it all had been.

After Melody was Phoebe, a senior Performing Arts major from Chicago; slender, with bobbed black hair. She recited Shakespeare while she stripped, backed up by cello music. Kate's closing monologue from The Taming of the Shrew, then Helena from A Midsummer Night's Dream. "Use me but as your spaniel, spurn me, strike me, neglect me, lose me; only give me leave, unworthy as I am, to follow you." Classy misogyny.

119

Phoebe was a fine actress, making the most of her limited role, but I sensed that the enthusiasm of the audience was waning. She moved into more modern pieces, some of which I didn't recognize, and began to bring out accoutrements like nipple clamps and a blindfold. Her thing was pain. She showed us the carefully applied pattern of crisscrossed whipmarks on her back and bottom as she pulled on a pair of long gloves, one black and one white. For her finale she sat sprawled forward in the chair with her legs spread wide, masturbating violently with the black glove while the white glove tried in vain to hold it back.

The applause was somewhat subdued this time, and I thought I knew why. It wasn't for lack of beauty or polish, or because she had gone last, after the motif of submission and degradation was already well-worn. Phoebe's act was just too intellectual. She wasn't a dumb cunt like Jill, or a bovine piece of ass like Melody, or a dancing marionette like me.

I liked her.

Nick bounded downstage onto the apron, grinning away, and the lights came up all across the stage. I stood up like the other contestants and faced out to the audience, wearing my brightest smile. This was it. I realized suddenly that I might win; I hadn't considered how that would affect my plan.

"What a show, huh, folks?" Nick oozed. "I don't know about you guys, but I've got a boner the size of Madagascar. Do we have some sluts this year or what?"

Woooo. Go, sluts.

"But of course, there can be only one SOTY. And the time has come to name this year's winner, who, as you know, will have the honor of personally servicing every single man on campus, from President Thornhill and the board of directors all the way down to the freshmen."

Shit. What if they chose me? Would I be expected to start right away, or would there be a grace period?

"I know you're about to come in your pants, if you haven't already, so I won't keep you in suspense. Drumroll, please."

Cue drumroll.

"The judges have spoken... and the winner of this year's contest...

Slut of the Year 2001... is... none other than... Miss Melody Thompson!"

Cue deafening applause. Deep, thumping bass from the speakers, vibrating through my body. Melody walked down center to the apron, smiling an Oh-my-god-I-won smile. I was surprised—my money had been on Jill—and relieved that it wasn't me. Nick took something from inside his jacket and lifted it to show the audience: it was a necklace, a silken black thread from which hung a large capital letter S made of silver. The throng was screaming their approval, hooting and howling and stomping their feet as Melody bowed her head and Nick slipped the necklace onto her. The noise was almost too much to bear. It sounded like a menagerie of demons, like the Coloosseum crowd spurred into madness by the sight of blood.

Melody's lips were moving. At last the roar began to subside and I could hear her saying over and over, "I can't believe it, I just can't believe it, oh wow."

"Believe it, baby," said Nick.

"Oh my god, this is such an honor, I can't believe it. I just, wow, I just want to thank the judges and the SBA, thank you so much, you don't know what this means to me, and thank you Dr. Thornhill and all of the faculty and the board of directors and thank you, thank you everyone who was so helpful this year, all my friends and Dean in the counseling department and my trainer Justin, I couldn't have done this without you. I was so shy when I first came here, and I really didn't have much experience, but I have learned so much over the years and I'm so grateful for the education I've received. I know I still have a lot to learn, and I can't wait to get started in my new duties as Slut of the Year. This is so exciting. Thank you for your support, thank you, all of you!"

Tears were running down her face. She was so happy.

"Blah, blah, blah," Nick cut in. "All right, then. You know, I'm glad you can't wait to get started, because I can't wait either. No time like the present, right?"

"Right, Nick," Melody said.

"Shut up. Get on your knees."

I could see her start to say "Yes, Nick," and stop herself just in time. She was a fast learner. She knelt before him and looked up expectantly.

Nick grinned and winked at the audience. "This is my favorite part," he said. Then he looked down at Melody. "Well, what are you waiting for, slut? Unzip me! Let's go!"

I looked away. I didn't need to see this. But I heard it; I heard the zipper come down, and Melody's small gasp.

"Now suck it," Nick growled. "There you go. Tastes good, doesn't it? Makes you salivate. Like a dog. There you go, bitch. Suck that cock. Lube it up good. You know where it's going next, don't you? That's right. Up your little — brown — fuckhole." He was holding the microphone down there, and the sound of Melody's slurping was amplified around the room.

It was disgusting. It was arousing. I felt sick and exhausted and angry. I was ready for this long night to be over.

"That's enough, slut." A soft popping sound, Nick pulling his cock out of her mouth. "Turn around and bend over. Stick that ass of yours way up in the air. Higher. I said higher, bitch."

Smack. Melody whimpered.

"Ladies and gentlemen, as president of the Student Body Association I hereby officially inaugurate this year's SOTY, Miss Melody Thompson."

Involuntarily, I turned to look. Twisted metal in strobelight on the shoulder of the road. His long, thick cock sinking into her ass. A low groan from deep in her throat. Her eyes closed, her mouth open, her voice husky into the microphone: "Fuck. Me. Nnnn." Her face flushed a deep red and she stopped talking. A strand of saliva dangled from her lower lip.

"Aw, here it comes. Here it comes, bitch." Nick's eyes were closed, too, and his pelvis jerked forward as if pulled by a string. "Take it all, you fucking cunt — take it — come for me now —"

And Melody began screaming, convulsing. Her arms gave way and she collapsed to the stage floor while Nick emptied himself into her with a bellow, holding on to her ample buttocks with his hands, thrusting blindly in and out of her hole. Two puppets joined ass to cock, no longer people, merely automatons now. Playthings of flesh and blood, sweat and skin and come.

I don't know why suddenly I thought of my sister, Olivia, who was about to turn nine. My beautiful pixie, full of innocence and fiery spirit. I missed her. I wanted to be back home, back with mom and dad in a safe place far away from here. I wanted not to know the things I knew. I wanted to go to sleep and wake up to find that this was all a terrible dream, fading out of memory. I wanted my old life back. I wanted Olivia's innocence.

But that wasn't going to happen. I could give up or I could keep fighting. Those were my only choices. If I gave up, if I surrendered to my fear, I would become a puppet again like the rest of them. For who knows how long. Maybe forever. If I wanted my life back, I'd have to fight for it.

Applause. The marionettes disengaged and bowed, curtsied. "Thank you all for coming tonight," said the man. "And if you haven't yet, you will be soon. Say good night, Melody."

"Good night, Melody," the woman echoed. Rim shot. The show was over. I turned and began to walk back toward the wings. It was time. Now, with the spotlight gone, in the chaos of the crowd, now I could make my move. Now I could find my ally. And I knew just who it would be.

Phoebe, the drama queen. The intellectual girl who was too smart for all this crap, even under hypnosis. I didn't know her, but then I didn't really know anyone here. It would be good to have someone intelligent on my side.

I saw Phoebe heading for the exit, and I followed her. I'd introduce myself, tell her how much I liked her act, then say that Dean had asked me to give her a present. A consolation prize. I'd put the chamsa around her neck, then—then we'd go for a walk out in the snow, and I'd tell her that my Master liked her too, that he wanted her for a ménage à trois. And maybe by the time we had walked to my room the chamsa would have begun to work; and if not, I'd make some tea and we'd sit and talk some more, and I'd do whatever I had to do until her mind began to clear.

That was the plan, but things didn't turn out that way. Because as Phoebe approached the door to the stairs, a short, barrel-chested man came through it and stood blocking her path. He wore black leather and carried a whip in his left hand. With his right he reached out and grabbed her by the wrist. "You're coming with me," he snarled as he pulled her to him.

"Yes, Master," Phoebe whispered, and together they disappeared down the stairs.

I could only stand and watch them go. Now what? Well, I'd just have to find another candidate. Maybe Jill. I'd—

"What exactly do you think you're doing?" a voice said quietly from behind me. I turned, startled, to find a boy my own age with sandy brown hair and dark eyes, regarding me with a displeased expression. "Have you lost your mind?"

I knew him.

It was my Master. It was Trevor.

Chapter 16

Guys and Dolls

Trevor

I couldn't believe it. After all the weeks spent in practice, memorizing lines and moves, rehearsing endlessly — and the audition for the SBA, which was flawlessly executed — after all that hard work, after coming so close, she blew it. I couldn't believe my eyes.

And I didn't understand. We'd been in perfect sync at the end of the semester. Grades were excellent. Sex was fantastic. Zöe and I were at the center of a thriving social circle; wherever we went, we drew admiring glances. I was strong and smart and popular. The best-looking girl on campus was my personal slave. I'd never been happier in my life.

There was no hint of rebellion in her. There never had been. I made my expectations clear, and she always followed them to the letter. What I wanted from her, she gave me willingly; it didn't matter what it was, or why. I never had a reason to punish her. Use her, yes; that was her purpose in life, to be used by me. And because she understood that, nothing I could do to her would ever be punishment. It would simply be my will, and she would accept it without question. We had the perfect relationship.

I, too, accepted without question this state of affairs. It didn't occur to me to ask myself why a girl like Zöe would do my every bidding, and it wasn't because I was afraid of the answer. I wasn't afraid of anything; there was no reason to be. My self-confidence remained undisturbed — until that night, the night of the SOTY Awards, when everything changed.

"What exactly do you think you're doing?"

Her head snapped around as if I'd given a command; I had surprised her. We stood there, a few feet apart, staring at each other through the backstage darkness.

"Have you lost your mind?" I said quietly. She didn't answer. "What's wrong with you?"

She blinked. Looked at her feet, then up at me. "Um. I don't know. I feel kind of st-strange."

I had gone from being startled (when the lights came up on her and I saw what she was wearing) to bewildered, then frustrated, and finally angry when that stupid cow Melody Thompson took the prize. Now I was furious. I took a step forward. "What did you say?"

I saw the fear in her eyes. "I—I'm sorry. Master."

My fist unclenched. "Damn right you are. I don't care how strange you feel, you'd better not forget how to address me."

"It won't happen again, Master."

"What the hell happened to you?" I hissed. "What? A concussion? How could you forget something so basic? How many times did we practice, and were you *ever* wearing *that?*" I poked a finger into the soft, dark red chenille between her breasts.

"I'm so sorry, Master. I know this is the wrong outfit. I looked in my closet but I couldn't find the—"

"Of course not, you silly cunt. I have it at my place. You were supposed to see me before you came here, remember? I heard you were on the last van up the hill, but that was an hour before showtime. I waited for you. I sat there and waited like a girl and I almost missed the fucking show. God damn it!"

I couldn't hold back. My hand whipped out and slapped her hard across the cheek. It turned her head and she gasped, stepping back involuntarily. Tears sprang to her eyes. "Please," she began, and stopped to take a shuddery breath. "Please hit me again, Master. I have disobeyed you. I am a bad girl and I deserve to be punished."

Like so much that night, it was a first. Oh, I'd slapped her around plenty of times, but not for disobedience. I did it because I liked it, and she liked it because I did. It was never punishment. Now—

"You'll get what's coming to you, don't worry," I said, lowering my hand. I still had an erection from watching the emcee fuck Melody's ass; most everyone did who had a dick, I suspect, except for those who'd already come. Dumb as she was, the bitch sure could take it up the rear. I was looking forward to sampling her myself, but that would have to wait—she had the board of directors to get through first, and the administration and faculty, before she began with the oldest of the male seniors. It would be weeks before freshmen like me had a crack at her. That was all right. She was nothing compared to Zöe.

I took her wrist and pulled her to me. Fear was in her eyes, but she came. "It's time you were reminded of a few things," I said quietly, withdrawing her collar from my pocket. It was a simple one, thick black leather with a silver clasp and ring for the nape of the neck and a silver O at the throat; I'd selected it myself from the catalogue. I placed it around her neck and cinched it, not too tight but tight enough to make her breathe carefully. As usual. Then I took out the leash and attached it, and turned her to walk in front of me. I gave her rump a slap, and we headed for the stairs.

"Trevor Ethan Bailey."

We had turned into the corridor behind the box seats and there was Dean, walking toward us with an easy smile. "Hi, Dean," I said.

"Hey there, Trev," he said as he reached us. "Zöe Willow Martin. Congratulations, you two. I'm not a bit surprised that you were nominated. Zöe, wonderful performance; Trevor, outstanding direction. But you don't look happy." He stopped, scanning our faces with his bright blue eyes. "Anything you'd like to tell me?"

Zöe's eyes were downcast. I knew Dean wanted us to be happy. He was always looking out for everyone, always there to help. I wanted to ask him for advice, but I could tell that he was distracted. Of course he was, on a night like this. So many people to help. And he probably wanted to find Melody and congratulate her personally; he didn't have time to stand around listening to me complain about losing. I'd tell him the whole thing later, in therapy.

"I guess we didn't train hard enough," I said with a tight smile, giving Zöe's leash a sharp tug.

"Lovers' spat, ah?" Dean clapped me on the shoulder. "Don't be too discouraged, you've got three more years to try. It's been a long time since a first-year team took the necklace."

"We'll try harder next time," I said. "Clearly the girl needs more discipline." I grabbed one of her buttocks in my hand and squeezed it hard. She made a small, quiet moan of submission.

"Well, I'm sure you're just the man to give it to her," Dean said with a broad smile. "Don't let me keep you." He gave my shoulder a final clap and moved past us down the hallway.

The snow had been falling since early afternoon and now, in the dark, the quad was submerged, lamps adrift in a slowly gathering sea. Our footsteps on the cleared pathway were the only sound as we walked through the muffled stillness. The air smelled of chimney smoke.

I began undressing as soon as we stepped into the vestibule of Kavner Hall: gloves, scarf, and hat, folded into my coat and handed to Zöe. Winter didn't fuck around up on the mountain; it wasn't like the cool breezes back home in San Diego. People died of hypothermia around here. I always made sure Zöe and I dressed warmly when we went outside. Always.

The hall was warm and silent. Most everyone was still at Fensler Auditorium, screwing and socializing and subtly putting each other down. If we'd stayed, there would have been no shortage of friends and admirers to congratulate us for the nomination, and of course any number of impromptu orgies to which we could have invited ourselves. Phoebe and Jill had their mouths full by now, I had no doubt, and Melody — if she was still conscious — well, she was the Slut of the Year, wasn't she? The board of directors would be so pleased. Her Master would be so proud.

But I wasn't proud, and I didn't feel like celebrating. It would have been one thing to lose because the other girls were better; that I could have tolerated. But to lose because of sloppiness, forgetfulness —

"Just leave it there for now," I said as we entered my room, gesturing toward the end table by the door. "You can put it away later." I shut and locked the door behind us, dropped my keys on the coffee table, and sat down on the couch. Zöe put the pile of clothing where I had indicated and turned to look at me, awaiting instructions.

I realized suddenly how long it had been since I'd eaten. There was no sense in disciplining on an empty stomach. "Get me something to eat," I said. "Something salty. Potato chips and olives, and a ginger ale. Hurry up."

"Yes, Master." She headed for the kitchenette, and I began to unlace my boots. I was hungry and tired, and all I really wanted to do was come, then go to sleep. But it wasn't that easy. First I had to find out what the hell was going on with Zöe, then I had to teach her a lesson. What a shitty way to start the new semester.

I felt a little better with my boots off. I stretched out and put my feet up on the table just as Zöe returned with the snacks. I took a handful of chips and was putting them in my mouth when she sat down on the couch next to me. Uninvited.

I nearly choked. Started to say something, almost slapped her down on reflex, but didn't; instead I held back, ate the chips and took a swallow of ginger ale. And watched her. She was waiting patiently for the next order, unaware of her faux pas. Something was definitely wrong. I took an olive from the plate and popped it in my mouth. "You've got some explaining to do," I said, leaning back.

"Master?"

"Don't play stupid." I swallowed. "I know you're not stupid, Zöe-girl. Tell me what's going on."

"I—I've been bad," she said, hanging her head. "I disobeyed my Master. I wore the wrong clothes tonight and I ruined the performance."

"I know what happened, Zöe, I was there. What I don't know is why you did that. Tell me why."

"I don't know," she said, and her face crumpled as if she was going to cry. "I don't know why it happened, I don't understand how I could have forgotten... I didn't mean to disobey you, Master. It was an accident."

"An accident. You just forgot." I glared at her. "You forgot all about coming here before the show. You wore a fucking bra. By accident."

"Yes, Mas—"

"Shut up. You still have it on, don't you? Well, take it off and give it to me. I'll put a stop to this right now. Yes, the shirt, too. Everything. You're not going anywhere tonight."

I ate some more olives and chips while Zöe undressed. The edge was off my hunger, now; other appetites were coming into focus. When the bra came away, my cock began to swell and straighten itself out. Her breasts were full and taut, tipped with dark rose nipples, and a piece of jewelry hung between them on a necklace of blue beads. Damn, the girl had nice tits. Not that I hadn't seen them before, many times before—not that she hadn't shown them to the entire school less than an hour ago, then fingerfucked herself to climax—but that was performance, and she'd been unreachable then. All I could do was want and wait.

Now we were alone. Outside the door was the rest of the world, Melody Thompson and her entourage, professors and classrooms and snow; inside it was just me and Zöe, with nothing to come between us.

"You forgot," I said again. "It just slipped your mind. And now you're sorry." I reached out and took her left breast in my hand. "It was a simple mistake, and you're very, very sorry, and it will never happen again."

"No, Master."

"And that's all you have to tell me."

"Yes, Master. *Aaah!*" Zöe cried out as I suddenly gripped her breast, hard, like juicing an orange. "Please—"

"Please what?" I snapped, squeezing harder. It had to hurt.

"Please forgive me, Master—please, I beg you!" Tears ran down her cheeks.

"But it isn't just one mistake," I said. "That I could forgive. But you keep making these mistakes. First you forget to meet me before the show. Then you decide to dress in a different outfit, without my approval, and you wear a bra underneath it, which has always been forbidden. Naturally you turn in an embarrassing performance, interrupting the steps we practiced to take off this new costume. Then you forget to call me Master. And now—" I let go of her breast, leaving a white handprint behind on the flushed skin. Her tears were flowing freely. "Now you're making another mistake, and you don't even know what it is, do you?"

Zöe looked terrified.

"No, you don't have a clue." I took a swig of ginger ale. "So it's not that you're being disobedient on purpose. And like I said, Miss Valedictorian, I know you're not stupid. You're not the forgetful type. But you come back from winter break and suddenly all your training is right out the window..."

Her eyes widened and she opened her mouth, as if she'd just re-membered something. "That—that's it," she said. "That's got to be it. Oh, Master—" Her hand went to her throat.

"What? What is it?"

"I *am* stupid. I can't believe I didn't think of this."

I sat forward. "The necklace? What about it?"

"It's this thing on the end of it," she said, lifting it over her head. "It's called a chamsa. My mom gave it to me for Christmas. Supposed-ly it's, like, this ancient talisman that magnifies your power or some-thing. What did she say?" Zöe frowned. "Something like... whoever wears it cannot be tamed, I think that was it."

She handed it to me, and I brought it close to my face to study it.

The chamsa was a piece of dark blue stone, carved into the shape of a hand. In the palm of the hand was an eye.

"I didn't think she was serious." Zöe shook her head. "I mean, I don't believe in magic. But now that I'm thinking about it... ever since I put it on, I've had a hard time remembering how to be obedient. It's like everything you taught me just started seeping out of my brain. I keep trying to be a good girl, but it's so hard, Master. There has been no one to command me for weeks, and this strange feeling in my mind that I'm an independent woman, that I should take charge of my own life—" She broke off suddenly and put her hands over her face. "It's horrible."

"Interesting," I said, rubbing the chamsa with my thumb. "A very interesting story. How long have you been wearing this thing?"

"Ever since Christmas, Master."

"Almost two weeks, then. You haven't taken it off?"

"Only for the performance, Master. When I took off my clothes."

The chamsa twirled on its string of blue beads, and we both watched it. *Whoever wears it cannot be tamed,* I thought. *All wrong for Zöe. But for me...*

"I don't believe in magic, either," I said. "Just because you don't understand something doesn't mean it can't be explained. Maybe this thing really does affect you, and maybe there's a logical explanation for why it works. Or maybe you only think it works. At any rate, it isn't doing you any good. I think you'd better stop wearing it."

Zöe was looking at me, and her expression lifted for the first time since I'd seen her today. "As you wish, Master," she said, wiping her tearstained face. "I—I think I'll feel better if I know it's in your hands."

"Or around my neck," I said, putting it on.

Zöe looked relieved. "Thank you, Master," she said. "I was hoping you would do that." She smiled. "I guess it's your Christmas present now."

The chamsa felt cool and heavy on my chest. I took a deep breath. "Well," I said. "If your disobedience was involuntary, as it seems it was, I don't suppose I can fault you too much. I was prepared to punish you severely, but that was when I thought you had defied me on purpose. Now..."

The truth was, I was glad to be relieved of the duty of punishment. I was exhausted; I'd taken the red-eye from San Diego, waited through two layovers, and arrived at school in the early afternoon, just as the snow had begun to fall. I had too much time on my hands. I ate lunch, got my ticket from Dean in the counseling office, showered and got dressed, unpacked, and spent the next five hours pacing my room like a jaguar in a cage. It was the night of the SOTY Awards, and my Zöe was in the running for Slut of the Year, only she hadn't arrived. I waited, checking my watch again and again, cursing under my breath, until I couldn't wait any longer. I ran to the auditorium, as best I could through the drifts of snow, and watched in shock as my beautiful slave took the stage and danced in the wrong clothing.

Then the rest of it. The loss of the SOTY necklace to that third-rate whore Melody Thompson. It had been a long day, full of bitter disappointments. Exhausting.

"Now," I said, "I have decided to forgive you. You may demonstrate your gratitude."

Zöe's cheeks glowed where she had rubbed away tears. The room was warm. She smiled at me, a shy, seductive smile. "Master," she whispered, and slipped off the couch to kneel on the floor at my feet.

At last. At last she remembered her place.

It was the first dream I'd had in months. I was in the sound booth at the back of my high school auditorium, sitting in front of the control board and looking through the window at the stage. It was faraway at first, too far to see clearly, but it was coming closer. Slowly, unevenly. Floating toward me through empty black space. I didn't know why, but I was afraid of it. I threw switches on the board, trying to find one that would make the stage reverse direction, but nothing worked. All the switches were mislabeled. The stage lights went blue, then pink that deepened into red, then violet. Then they went dark.

I was still afraid, because I knew the stage was still approaching. I tried to stand up, but I couldn't move from my seat. I couldn't even turn my head. Suddenly a searing white light filled the window and was gone again in an instant. Then again. Again. A strobe. My eyes seemed to have no lids, or else they simply wouldn't close; I couldn't look away.

It was the set from *Guys and Dolls*, the play I'd done tech for in my senior year. Downstage left, near the apron, a rowboat was tied to the pilings of a wharf. Someone was crouching in the boat, her back to me.

Her.

Curly hair that I recognized. Rising slowly to her feet. Dread rising inside me like a dark tide, nameless dread because I knew that I knew her and didn't want to know, didn't want to see the face turning toward me. I didn't want to remember. There she was, looking me straight in the eyes through the stutter of light and dark. It was her. My heartbreak. Sarah.

Her face bore an expression of disdain and disappointment. There was no sound, but I could read her lips perfectly. *What have you done?* she said, shaking her head.

I tried to speak, but no sound came out. Desperately I mashed the board with my hands, pushing switches that did nothing to make this vision go away. I was powerless. I could feel myself beginning to weep because I knew that I was guilty, that I had done something terrible even if I couldn't remember what it was.

But then suddenly the strobe was gone, the sound booth was gone, and the girl in front of me wasn't Sarah anymore.

It was Zöe, and she was naked.

Naked and gleaming with oil, wearing only a black collar and a pair of stiletto heels. Hands clasped behind her head. Dark red lipstick. Jutting breasts. Looking straight ahead, blankly, like a mannequin.

"She awaits your command," said a voice from behind me. I was sitting on a soft, comfortable couch, and a man's hand was on my shoulder.

"Begin," I said. As I spoke, I felt my consciousness shift, split into two perspectives. I saw myself from the outside, and at the same time I continued to look through my eyes, watching as Zöe's arms fell and she began to move into a dance.

"You've done well," said the other voice, the man standing behind me. Dean. I couldn't see him clearly, but I knew it was him. I felt a rush of pride at his words. I had done well. My choreography was inventive, and Zöe executed the steps perfectly. I'd seen it a hundred times, and still I could feel my cock stirring and swelling as I watched her caress her breasts, pinch the nipples into stiff peaks.

Yet something was wrong.

Perfect, but wrong.

"She's a natural," I saw myself say with a smirk. "Born to take orders. Arntcha, bitch?"

I felt a twisting in my gut. The words — it was me saying them, my face wearing that contemptuous expression. I looked ugly. I sounded ugly.

"It's like flipping a switch," said the Zöe-doll dancing before me. "Something inside me just surrenders. I have to give in. I have to obey every order."

"They'll be coming in their pants," I said. "She can go all night, you know."

"I know," said Dean.

We watched her stroke her oily skin, stroke and spread and writhe as she recited her script. I was aroused and at the same time disturbed by what was happening. It was sexy, but it didn't seem right.

What have you done?

The words were there in my mind. I felt the pit of my stomach lift, as if I was in an elevator that had begun to fall.

"I want to be your sex toy," Zöe said calmly. "I want to be your fuck doll."

No. It wasn't right. It wasn't right. I was falling, and there were dark waters below me; nothing to hold onto, nothing to break my fall. I watched her bend over, ass upthrust toward me, fingers stroking the wet petals of her cunt. My cock was rigid. I wanted to throw up. I wanted to take her by the hips and impale her, pump her full of come. It wasn't right.

"I have no control."

My heart lurched. The darkness rushed up to swallow me. I closed my eyes and screamed

"STOP!"

and smashed through into waking, up from the pillow into a body slick all over with sweat and yelling wordlessly, not knowing at first where I was.

"Master?"

I gasped for air, my heart raced; the darkness was absolute.

"What is it? What's the matter?"

With a click the bedside lamp came on, and there was light, and I was in bed. Awake. I felt a hand on my arm and turned to see Zöe there beside me, hair disheveled, a look of sleepy concern on her face.

"Master? Are you all right?"

I took a deep breath and let it out shakily. "Oh God. Yes. I'm all right. Just—had a really bad dream."

"Will you... tell me about it?"

I rubbed my face. "Mm. Jesus. I don't know, it was—"

Master.

"It was so real," I said. "You were in it. And Dean was there." I shivered. The sweat on my skin was chilly. "I was making you dance, and he was w—"

She called me Master.

I jerked away from her in sudden panic as my heart gave another lurch and the shiver took hold of my spine.

"Wait a minute. Wait a fucking minute."

She was naked. She was wearing the black leather collar.

The SOTY Awards. Slut of the Year. Zöe's dance.

"Oh my God," I muttered through my fingers. It wasn't a dream. No, and now the memory of the evening came rolling in on me: the girls on stage, Melody Thompson getting ass-fucked by Nick Hallo-

135

way, my anger, my hand slapping Zöe across the face. Then the walk back to my room. Squeezing her breast in my fist. Putting on the necklace. Zöe down on her knees, sucking me off. My hands in her hair. Pulling her toward me, hearing her gag as I came down her throat. Falling into bed with her nestled against me. Then sleep, and visions.

"What did I do? What the hell is going on?" I whispered.

"You're coming to your senses, Trevor," Zöe said.

"What?"

She got up from the bed. "Stay there," she said quietly. "I'll put the coffee on, and we'll talk."

Chapter 17

Empathy

Trevor

I think it's the safety of horror stories that makes them so popular. We like the thrill of being tourists in the country of evil, taking mental snapshots of ugliness from behind the guardrail. We can close the book or stop the video whenever we like, and because we can, we don't—not if it's any good, not if it works. We like to have control over the things that frighten us.

"You're going to think I'm awful for saying this," I said, "but there's a part of me that just wants to go under again. I mean, I know it's terrible. But I don't want to know."

"I don't think you're awful," Zöe said. "I understand. I felt the same way at first."

We were sitting on the couch with cups of coffee that neither of us were drinking. I held mine in my hands even though it was painfully hot. The pain kept it real.

"It's not just that it's terrible, it's also hard to believe," she continued. "You know, things like this just don't happen. Our rational minds aren't conditioned to accept it, so we try to pretend it isn't happening."

"Yeah. Right." I looked over at her. "You're pretty smart."

She smiled and looked away. "Well. I'm not stupid, anyhow."

"Listen," I said. "I mean, there's nothing I can say that won't sound lame, and I know it's not enough by a long shot, but I—"

"It's okay," she said. "You don't have to say it."

"But I want to."

"Look, you were just as much a victim as I was."

"That's not true," I said, putting my cup down on the table. "Nobody raped me. It's not the same."

"It's not the same, but it wasn't your choice."

"No, it wasn't," I said. "But still, it was my body doing it to you. You heard me saying those things. I mean, I wouldn't blame you for hating me."

"I don't hate you," she said. Her eyes were kind. "I don't blame you. It's not your fault."

"I'm sorry," I said, and I was crying: crying for the first time in months. "I'm so sorry, Zöe."

She leaned forward and took me in her arms. "So am I," she whispered.

The dam inside me burst and I wept openly, sobbing onto her shoulder, while we held each other. I was so ashamed. I was ashamed of what I had done, ashamed for wanting to forget what I had learned, ashamed for crying and for wanting to be held by this beautiful, warm, fragrant girl whose forgiveness was almost unbearable. It was too much to contain.

Imagine discovering that for the last two months, everything you have done and said and thought has been controlled by someone else. Imagine finding out that you have had no will of your own, and no idea of your enslavement. Imagine learning this from a girl you raped just a few hours ago, a girl you've been abusing and humiliating for weeks without the slightest flicker of conscience. Imagine that.

It was the chamsa that brought us back to ourselves. Zöe had told me the truth, accented only slightly to spark the interest of the Master I had been. The chamsa didn't magnify one's power so much as protect it, insulate it from the persuasion of outside forces.

Namely, Dean.

"You think he's the only one doing this," I said. It wasn't quite a question.

"Well, he's got help," Zöe said, folding her legs into a half-lotus. "But yeah, I think it's just him. I'm guessing. The way this is set up, from what I can see, it looks like it's one guy amusing himself."

"So nobody else knows what's really going on?"

"I don't think he can afford to let anyone know," she said, sipping her coffee. "Too big a risk. That's probably why he chose this place, because it's so isolated. Up here, it's not that hard to keep security tight as long as you've got the cops working for you. Someone finds out, you just take them in for questioning and..."

"And what?" I asked. "What does he do?"

"I'm not sure," Zöe said slowly. "It's got something to do with his eyes, I think. Did you notice how weird they are?"

"Not really," I said. "They're blue, right?"

"No, I guess you wouldn't pick up on that," she mused, half to herself. "You were already part of the program. I saw him right before the show, and he gave me this look, like... like I don't know, like he was telling me someth—"

She stopped suddenly, the cup halfway to her lips.

"What is it?" I asked.

"That's it," she said excitedly. "That's why I—listen, can you remember what happened before the winter break? Like, details of things, like what you did with me? Do you have memories?"

I had memories. I didn't want them, but they were there. Zöe on her hands and knees on a tabletop in Dean's office, naked. A long black dildo in my hand, probing the depths of her—her cunt, that was the word I used, and my cock easing slowly into her ass. That was the day we first met. I slapped her face and made her cry and she told me she liked it, asked me to hit her again.

"Sure," I said.

"Do you remember what classes you're taking?"

"Well—yeah."

"See, and I don't," she said. "I mean, I remember basic things like my room number and what hall I live in, but I can't remember being in a classroom. Not really. It's like, I know that I went to classes, but the specifics aren't there. Same thing with you. I know we've been, uh, going steady, but I can't remember meeting you. I didn't even know your name until they announced it at the show. All I could remember were these dreams I had when I was wearing the chamsa."

"Like the one I had."

"Right. Only they're not really dreams, of course. I'll bet you saw Dean yesterday, didn't you?"

"Uh huh. I went to his office to get my ticket."

"That's it," she said again. "Listen, here's what I think happened: before we all went home for the holidays, Dean made sure we'd forget the details of our lives here. Just in case anyone asked us what school was like, he made sure we wouldn't have much to tell them."

"Why not just make us lie?" I asked.

"I don't know." Zöe's forehead wrinkled. "That's a good question. Maybe it's easier to take memories away than to add fake ones."

"Or maybe it was just safer," I suggested. "If you don't lie, you don't have to keep track of your story."

"Good point," she said. "Anyway, he didn't erase our memories, he just buried them. Then when we came back, he brought them up to the surface again. That's what all this crap with the tickets was about. You couldn't get into the auditorium without a ticket, and you couldn't get a ticket without seeing Dean."

"Reestablishing security."

"Right. Only I was wearing the chamsa when I saw Dean, so his influence had no effect on me. That's why I still can't remember very much about last semester. I never got reprogrammed."

"Okay," I said. "That makes sense. But why was I expecting you to come here before the show? If you didn't remember that I was your, uh—"

"My Master," she said. "It's all right, you can say it."

"Uh, yeah, okay. Then how were you supposed to know—"

"Mmm. I see what you're saying. Oh! My flight was delayed, that's why. That wasn't part of the plan. I got here late, so I didn't get a chance to see Dean until the last minute."

I nodded. I took a swallow of my coffee, which had gone lukewarm. Suddenly I couldn't think of anything to say. I was embarrassed again, and very tired. It was four in the morning.

"So," Zöe said.

I rubbed my face. "So. What now?"

"Exactly. Well." She yawned. "Mmn. I had some time to think about it during the show, after I did my little dance." A dismissive flutter of fingers. "I was going to try to handle this myself, but there's just no way to do it alone. It's going to be hard enough with two of us."

"I was wondering about that," I said. "Why did you pick me?"

"You weren't my first choice," she said. "No offense. I was going to slip the chamsa onto one of the other girls, but she got taken away before I had a chance to talk to her. Actually, it's a good thing that didn't work out. It would have been way too suspicious, two girls together without a guy. We'd've been missed right away. But no one's going to think twice if you and I go off by ourselves. It's the perfect cover."

"But how did you know?" I asked. "About me, I mean."

"How did I know what?"

"Um. Well, you got me to put on the chamsa. And I had a bad dream and woke up, and then you told me this weird story, and... what I mean is, how did you know I wouldn't just—" I stopped. I was blushing. "Look, I'm not a total dick, but I know a lot of guys who are. This whole setup—it's wrong, okay, obviously it's wrong, but it's basically every teenage boy's wet dream. What's to stop me from turning you in and going back to, uh—"

"To fucking my brains out?" Zöe finished for me.

I couldn't meet her eyes.

"That's a good question, Trevor," she said softly. "I can't answer it for you. All I can say is that I hope you won't. I don't like being brainwashed, and I have to take a risk and hope that you don't, either."

"No," I whispered. My cheeks were hot.

"I have to trust you," she said.

I couldn't speak. I felt her hand touch my chin and gently lift it until I was looking at her.

"We barely know each other," she said, a slight smile playing on her lips. "It's funny. Well, it's not funny, but. You know. Considering the things we've done together for the last, what, eight weeks? Ten?"

"Can I just say something?" I managed.

"And I still don't have any idea what kind of person you are. Shit, I barely know what kind of person I am. I've been kind of a stranger lately."

"You can trust me," I said. "I mean. I won't, uh—"

"I didn't even know you were my boyfriend until last night."

"Can I just say something?"

"Uh huh," she said, smiling. "Go ahead."

"Look, don't take this the wrong way," I began.

"No, not at all."

I started to speak again and stalled. I took a deep breath. "I guess I can't get any more embarrassed than I already am," I said. "The thing is, obviously you've heard this before, but you're really, really, uh, beautiful. Amazingly incredibly beautiful. It's a little weird that I'm even talking to someone like you. Then this whole thing with, you know, the whole sex thing — it's — " I stalled again. I felt myself getting stupider by the second. "Okay, I guess what I'm trying to say is that I like you and I'm, uh, I'm really attracted to you, and I hope that doesn't creep you out. I'm on your side. Just so you know."

I shut up then. Zöe's hand had left my chin and was stroking my cheek, slowly and gently. She was still smiling, looking at me.

"You know what?" she said. "I think I'd like to kiss you now."

I had no comment. It was all I could do just to keep breathing. Zöe leaned closer, and everything in me was doing a crazy dance of anticipation, dread, guilt and horniness.

Then her lips were touching mine.

I felt unreal. I would have floated away if it hadn't been for the touch of our lips, the tether holding me down to earth. Something worth staying for. Soft electricity.

"That was nice," she breathed.

"Yeah," I said. "You could do it again."

She did.

"It's nice to meet you, Trevor," she said a moment later.

"Delighted, I'm sure," I said, and we both started laughing, and kissed a few more times, then Zöe fell back against the couch and exhaled noisily.

"Well, that broke the ice, anyway," she said.

"Wow," I said.

"Yeah. You're a good kisser."

"Am I? Thank you. I didn't know that."

"It's true. What, don't tell me I'm your first."

"No," I said.

"Well, then."

"No, but she..."

She. Suddenly the trippy sense of elation was gone, and I was left with the old ache of Sarah.

"What is it?"

"She just never told me that, is all," I finished.

Zöe turned toward me, resting her head on her arm. "Really?"

"Really."

"Then she didn't deserve you," Zöe said quietly.

I felt an icy tug in the pit of my stomach, and almost started crying again. I remembered how it had been in the fall, when I was crying all the time. When I wore the mask of tears. How exhausting it was to hurt so much, and to hate myself so much, but I couldn't make it stop. I couldn't fix the leak in my heart that was driving me mad, keeping me awake all night with its dripping. Water torture. Sarah's ghost.

And Dean fixed that for me. Fixed it right up and sealed away the memory of her so I didn't have to cry anymore, so there was nothing to cry about. Gave me a different girl, one who'd always adore me and never change. Took away the part of me that cared how other people felt. My empathy.

"I'm pretty high-maintenance, as guys go," I said. "I get, um, emotionally involved. I think I kind of wore her out."

Zöe raised her eyebrows. "Yeah, well, those are the kind of guys I go for," she said, yawning and rolling her shoulders back. "The basket cases. They tend to be more interesting than the strong, silent types. I'm not one of those chicks who use guys as security blankets, you know, so they don't have to face shit for themselves? Ugh, I hate that."

"So you've had a lot of boyfriends, then."

"I don't know," she said. "What's a lot? I've had a lot of guys come on to me, based on the way I look, but I'm pretty good at brushing them off. Serious boyfriends, let's see... five, not counting you."

I smiled ruefully. "Yeah, I guess you can't really count me."

"Not in a serious way, no," Zöe said, and she reached out to stroke my arm lightly with her fingertips. "But it's nothing personal. You know that, right? Actually—" She exhaled through her nose, a little snort of realization. "That's the problem. With all of this. It's impersonal. It's like a big porn video where everyone's just fucking because it's their job."

"Only they're not getting paid," I put in.

"Right. And they don't have a choice. It's just so... God! It's just so lame."

I laughed. We both did. It was a relief.

"So what are we going to do about it?" I asked her.

"Right," she said again. "I was about to tell you my big plan when we, um, kind of got sidetracked."

"Well, you have my full attention now."

"That's good. Okay. So the first thing I realized is that ordinary methods aren't going to work. I mean, normally in this kind of situation—not that there is this kind of situation, really, at least not that I've ever heard of—but you know, if I was faced with a sexual predator, and that's basically what Dean is, normally I would start by telling my mom and dad, and then I'd call the police."

"But you think he's got the police under his, his spell."

"Or whatever it is. Yeah. Wouldn't you, if you were him?"

"Yeah, that makes sense. But why not call your folks? You don't think they'd believe you?"

"It's not that. I just think we can't be too paranoid. If it was that easy, this whole setup wouldn't last very long. There's got to be really tight security, and I'm willing to bet that includes the phones. How hard would it be to have the lines tapped?"

"So someone makes a long distance call—"

"And maybe it never goes through, or maybe it trips an alarm and the operator starts listening in, and if you say anything suspicious the line goes dead."

"By which time the goon squad is on the way to your room."

"Exactly. So no phones."

"What, then?"

"We have to start by taking him out of the picture," Zöe said. "As long as he's out there, he can screw up whatever plans we make. We deal with him first, then we make our getaway."

"So, what, we kidnap him?"

"I think we have to."

"And stick him in the trunk and drive away? That's not going to work," I said. "If he's got the phones tapped, he'll have the roads watched, too. We'll get pulled over."

"Okay, so we don't put him in the trunk. We have him sitting up front with a knife in his back, and if we get stopped we make him tell the cops that everything's fine."

"Still seems pretty risky," I said. "We don't know how he does this... thing. You said you thought it was his eyes. Maybe he's telepathic. He could say one thing and think another."

"Then we'll blindfold him."

"Oh, that's not suspicious."

"All right, what do you suggest?" Zöe snapped.

"I'm sorry, I didn't mean to be sarcastic—"

"No, you're right," she said, waving her hand. "It wouldn't work. I'm sorry, I'm just tired. Seriously, though, what do you suggest?"

"Well," I said, "I'm just thinking out loud here. If we think he hypnotizes people with his eyes, then we definitely have to blindfold him or find some way of keeping his eyes closed. Right? Otherwise he's too dangerous. So that's the first thing. Second thing is, like you said, he's probably got security up the wazoo. And they'll all do whatever he says. So if we want to get out of here without being stopped, we have to make them think that Dean wants it that way."

"How?"

"I don't know."

We sat in silence for a while, mulling over the problem. Then Zöe stretched and stood up. "I need more caffeine. You?"

"Okay," I said. She took our cups and walked over to the kitchenette. I watched her blankly. The few hours of sleep I'd caught had only whetted the edge of my exhaustion, which made the already surreal situation in which I found myself just that much weirder. I could barely understand what was happening, let alone make plans. What a bad fucking dream. I wanted to go to sleep, like my body was screaming for me to do, so that I could wake up and forget all about this.

Zöe was saying something. I turned my head. "Huh?"

"We go see him in his office," she repeated, pouring coffee. "You know, for a counseling session. It'll be just the three of us. We knock him out, tie him up and blindfold him. When he comes to, we call the cops and make him say that he's sending us out on an errand to the next town."

I thought about that while she came back, setting my cup down on the table next to me. I picked it up and took a sip. "Where do we get the car?" I asked.

"Hmm. We use his? If he has a car."

"He probably doesn't."

"Okay, so we get him to call someone who does. That's not the part I'm worried about." She gulped her coffee. "The part I'm worried about is what happens after we get away."

"Why?"

"Because then we've got two big problems. Number one, how are we going to make anyone believe us? And number two, assuming we get someone to believe us, how are they or we going to fix this situation without making it worse?"

I groaned. "My brain hurts. I don't have any answers."

"We need evidence," she said. "Something on tape. Pictures."

"I'm falling asleep, Zöe."

"We need supplies."

"We need sleep."

"How about a shower instead?"

I perked up a little. "Together?"

"Why not?" She smiled. "If it keeps you awake."

"It might help," I said. "Who knows. Maybe I'll get my second wind."

"It just isn't a good idea to sleep right now. It's already, like, a quarter to five, and we have to be ready to go by the time classes start. The longer we wait, the more dangerous it's going to be."

"Yeah, all right."

"Trevor," she said, putting a hand on my knee, "I know this is a lot to take on. I'm sorry if I'm moving too fast. It's just... I'm really scared, but I'm also really mad, and I don't want to go back to the way I was before." She took a deep breath. "I—I'm asking a lot of you because I don't have a choice. It has to happen now, and you're the only one who can help me do it."

I'd been looking at her all night, having this impossible conversation with her. I wasn't seeing anything new. But somehow I was mesmerized as she spoke, as if I had suddenly remembered how to see, or how to respond to what I saw. Zöe was amazing to behold. Such a stupid, inadequate word, beautiful; so unoriginal, so misused. She was beautiful beyond words.

And she was real.

And I was falling in love.
"I need you, Trevor. I need your help."
"There it is," I said.
"What?"
"My second wind."

Chapter 18

At the Gates

Trevor

The dawn was drowned in clouds, a sullen, hungover light that gave no shadow. Our mouths made clouds of their own that hung in the air for a second, then vanished.

The silence was eerie. Under our feet the snow squeaked and crunched, and that was the only sound. It was early, much too early to be up and about after last night's revelries, but it couldn't be helped; we had to risk it. We needed supplies from town, and the fewer witnesses, the better.

Zöe wore a calf-length black rabbit coat, and underneath it the black vinyl bodysuit that was her Master's favorite. We'd found them both in her closet, along with a pair of four-inch stiletto heels. Black, of course, like her suede arm-length gloves, the thick leather collar around her neck, and the leash that I held loosely in my hand. I walked five paces ahead, moving slowly, keeping my eyes open for signs of life. The chamsa lay cool against my chest.

"How are you doing?" I muttered.

"These are the stupidest shoes in the history of the world," she muttered back. "Whoever designed high heels should be drawn and quartered. My feet are freezing."

"At least the coat's warm."

"Yeah, the coat I like," she said. "Not that I'd ever wear fur under normal circumstances, but... I can definitely see the appeal."

We came around the corner of the science wing and started up the main road toward the front gates. Just past the gates, the road began to slope down and around the side of the mountain, making a series of switchbacks before it reached the valley floor and headed out to the town of Ferngrove.

"Heads up," I said. The light in the gatehouse was on, and through the window I could see a guard reading a book. As I watched, he looked up and caught my eye. "We're on."

"Remember, you're doing all the talking," Zöe said. "I can't help you now."

"Shut up, bitch," I snapped.

"Yes, Master," she said quietly.

The door to the gatehouse opened and the guard stepped out, blowing on his hands as we approached him. "Morning," he called. His nametag said GUS.

"Good morning," I responded coolly, channeling my inner sadist. I could do this. No problem.

"Where you folks headed?"

"Where does it look like we're headed?" I said. "Down the hill."

"Mind if I ask why?"

"Tell him, slut," I growled, and pulled on the leash. "Tell him why we're going to town."

"I—I've been bad," Zöe said in a guilty little-girl voice. "I've been very bad and—and Master needs to punish me. We need some things from the general store."

"Uh huh." The guard shifted his feet. "Well, I haven't been notified of any trips. Why aren't you going in the van?"

Van?

"It's cold out, you know."

"Exactly," I said. "This is punishment. It's not a trip. It's not an outing. My slave has displeased me, and now she must suffer."

Behind me, Zöe let out a little whimper.

"Yeah, well, like I said, I haven't been notified. Did you request clearance from counseling?"

"Look, Gus," I said icily, taking a step nearer. "I'm in a really bad mood right now, so I want you to listen carefully. This little slut has *fucked up*. She has embarrassed me in front of the entire school, and I have no desire to repeat the experience. That is why we are making this little excursion before breakfast, before classes, without a van and without a fucking passport. We are simply going to the store to pick up some duct tape and a few other essentials, after which we will return to my room and this stupid whore will be taught a lesson she'll never forget." I yanked the leash, and Zöe whimpered again, tottering forward in her heels. "Are you getting the picture, Gus?"

"Yeah, I get the picture okay," Gus leered over my shoulder. "Sounds like fun." His smile disappeared abruptly. "But I still got a job to do. Doesn't matter what, I can't let anyone through without clearance. I'm gonna have to call it in."

I hesitated. What now? Gus took a walkie-talkie from his belt, and in a flash I saw the holstered gun beside it. I squelched the urge to turn and look at Zöe for help. Should we run? Tackle him? Or keep bluffing?

"Control, this is 82, over," Gus said.

"Go ahead, 82," the receiver squawked.

"Got two kids here requesting individual 220. No clearance. Please advise, over."

There was a pause. I arranged a scowl on my face. Then the receiver crackled. "You have their names?"

Gus looked crestfallen, but only for a split second. "Full names, please," he said, looking at a spot just over my head.

I had to think fast. "Look, forget it," I said. "If I'd known it would be such a hassle, we wouldn't have come here. Tell your boss it's a false alarm. Come on, slut." I turned to go, tugging the leash.

"Hold on, there," he said. I stopped. Zöe and I glanced at each other. "I still need your names." She gave an almost imperceptible nod, and I turned back.

"Trevor Bailey," I said. "And Zöe Martin."

Gus repeated our names into the mike and we stood waiting for a response. My mind was racing. How defiant was I expected to be? How far could we push it before our cover was blown? Could I grab the gun away—and if I could, then what? No car in sight. No way to escape on foot. I fought back the rise of panic, and with my free hand I felt for the reassuring lump of the chamsa under my shirt. At least we still had this.

"Okay," said the receiver. "Big D's in the loop. Word is to keep them there and he'll be out in a minute to authorize."

"Copy that," Gus said, and stuck the walkie-talkie back on his belt. "We just need to hang tight for a few minutes," he informed us, as if we hadn't already heard. "We'll get this thing straightened out and you folks can be on your way." I gave a curt nod, which he returned, and we fell silent again.

The best-case scenario, I figured, would be that "Big D" bought our story and okayed our trip to town. Then we'd go get the duct tape, the tape recorder and the knife—assuming we could find all those things in Ferngrove—and we'd proceed to the counseling session as planned. If he believed us but didn't let us down the mountain, we'd have to improvise. Maybe we didn't need the tape; maybe he had restraints in his office. And a weapon. We had to find a weapon somehow, or how would we ever persuade him to do what we wanted?

And something else: assuming we found a weapon, what if he called our bluff and made us use it? What if we had to hurt him?

Or kill him?

The sound of an engine cut through the stillness. A Jeep was coming up the road toward us, and I felt a chill that had nothing to do with the cold. It was him. All my questions were about to be answered, one way or another.

Breathe, I told myself from a place inside that was strangely calm. *You're doing fine. Just remember to breathe. You are strong and confident. You are a Master. You have nothing to worry about.*

The Jeep pulled to a stop about ten yards away and I saw him through the windshield, sitting on the passenger side. Dark hair flecked with salt and graying at the temples. Eyes a cold blue that held me transfixed as he opened the door and stepped out into the snow, the driver coming around the other side to join him. I didn't recognize the driver, but he wasn't the one who mattered. It was clear who mattered. There was only one place to look now.

Cold, cold blue. Winter sky with nothing behind it but the absolute zero of outer space.

"Gordon Augustus Heineman," Dean said. "Trevor Ethan Bailey. Zöe Willow Martin. Good morning, Trevor."

"Hey, Dean," I said, remembering to breathe.

"I'm surprised to see you here," he said. "Rough night, was it?"

"You could say that, yeah."

"What's this I hear about walking to town?"

"We just need some supplies," I said. "A few things for training. Zöe's been very stubborn, so —"

"Stubborn?" Dean's eyebrows lifted. "Our little Zöe?" His gaze shifted to her. "That's most unusual. I don't recall any stubbornness in the past. What seems to be the problem?"

"I don't know," she whispered, eyes downcast. "I'm so ashamed that I've displeased my Master."

"Look at me, Zöe," Dean said kindly, with a warm smile.

Shit.

"Master has forbidden me to look at anyone," she murmured. "I'm not worthy. Until I have suffered —"

"Until you suffer and repent," I snarled, "you're not worthy to lick his shoes." *Good save.* "We're going to set this thing straight if it takes all day. We just need some duct tape and —"

"That won't be necessary." Dean turned his smile on me, and despite the alarm bells going off inside, it was easy to smile back. "I think if we all head back to my office, where it's warm, we'll be able to sort everything out. What do you think, Trevor?"

Shit shit shit. A direct question. Dean had made a suggestion, and he was asking for my opinion. There was only one thing I could say.

"I think that's a good idea, Dean," I said. "Let's do that instead."

Plan B.

"You see? There's nothing to worry about. I'm sure once we all have a chance to talk, you'll both be feeling right as rain. In fact, Trevor, you don't mind if Zöe looks at me right now — do you?"

"No, I think that would be okay," I said. Gus was standing a few feet away. I could see the gun in his holster. He wasn't paying much attention to it. Maybe —

"Zöe Willow Martin," Dean intoned. "Look at me."

"Yes, Dean," she said quietly. Her face lifted to his.

"That's better," he said. "Much better. You've got pretty eyes."

"Thank you, Dean."

"It's cold out here," I said. "Let's get back to your office."

"Thank you for your help, Gus," Dean said.

"No problem, Dean," he said. "I'm gonna head back inside myself, if you don't mind, before I freeze my nuts off."

"I don't mind." Dean was still looking at Zöe. "Keep up the good work." Gus walked over to the gatehouse, opened the door, and was gone.

No matter. We'd all just head back to the office for a quiet little session. I'd keep my eyes open for heavy blunt objects... and somehow, before the truth came out, I'd find a way to smash old blue eyes over the head. Hard. Hard enough to do the job.

"You're done with all that stubbornness, aren't you, Zöe?"

"Yes, Dean."

"I think if you look deep inside yourself, you'll find that you understand the cause of your disobedience."

"Let's *go*," I said.

"Do you feel ready to speak honestly about it?"

"Yes, Dean."

"So what seems to be the problem?"

He couldn't wait. The bastard just couldn't wait, and now —

"The problem is that I know what you've been doing," Zöe said. "I know the truth about what's happening here. I found a way to break the hold you have on me."

Now we were fucked. Now it was all over.

"I see," Dean said calmly, his eyes flashing. You could cut yourself on that blue. "And what might that way be?"

"It's called a chamsa," Zöe said flatly. No emotion, no expression at all. "Trevor's wearing it right now."

The instant that she said it, I bolted for the Jeep, knocking the driver out of the way. I yanked the door open, slammed it shut behind me — thank God, the key was in the ignition — turned the key, and the adrenalin blaring like sirens through the wires and arteries inside me wound to a freakishly high pitch as the windshield shattered — gun, the driver had a gun — and I ducked low in the seat, jerking the stick into reverse and flooring the gas pedal as I heard a voice, Dean's voice, yelling *the tires, shoot the tires*. I hit the brakes and turned the wheel, hearing the crack of shots, feeling the Jeep slide into the turn as I jammed the stick back up to drive and floored it again. I raised my head and saw ahead of me a long field of white, a lowering gray sky, and where they met in the distance, a row of buildings.

I didn't know where I was going. I didn't know what to do. And now from all around me I heard the rising scream of sirens, real sirens, drowning out the noise in my blood.

Chapter 19
The Smell of Curry

Dean

I've seen a lot of things in my time.

In the summer of 1981 I was riding the tube beneath London on my way back to a hotel, after a day of sightseeing around Canterbury, when I encountered Mira Nagaraj. She was laughing with another girl, a friend of hers, and the laugh was what caught my attention at first: a feathery ululation, a bright cascade of glottal stops like a rice curtain in the wind. I turned around and caught the smell of her, the clove-scented musk of her body, at the same time I saw how strikingly beautiful she was. Dark hair and eyes, dazzling white teeth as she smiled, and the pinpoint glitter of a rhinestone in the lobe of her right nostril.

I was enchanted. Mira's laugh was older than she was; it had a gentility that belied her obvious youth and far outclassed the discordant whinny of her much less attractive friend. Even her speech was unusually mature, not in vocabulary but in tone. I wondered what she sounded like when she was coming, and I resolved to find out.

Not in the tube, of course; too many people crammed in cheek by jowl around us. Even my standard induction might arouse suspicion, or at least curiosity. I was always more careful than I needed to be, for the challenge of it as much as for safety's sake. The days of sloppy work were far behind me.

So I waited until the girls disembarked at Temple Station and followed them at a discreet distance, through the underground and up a long flight of stairs into the warm purple evening. If you know what you're doing, it is remarkably easy to follow people without being observed. Unless a person already has reason to believe they're being watched, they generally don't look behind them, especially in a city. Try it sometime. You'll see.

I caught up with them at Blackfriars Bridge. "Excuse me," I said. "Don't I know you?"

Eye contact. That's all it took. That's all it ever takes. Humans are such visual creatures; sight is our primary means of interaction with the world around us, the way we process the vast majority of the information that comes our way. Seeing is believing, and the rest is guesswork.

Mira was no exception. "No, I don't think so," she said, but already she was beginning to feel how pleasant it was to be in my presence. My record was two seconds. Mira took about six.

"What's your name?" I asked her.

"Mira Nagaraj," she said. "And this is my friend, Pris."

"Priscilla Staples," said her friend. "Pleased to make your—"

"Priscilla Staples," I repeated, shaking her hand. "Charles Andrews. I'm sorry to keep you. You were just about to leave, weren't you?"

"Well, no... I mean, I didn't think I was... it's... see, this is... girl's night..." Priscilla was struggling to find the right words. "But Mira, I'm sorry, luv, I meant to tell you, it's just I've got so much to get done at home and—well—do you mind terribly?"

"No, that's all right, Pris," Mira said, looking at me. "I understand. Next weekend, right?"

"Absolutely," Priscilla said. "Anyway, I don't want to be a third wheel now you've got a fella. I'll expect a full report, though, I'm warning you!"

"Bye, Pris," Mira said, rolling her eyes.

"Call me. Pleasure meeting you, *Charles*." She squeezed Mira's shoulder and walked away down the path.

"Sorry about her," Mira said in her delightful accent. "She's all right, she just doesn't know when to shut it."

"She doesn't matter right now," I said. "I'm much more interested in you, Mira Nagaraj."

Mira blushed and didn't know what to say.

"You must think me very rude," I continued. "A strange man coming up to you on the street. Although I expect you get a lot of it, looking the way you do."

"Well," she managed, but was too flattered and embarrassed to go on.

"It's just that your beauty is quite remarkable, and I know I would always have regretted it if I hadn't introduced myself."

"Thank you, Charles," Mira said. She found it hard to meet my eyes, but it wasn't really necessary any longer. I'd made contact.

"So, have you actually got a fella?" I asked.

"No — well, there's Jalal, this bloke I've been seeing, but it's not serious. Not really." She flashed a quick, nervous smile at me. "Just for laughs, you know."

"You live alone, then."

"Nah, with the family. Up North Finchley in a flat. I can show you — I mean, if you're interested."

"What a wonderful idea," I said mildly. "Let's take a cab."

I was rolling high from a score near Piccadilly that morning, an ad man who wore Bill Blass and Rolex and a ridiculous pompadour. He was one of the easy takes, the yes-men who make their living by greasing palms and flattering their superiors. I touched him for nearly £1,000 and he thanked me for it, invited me to lunch. Which I politely declined. But I was happy to spend his money.

I'd been tipping handsomely all day, and the cabbie was no exception. His smile of surprise and gratitude was genuine, since I'd left his mind undisturbed, and I got a special satisfaction from that. Playing Robin Hood was one of my more virtuous hobbies. Mira barely noticed, as I'd been stroking her thigh the whole way there and planting seeds of suggestion in her subconscious. She was well-primed when the cab pulled up in front of her building.

The street was a row of red brick tenements, too tidy to qualify as a slum but clearly a rung or two below middle class. Mira led the way up the front steps and into the foyer, then up three flights of stairs to the front door of her flat. She turned the key and we went in.

The first thing I saw was a man with a thick black mustache and a stocky build, sitting on a couch with his stockinged feet propped up on a coffee table. His eyes were fixed on a television set next to the door. He glanced up as we came in.

"What are you doing home so early?" he said to Mira. "And who is this?"

"Dad—" she began, but I cut in, moving forward with my hand extended.

"Charles Andrews," I said. "Pleased to meet you, sir."

You will tell me your name.

"Asher Nagaraj. To what do I owe—"

"It's nothing, Asher Nagaraj," I said. "Really nothing to worry about. I'm going to spend some time with your daughter, but it has nothing at all to do with you. Don't allow us to distract you from what you're watching."

"A pleasure to meet you, Mr. Andrews. I hope you don't mind, I'm just going to finish this programme."

That took care of him.

We found Mira's mother in the kitchen, stirring a pan of pungent curry. I introduced myself and told her not to give my presence in her house another thought. I also suggested, wordlessly, that she might feel moved to make herself sexually available to her husband later that evening. A tip of the hat to old Asher, in return for the loan of his lovely daughter.

Now that the parents were under control, I was inclined to dispense with further pleasantries. It had been nearly twenty-four hours since I'd last had sex, and my ever-hungry libido was straining at its leash. At first I prompted Mira to invite me on a tour of the flat, leading naturally to her room, but almost immediately I changed my mind. While fucking teenage girls in their pink, fragrant bedrooms was an experience I enjoyed on a fairly regular basis, there was also something very pleasurable about fucking them in the presence of their families.

"No," I said. "I don't give a shit what your home looks like, quite frankly. The only thing I'm interested in is what you sound like when you come. Have you ever had sex, Mira?"

I had set the level of her awareness rather high, which allowed for a greater degree of anxiety. I'd already established arousal, but also had maintained the pretext of respectability—the overlay of social conditioning that dictates what kind of behavior we expect from ourselves and others. Mira was attracted to me, desperately so, but she felt compelled to sublimate her responses because of who and where she was.

"Well? Have you?" This was the first time I had been so blunt in my speech. Mira shot a glance at the couch where her father reclined. "Answer me." No mental nudging this time. Freestyle.

"I — no, of course not."

"Never? Not even with this, what was his name, Jalal?"

"Please — it's not like that. I'm a good girl."

"I'm sure you are," I said. "Be a good girl now and take off your clothes."

"My bedroom is just down the — "

"Did you hear what I said?"

"But — my father — "

"Do it."

"Yes, Charles," Mira whispered.

She turned away from me, shyly, slipping off her shoes and lifting her shirt over her head. Her bra was lavender and clasped in the back. She reached behind to undo it.

"Allow me," I said. With one hand I unhooked the clasp. Hungry. Impatient. I flipped away the straps with my index finger and took her by the arm, turning her around. Put my hand on her soft, warm belly and pushed her back against the wall.

"I can't do this," she said in a shaky voice, crossing her arms over her chest. "Please don't make me do this."

She wanted it. She wanted me so much it hurt. It was so hard to hold back, to do what she felt she had to do.

"Little slut," I murmured. "You'll do what I tell you, and you'll like it." Not a command. Just ordinary, run-of-the-mill persuasion. The confidence I'd summoned from a decade of having everything — absolutely everything — go my way. "Now drop your arms."

Her lips were trembling. Her eyes were fixed on me in fear and wonder and desire. She dropped her arms, and the bra came away from two lovely chai-colored breasts with dark brown nipples, falling to the floor.

"That's better," I said, caressing her smooth skin. She shuddered when my fingers trailed over the hard little nipple. I was just leaning forward to take it in my mouth when someone spoke from behind me.

"What on earth do you think you are doing, sir?"

I spun around. In the hallway stood an old woman with gray hair, very short, dressed in a sari and what looked like twenty or thirty bead necklaces. Her head was cocked a little to one side, and she regarded me with a strange, motionless stare.

My heart was hammering at my ribs. She had no shoes on. I hadn't heard her coming.

"Who are you?" she asked sharply.

I found my tongue. "Charles Andrews," I said. "And your name is —"

"What are you doing in my home?"

"Just visiting a friend," I said, motioning to Mira. "I'm sorry. I didn't catch your name."

You will tell me your name.

"This is not right," the woman said, shaking her head. "Something is not right here. You are not being honest with me."

"I don't know what you mean," I said. "There's nothing to worry about. Everything is perfectly normal. In fact, you can forget all about this and go back to — to wherever you just came from. There is —"

"You are not being honest with me," she said again in her thick Indian accent. "This is all wrong."

It was wrong. I didn't understand what was happening. This was the first time in more than ten years that anyone had failed to respond to my suggestions.

"Mira Nagaraj," I said, turning back to her. She had crossed her arms again, covering those luscious breasts. "Who is this?"

"That's my auntie," she said.

"Her name, her full name," I snapped impatiently.

"Nandita Singh."

"Nandita Singh," I said, looking straight at the old woman. "You are very tired now and you want to take a nap. You will forget everything you have seen here. You have already —"

But as I said it I suddenly knew, even before the woman opened her mouth and snapped: "I haven't seen anything, you fool. I'm blind."

Of course. That was it.

"And I'm not tired in the least. Now for the last time, why are you here and what are you doing with my goddaughter?"

She couldn't see me. My eyes had no effect on her, and without them my words were just ordinary language, powerless. I couldn't control her.

"I told you, I'm just visiting," I said.

"I'm blind, young man, not deaf. I heard what you were saying a moment ago. Calling my goddaughter names."

"It's all right, auntie," Mira said, with a little help from me. "We're just playing. Please don't worry, I'm fine."

Nandita pursed her lips and frowned. "Taking off your clothes in the drawing room is not fine, child. This man is taking advantage of you." She turned her head slightly toward me. "But I will not allow it. Do you hear me? I will not allow it."

"Suppertime," Mrs. Nagaraj sang from the kitchen.

"I think you had better go, Mr. Andrews," the old woman said quietly.

My erection had wilted. I was suddenly aware of how hot and stuffy it was in the flat, how overpowering the aroma of curry and boiled cauliflower had become. I felt a sickening wave of revulsion pass through me, and thought for a moment that I was going to vomit.

She was just an old blind woman, five feet tall with bones like twigs and skin like paper that had been crumpled and smoothed out again. I could have snapped her neck as easy as pie if she'd gone for the phone. I could have fucked Mira right there in front of her and the parents, and there wouldn't have been a goddamned thing she could have done to stop me. Not a thing. I could have stayed.

Could have. But didn't. Instead I muttered something and stumbled through the front room and out the door, down three flights of stairs clutching at the railing, stomach heaving, vision blurring with sudden, inexplicable tears. I never again saw Mira Nagaraj or her family.

In my time I've been to six continents and 82 countries, traveling by yacht, balloon, private jet and other more conventional forms of transportation. I've walked through palaces and mansions and executive residences. I've seen the sun breaking over the Himalaya and settling into Tahitian waters. I have heard concerts from orchestra circles, tasted the finest cuisine, worn the sharpest clothes. Whatever could be bought I had for the asking, and what I asked for was never refused. Money was incidental. My desire was the only real currency.

I've seen a lot of things in my time, met many thousands of people. I have dallied with women of every kind imaginable and I have made every one of them melt with yearning. I have had, as the saying goes, my way with them. In the balm of their mouths and their derriéres and their sweet vulvae, I have found release and felt the most exquisite pleasure.

But on that warm summer evening in 1981, it had been more than ten years since I had felt anything resembling fear. I was afraid of Nandita Singh for reasons I could not identify.

It would be twenty years more before I felt anything like it again.

Chapter 20

Staredown

Dean

At first I was only surprised, which was surprising in itself. Merely to be involved in a situation that I had not choreographed was unusual enough, but to be faced with a sequence of events that I could not have predicted—to bear witness to something truly unexpected, over which I had no immediate control—to feel the sensation of true, unfeigned astonishment: that this was even possible was astonishing. I stood motionless as Trevor bolted for the Jeep, knocking Phil aside and yanking open the door, while Zöe's fresh words echoed in my mind. *I know what you've been doing. I know the truth about what's happening here.* But Phil, one of my favorite lackeys, didn't hesitate. He'd been a cop before I came to the university, a good cop with fast reflexes. Astonishment wasn't part of his programming. He was pulling out his .38 as the door slammed shut, cocking and aiming as the engine thrummed into life.

The windshield shattered. I came unstuck from my little trance. "The tires, shoot the tires," I shouted. Gus slammed out of the guardhouse behind us yelling something incoherent, and a mound of snow near Phil's foot exploded into a squirrel-tail of spray as a report cracked the still winter air.

"Son of a bitch!" Phil jumped as if he'd been stung and whirled around. "The fuck was that?"

Gus was managing to look both shocked and sheepish. "Oh, man, I'm sorry. I was, uh, aiming for the..."

Ignore him, I thought at Phil. *The tires!*

Phil turned around again, drew a bead, and fired at the retreating Jeep. Another crack and the rear fender buckled. "Shit," he hissed through his teeth, squinting. Exhaled. "Naw. It's out of range. You dumb motherfucker." Clearly not directed at me.

I forestalled another apology from Gus with a flick of my mind and took Phil's walkie-talkie; I'd left mine in the Jeep. "Control, this is Big D," I said. "Code Red. I repeat: Code Red. All units to pursue official Jeep now heading... north-northwest across main quad. Driver is Trevor Ethan Bailey, freshman student, caucasian, brown hair, slender build. Extremely dangerous. Contain and capture, wound if necessary, but do not kill. Repeat: do not kill."

I said all this without thinking, it seemed, on auto-pilot, even though it had been a long time since the last security breach of this severity. I was accustomed to clearing up any unpleasant misunderstandings with a simple conversation. Like the one I'd had just last month with the parents who came to school unannounced, and saw Trevor parading Zöe through the snow in her topless bodysuit, and quite naturally went to the police. That was the way it was supposed to work.

"Dean." It was Phil. I glanced at him and he motioned with his head; I turned to see that Zöe was across the street and backing slowly away. When she saw me looking she broke into a run — more of a trot, actually, because of the high heels she was wearing.

"Zöe Willow Martin," I called. "Stop right there."

She came to a sudden halt, teetering and nearly pitching forward into the snow. Moments before, I had looked into her eyes and compelled her to tell me the truth; but I had said nothing about remaining still, or about fealty to me. I'd had no idea what truth was about to be told. Clearly, it was time to get specific.

"Gordon Augustus Heineman," I said. "No one enters, no one leaves. The gate stays shut until you hear otherwise from me. If anyone tries to get through, shoot first, then call."

"Sir." I hadn't told Gus to salute me; that was his idea. He'd spent a few years in the army when he was younger, but, alas, couldn't shoot for shit. I returned the salute and motioned to Phil to follow me across the street. In the distance, I heard the sirens winding up. Code Red.

Zöe was shivering. I took her by the chin and looked her in the eyes. "Fuck you," she whispered.

"You will not speak except to answer a direct question from me," I said. "You will tell me only the truth. You will remain within ten feet of me at all times. You will not attempt to harm me in any way. Do you understand?"

"Yes, Dean."

"Good. That thing Trevor's wearing—what's it called?"

"A shoe."

I smiled. This was fun. I tugged the glove from my right hand, pulled back and slapped her across the cheek. Not nearly as hard as I could have done, but not a love tap, either. Enough to make her wince. "I think you know what I mean, Zöe," I said, carefully putting the glove back on. "The thing that broke my hold on you, as you put it a moment ago. What is it?"

"A chamsa."

"What does this chamsa look like?"

"It's a piece of lapis lazuli carved in the shape of a hand," she said dully. "There's an eye in the middle. It's on a necklace of blue beads."

"And how does it work?"

"I don't know," she sneered.

Specificity. "What effect does it have on the person who wears it?"

"It keeps their mind clear."

"Clear from what?"

"From whatever it is you do to people."

"I see. Tell me where Trevor is going."

Zöe said nothing. It took me a moment to remember my previous command that she speak only when asked a question. "Where is Trevor going?" I asked.

"I don't know."

I grunted and turned to look out at the quad where the Jeep had gone. It didn't matter, really. There was only one official exit, and Gus, poor shot that he was, would have no problem putting down anyone stupid enough to use it. Trevor would know better than that. If he wanted to leave the plateau any other way, he'd have to do it on foot, leaving nice clear prints in the snow for my men to follow. And if he stayed...well, the campus was a finite space. He had a head start, but it was only a matter of time.

"Big D to Control," I said into the walkie-talkie. "Send a car to the front gates, picking up three passengers. And open a channel between me and all units."

"Ten-four," it responded.

I clipped the walkie-talkie on my belt and turned back to Zöe. She was trying for a poker face, but it wasn't working very well. Too much fear behind the eyes.

"I had a rather late night," I said. "Fun and games, you know. That Melody Thompson is a spirited girl. Amazing stamina. And now here I am, standing in the freezing cold at dark o'clock in the morning, having been woken out of a sound sleep because you and your confederate decided that now was the time to make a break for it. I haven't had my coffee. So you'll understand, I hope, if my manners leave something to be desired."

I reached out with a gloved finger and stroked the line of her jaw. It trembled a little.

"It probably won't do any good to tell you this, but you might as well relax," I told her. "The hard part is over now. We're going to head back to my office and warm up a bit, and I'll have my coffee, and then you'll tell me what I need to know. After we're done, you won't remember that any of this ever happened."

Of course I could have made her relax. But I didn't want to do her any favors. After all, it was her fault that I had to deal with this now; let her sweat for a while. Until all my questions had been answered.

We waited there in the chilly half-light while the sirens wound up and down, until another Jeep arrived. The three of us got in, Phil riding shotgun with the driver while Zöe and I shared the back seat. As we took off, I went over in my mind the procedures for a Code Red, which had happened only once before in the twelve or so years since I'd finally got the school up and running the way I wanted it. Everyone on campus and down in Ferngrove knew what the siren meant: a dangerous intruder was in the area. Those who were outside must go immediately to the sculpture in front of the library, and those who were inside must immediately lock themselves inside the nearest room, get away from the windows, and await further instructions. Police were to block all roads leading out of town. The helicopter had never been used in an emergency — I'd acquired it shortly after the first Code Red, involving an out-of-state boyfriend who paid a surprise visit and managed to get nearly 50 miles away before we brought him down — but it was taken for test flights on a regular basis, and in theory it should be ready to go within minutes. This was, in a way, a good thing; hunting down Trevor would give me an opportunity to test the efficiency of my security system. And I couldn't deny that it was exciting to experience real danger, or at least a hint of it, for the first time in a long while.

The radio crackled. "Big D, I have a visual on the subject. Jeep is stopped outside Wynant. Subject just entered the building through the south side entrance. Please advise, over."

I grabbed my end. "All units, this is Big D. Proceed to Wynant Hall immediately. Units 12 and 14, cover main entrance; 16, 18, you've got the rear doors. All others proceed to south side entrance. Remember, I want him alive."

Not that they needed the reminder — once was always enough — but this was important, and I wasn't taking any chances. Death is tricky to cover up, even for me. Besides, there was no need to take such extreme measures; as long as we could contain Trevor, he was only a short-term problem. And I was curious. I wanted to know where he'd found this thing, this chamsa.

Phil was a good driver. He had us there in less than three minutes, ahead of the pack. The Jeep was parked with its front wheels up over the low brick embankment near the cleared pathway, driver's side door hanging open, a stream of smoke purling from the exhaust pipe into the cold air. Trevor was gone.

"Got him now, boss," Phil said. "He's up a tree."

I nodded. *Seal it off*, I thought into him. *Two snipers at every door with tranq guns. Floor-by-floor search in two staggered teams, and when you find him, approach with extreme caution. He's got something on a chain around his neck that's very dangerous. Get it away from him first, then call. I'll sit back on this one, see how you do.* Phil was gay, and although I wasn't interested in him sexually I played, subtly, on his fear/worship relationship with father figures. His need to prove himself to older men had spurred him to a stint in the army, a bout with alcoholism, a renewed faith in Jesus Christ, and a respected (if not exactly beloved) role in the community, all before I met him. I'd done a little cosmetic surgery to his personality — streamlined it by eliminating the threat of addiction, for example — but had found relatively little that needed tweaking. Phil was a natural guardian: good reflexes, attention to detail, and a natural tendency toward obedience when it came to his elders. Meaning me. I just gave him a pat on the head now and then, a reminder that I was evaluating his performance and finding it satisfactory.

I sat in the back seat with Zöe and watched him bark orders to the rest of security, setting up the snipers and teams. Just above the treetops on the ridge across the valley, the sun had risen, a pale disc in an ashen sky.

"It was a good try," I said. "You nearly made it. Gus isn't the sharpest cue in the rack, as you probably noticed, but he knows how to follow orders. Shouldn't have let him make that call." I paused, waiting for her reply as I watched the first search team slip inside. Then I remembered the restriction I'd placed on her. "You may speak freely, but you'll stop when I snap my fingers. Tell me what's on your mind."

"The satisfaction I'm going to feel when I see you dead."

"My, my," I said. "Such a bloodthirsty impulse in one so young. When I was your age I was busy trying to prevent death, not cause it. In case you haven't noticed, I don't want to kill your master. I'm trying to save him."

"He's not my master," she said through her teeth, "and the only thing you're trying to save is your own ass."

"The fate of my ass determines the fate of every other ass at this school," I replied dryly. "And the instinct for self-preservation is universal, which is why I'm not angry. I understand why you did what you did. I happen to be more powerful than you, that's all. You tried and failed because you couldn't win."

"You must be one hell of a failure to want to win this bad," she said. I had to hand it to her: she was good with the comebacks. Not to mention a solid performer in bed.

"Sour grapes, my dear. It's easy to feel righteous when your luck runs out. But you really have no reason to complain; once we've cleared up this little matter I'll reorient your perspective, and then you'll have nothing to worry about. You remember the importance of keeping perspective, don't you, Zöe?"

She didn't answer. After a moment I glanced over and saw her looking at me with something like pity in her eyes. Her head shook slightly from side to side. "You sad little man," she murmured. "You sad, pathetic, lonely little man. Fuck me in the ass like the mindless whore I am." The last sentence was a suggestion of mine; I didn't care for the way the conversation was drifting.

"I might just do that," I said, "if you ask nicely." I showed her a big warm smile, the kind I give to parents and investors, and snapped my fingers. "But that'll do for now."

Then I opened the front of her fur coat. She was wearing the vinyl bodysuit I'd special-ordered for her from a fetish designer in Ontario. It had become Trevor's favorite, and it was easy to see why; she looked like Catwoman, except for the exposed breasts. Her nipples were stiff from the cold. I brushed them with the back of my hand.

In the wake of last night's orgy I had felt pleasantly depleted, drifting off to sleep on a pile of velvet pillows and warm female flanks in the basement of Fensler Auditorium. I hadn't planned on any further fornication for at least a couple of days, but now I was ready again. My rapacious appetite for sex, never far from the surface, had been stimulated anew by the sight of Zöe's breasts in their shiny black frame and by the prospect of bringing her back under my thumb.

Trevor was up a tree. I was aroused, tired, cold, and in need of caffeine. I decided to let the boys handle him.

"This is Big D, heading for home," I told dispatch. "Taking the girl with me. Turning off radio. Page me when they find Trevor Bailey, or if any complications arise."

I got the ten-four and switched off. Zöe and I moved from the back seat to the front, and I started the Jeep.

Chapter 21
Breaking the Girl

Dean

When I have a cup of coffee, especially first thing in the morning, I often think of Brigitte. She was a young upper-class girl I found in Denmark in the Seventies, on my first trip across Europe. I stayed with her for a week, sending her parents to stay in their summer cottage while the two of us occupied the family's modest small-town estate. Every morning I would sit for fifteen minutes in the sauna, take a long, hot shower, and slip on a terrycloth robe before going into the sitting room beside the kitchen. Brigitte, who had just turned seventeen, would be standing in the kitchen wearing only an apron, grinding Blue Mountain beans at the counter. She had a buoyant, lightly fuzzed rump the shape and color of a large peach, and I'd stroke it on the way to my favorite chair. After the coffee had brewed in the French press, she'd serve it to me in a white cup on a white saucer with a chocolate croissant and a flower picked from the garden outside. I'd sip my coffee slowly, looking out over the lawn that sloped down to a pool while Brigitte knelt and made obeisance to my cock. Sometimes I'd allow her to suck me off; other times I'd have her straddle me just before I came, bouncing up and down in time to the rhythm I'd establish by grasping and tugging on her breasts. She was wonderfully receptive. A clean vessel. Brigitte in the morning.

But I was older now, feeling the drag of years behind me. Fifty of them. Not that my vigor had diminished — well, maybe a little. Not much. There was no question that I still could get it up, still hungered after the same things. But they were the same things. It had taken me years to establish perfect dominion over this castle on the hill, and now that I had everything I wanted... well, now things were too easy. I was putting on weight. My hair was going gray. I was slowly becoming an old man.

I contemplated this while I drew a double shot of espresso and poured it into my favorite blue mug, filling it up the rest of the way with coffee. A red-eye, they call it out west. While it cooled I went to stand by the sliding glass door to the patio, looking out across the snowy quad at the cluster of Jeeps around Wynant and listening to the thrum of the helicopter that circled overhead.

The second-story apartment above my office was the place I called home, because it wasn't in use by anyone else, but I spent relatively little time there. In any given week I probably slept in it two or three times at most, generally preferring to browse the dorms and single residences instead. I'd never mastered the art of settling down, and it is an art; I was fascinated by how other people feathered their nests. One sophomore boy I visited had no furniture in his room except a burnt-orange sofa, a television that sat on top of a mini-fridge, and row upon row of empty beer cans stacked neatly from floor to ceiling. Old Style wallpaper. Others had more elaborate altars — thumb-tacked constellations of photographs, mysterious graffiti, mandalas of china horses and glass swans, fishbowls of loose change. Their rooms smelled of sweat and incense and dirty laundry.

My own apartment had no smell. It was kept spotlessly clean for me: bookcases dusted, bulbs replaced, bedsheets washed three times a week whether they'd been used or not. Even the small patio deck outside had been swept clean of snow this morning, and the newspaper had been placed on the endtable by the door, just in case I came by. Everything made ready for me.

I lifted the mug, inhaling the fragrant steam for a moment before bringing it to my lips.

Ahh.

It was the taste of the world of the living, earthy and definite. The flavor of all those dormitory rooms with their disparate lives that I walked invisibly through, observing, manipulating, sipping at slowly for four years before letting them go.

"That's better," I said, turning away from the window. "Now, my dear, I want you to tell me all about your little rebellion."

Zöe was sitting on the bed, hands at her sides, stone-faced. She said nothing. I came over to where she sat, angled a nearby chair so that it faced her, and settled into it. "Everything. From the beginning. Now, if you please."

"Dude, if you want something from me, then take it." She looked directly at me for the first time. "Let's not fuck around. Rape my head and get it over with."

"I appreciate your suggestion," I said. "But I have another idea." Zöe gasped as a migraine suddenly exploded in her brain, the most severe headache she had ever experienced. My own suggestion. "We're going to engage in some aversion therapy instead. Each time you fail to answer a question, or give an answer you know is false, or dissatisfy me in some other way, you will feel pain. This is just a soupçon of what's in store. On the other hand, each time you respond truthfully and with respect—" The migraine vanished and was replaced by a small glow of pleasure in her clitoris. "You'll be rewarded. Give me what I ask for, of your own free will, and you will find that I can be quite generous."

I took a sip of coffee. I waited her out. At length she said: "Why does it matter? Why not just make me tell you everything? *Aaah!* Shit-shitshit, make it stop make it stop—Jesus Christ. Okay, you're a sadist, I get it. Fine."

"You don't get it," I said, "but that's not really important. I'm not interested in your opinion of me. Just the facts, please."

"Fine," she said again. "What do you want to know?"

"How did Trevor come into possession of the chamsa?"

"I gave it to him."

She was telling the truth. If she had been lying, she would have felt wasps crawling over her face, stinging. "And how did you come to have it?"

"It was a Christmas present."

"Go on."

Zöe sighed. "I got it from my parents. It's a family heirloom. My mom said it would protect me from the Evil Eye. *Mmmn.* I started, um, wearing it around my neck. I know what you're doing, by the way. You're making me feel horny, because sex is all you think about, and we'll probably fuck in a minute and—"

This time it was motion sickness she felt. She put a hand over her mouth, swallowed, and went on quickly.

"And I just want you to know you're kind of ugly and notmytypeatallyousickfuck, okay, so I was wearing it around my neck. Like a necklace. And I started having nightmares, only they weren't really nightmares, they were memories. Stuff you told us to forget while we were home from school; that's my guess, anyway. Can I have a glass of water? No? All right. Anyway, I thought I was going crazy, so I didn't tell anyone about them—"

"Tell me about the dreams, Zöe."

"Well, memories, like I said. I was being slapped around by someone; I think it was Trevor, but it might have been you."

"Slapped where?"

"Everywhere. My face at first... then my ass... then all over."

"How did it feel?"

"Um. It hurt. It hurt a lot. But it felt good."

"Just as telling the truth feels good. Doesn't it?"

"Yes..."

"Yes. It's so much easier, and it's going to keep getting easier the more you do it. I want you to take off your coat and gloves, and while you do that, tell me more about this dream that was not a dream."

Eyes downcast, Zöe opened the curtain of soft fur to reveal those outstanding breasts of hers, framed in glossy black. "There was... there was a... cock. Um. I couldn't see who it was because I wasn't looking at the face. I had to suck it. Wanted to. It was really..." She paused. Swallowed. "Really big. Around, you know. And it just kept coming. God... *damn* it." She stopped with her gloves bunched in her left hand. She was blushing. A tear broke loose from her eye.

"It's all right," I said gently. "I know you're trying to resist this. I understand. You've worked hard, and you don't want to see it all come to nothing. But you'll feel better soon, I promise. Much better. Now take a deep breath—that's it—and continue."

"Okay. So I was, uh, sucking this... yeah, and it was so big it made my jaw ache, but at the same time I really wanted it. Like, *really* wanted it. But I also really didn't. It was like I was in two places at once, two minds at once. There was the part of me that hated what was happening, and the part of me that wanted to obey. God." Zöe's thighs were shifting slightly, rubbing against each other. "And it just got more intense, and then I—woke up."

"I see. And you didn't tell anyone about it."

"No."

"What did you do?"

"Nothing. Until I came back to school last night. The plane was delayed. Got here late." Her left hand stroked her upper leg as she sat there on the edge of the bed, squirming. "I just had time to eat and change into something nice. Only it wasn't the right costume. I didn't know..." She broke off, caught up in the fever of sexuality that was taking over her mind. I gave her a mild electric shock that made her jump. "I'm sorry, Dean," she said, breathing heavily. "Um. So I got there, and I saw you at the ticket booth—"

"But you didn't get with the program when I looked at you," I said, "because of the chamsa."

"Right. Then the show started, and I realized what was happening."

"And you had to act the part."

"Yes."

A grin widened my mouth. Oh, this was too good! "Tell me," I said, "how did it feel to dance that way?"

"It felt sexy. And wrong. Scary."

"Why?"

"Because... it turned me on." A deep flush had spread across her cheeks. Her mouth was open, and her hand was delving closer to her inner thigh with each stroke.

"But Trevor wasn't happy."

"No. Because I had the wrong clothes on. And I lost."

"So he took you back to his room and... punished you."

"He—he started to. He hurt me. But then he forgave me when I told him about the—the chamsa." Her voice broke off and she exhaled. She was rubbing the crotch of the bodysuit, furrowing the gleaming vinyl with two determined fingers. "I said it made me, mmm, made me strong and assertive. So that he'd want to put it on. And he did. And then he forgave me. He let me... show my gratitude."

"You sucked his cock."

"Uh huh."

"Did you want to?"

She hesitated. "Um. Kind of, yeah. Yes. It was exciting. It was like playing a game. I liked pretending to be his slave. I liked making him come. Didn't like the taste, though."

"And by that time the chamsa had, uh, cleared his mind?"

"No... I don't think so. He was pretty tired. We both were. We went to sleep, and a little while later he woke up screaming — and he wasn't your puppet anymore."

I smiled. "Are you my puppet, Zöe?"

"Yes, Dean."

"Does that bother you?"

"Sort of. Not really."

"Not as much as it did before?"

"No. I'm getting used to it."

"That's good," I said. "I told you it would get easier, didn't I?"

"Yes, Dean."

I sent a shiver running down her back and over her buttocks, turning to a warm, tingling sensation that lingered there, like champagne fizzing in the throat. Her lips parted. She was looking me steadily in the eyes, no longer fighting, acquiescent. It was time.

"Stand up," I said. "And turn around."

Without hesitation she stood and turned. I drank the last of the coffee, set down the mug, and rose behind her.

"You're doing very well," I told her. "I'm pleased with your progress, Zöe."

"Thank you, Dean," she said huskily. My compliments meant so much to those who earned them. I took the zipper at the place where it began between her shoulder blades and peeled slowly downward, parting the vinyl to reveal smooth, pale flesh.

"We're almost finished now. You spoke with Trevor, told him your theories, then the two of you made a plan. Is that right?"

"Yes, Dean."

"Tell me the plan." The bodysuit came away from her slender waist, and I slipped my hand inside to lift it over the parabola of her ass. Her skin was warm. I felt saliva spring into my mouth, my cock surge and stiffen.

"We were going to come to your office," she said, stepping out of the pile of vinyl. "After we got supplies from town. We were going to catch you by surprise and hit you over the head. Then we were going to blindfold you and make you tell the cops to let us go."

"Mm. I've heard worse," I muttered. "You still didn't have a chance, though."

"I know that now."

Turn around.

She turned to face me. Her face was lovely, suffused with desire and submission. She had nothing on but the collar.

I held her gaze, sending a few key suggestions as I skimmed the back of my hand across her nipples. So taut, so definite. *Like little tooth-paste caps,* I thought, which reminded me that I hadn't observed proper oral hygiene in the midst of last night's exertions. I ran my tongue over my teeth. After I fucked Zöe, I'd brush and shave and take a hot shower; then I'd have her make me a proper breakfast. A la Brigitte.

"I see now that it was a mistake to fight you," she said. "I let myself be confused by thoughts of freedom, and I forgot that it is in my nature to be a slave. I confused my Master and I almost hurt you. I'm so ashamed. I offer my humblest apologies for the things I've said and done. Do with me what you will."

I began unbuttoning my shirt. "That's a pretty speech," I said. "I have a feeling you'll do much better at the SOTY Awards next year."

"Thank you, Dean."

Get on the bed. Third position. She sat, scooted back onto the mattress and turned to kneel facing the foot of the bed, coming forward onto her hands. I emptied my pockets onto an end table. "Soon," I said, "that pager will ring to tell me that Trevor has been captured. He will be brought here in handcuffs, and he will be angry and defiant, as you were a moment ago." I unzipped my pants. "He will talk to you and try to persuade you to resist me. Just ignore him. He's sick, and he needs help before he can become your Master again."

"I understand," Zöe said softly.

"Good girl." I stepped out of my clothes and walked across the room to the kitchenette, where I opened a cupboard above the stove and took down a small green bottle of extra virgin olive oil. I brought it with me as I came back around the half-wall to the bed. "You remember this, don't you?" I asked her.

She nodded. Of course she did. She remembered everything; it was all back in place now, the slavegirl programming I'd overlaid so painstakingly, resculpting the surface of her persona. Like the bodysuit, it fit her closely, accentuating certain features and minimizing others. Impossible to remove or reapply on her own, but with my help—the work of a moment. As easy as looking into my eyes.

This Zöe knew what the green bottle signified, and was not afraid. Did she shiver? Only with desire, the filament of need that shimmered in her spine, the anticipation that raised gooseflesh over her arms and thighs and buttocks. Fever and ice.

I stood beside the bed and opened the bottle, tipping a measure of the thick, green-gold oil into my palm. I rubbed my hands together and touched them lightly to the small of her back, sliding them toward me up and over the smooth full-moon curves of her rump and then pressing slightly into the resilient flesh as I slid away, up and over again, and back to hold each cheek firmly in the splayed fingers of my hands.

The aroma of olives rose from her warm, gleaming skin, blended with the musk of her arousal, and I took in a deep breath through my nose. I adored this smell on women, had done ever since the dusky-hued young mother in southern Italy whose name I can't remember, who needed only the slightest push to awaken her smoldering appetites. (I took her from behind in her kitchen, lifting her skirt and slathering her backside with oil from a stone mortar, fucking her while she held onto the windowsill over the sink, her breasts dipping in and out of warm, soapy water.) Zöe's breathing was coming more quickly now. Slowly I parted the hemispheres of her ass to reveal the dark, pulsing star of her hole. Then I said: "One finger."

Zöe whimpered. Lifted her left hand from the bed. Moved it up and behind, drawn like a magnet by my command. Touched down. Slipped in. And in. Her breathing stopped for a second, then broke out again, a hard exhalation. All the way in.

"Two."

It came out halfway, and her index finger slid in beside it. They moved in together, more slowly this time.

Stay there.

I let go of her cheeks, admiring the way they sprang back into place with her fingers caught between them. She really did have one of the best back ends I'd seen in years, not quite as voluptuous as Melody Thompson's but still marvelously full and supple. I slapped her right cheek, not very hard, not really thinking about it, just to watch the shimmying of taut flesh. She gasped.

"You have inconvenienced me," I murmured.

"I'm sorry—"

I pulled back and slapped her for real, a good hard smack that left my hand tingling. "You have already apologized," I said. "It is not necessary to repeat yourself." Just to be symmetrical, I slapped the other cheek as well. She made a cry with her mouth closed, squirming, as the mark of my hand went from white to red.

I came around to the foot of the bed and took a moment to drink in the sight of her, down on her knees and one hand with her eyes closed, her breasts hanging like ripe fruit on a low branch. I leaned forward, took a nipple in my slippery fingers and pressed. Her lips parted and she drew in her breath sharply.

"All that is necessary," I said, "regardless of the circumstances, is absolute submission to my will." I took the other nipple, held and pressed it between my other fingers. "To obey me without hesitation and to please me. You want that, don't you?"

"Yes. Yes." Her face was flushed.

"Good girl. Now. Fingerfuck your ass."

"Yes, Dean." There was no hesitation. Her left arm began moving behind her. I pulled on her nipples as she hit the downstroke, and she made a strangled noise in the back of her throat.

"There is no penance, Zöe," I said. "No punishment. You are a slave, and you exist only to serve. If I wish to cause you pain, for whatever reason, you will take the pain gladly. If it amuses me to give you pleasure, you will feel pleasure. Whatever I decide, you will accept completely. Punishment exists only for those who are free. Do you understand?"

I had continued to pinch and pull her nipples as I spoke, setting up a rhythmic pace as if milking her. She was breathing heavily. Instead of speaking, she nodded. I slapped her face. It felt good.

That felt good. Beg for more.

"Please... hit me... hit me again..."

"What did you say? Didn't quite catch that." I pulled hard on a nipple.

"*Nn.* Please. Hit me. Again. Hard. Hurt me. I... beg you."

I slapped her cheek so hard that she lost her one-armed balance and fell on her face on the mattress. I laughed. "Clumsy cunt." Her fingers were still sliding in and out of her rectum; they hadn't paused for a second. I toyed with the notion of having her add a third finger and a fourth, of telling her I wanted to see how far up her ass she was capable of sticking her fist. Wouldn't really have her do that, of course—I didn't want to risk any permanent damage. Just tease her, that's all.

But then I decided against it. As entertaining as this was, it hadn't been part of my schedule for the day. Classes were back in session, and I had business to attend to. So I'd come, freshen up, eat a quick bite and maybe come again if I was still in the mood, then go finish with Trevor so I could get on with things.

"Take your fingers out," I said, "and lie on your back. Cross your wrists above your head." As I gave these instructions I came around the side of the bed and moved up onto it, stroking my cock. Zöe turned over and crossed her arms as directed. She looked appealingly disheveled with hair in a tangled fan across her face, so I left it that way. Her nipples were still hard. Toothpaste caps. Breasts rising and falling with each breath.

I put my hands on her thighs just above the knees and pushed them firmly apart. She moaned, but offered no resistance, leaving her legs spread open. The lips of her cunt had already parted slightly, like a steamed shellfish, revealing a glimpse of the moist flesh inside. I leaned forward and, with the head of my cock, stroked that gleaming line. Zöe cried out.

"Little whore," I grunted, and entered her.

Immediately she began to scream. Her cries almost startled me at first, but I had heard them before—from her, and hundreds like her. They were sounds that women make when they are on the edge, riding the sharp rim of pleasure that has been denied them, so near to fulfillment that they are no longer capable of thought. I thrust my full length into her and felt her cunt clenching uncontrollably around me, helplessly in thrall to the instrument of her release. I kept her there, balanced on the point, screaming, tears running down her face, eyes wild and random while I reared and plunged, again and again, savagely, lifting her pelvis with each fresh impalement.

"Stupid—fucking—cunt," I growled. "Cocksucking... fucktoy... slut..." As I felt the tension rising within me, I raised the pitch of her agonized screams, and as I lost control I bellowed: "Now!"

Zöe came like an avalanche as I flooded into her. We hung suspended together in that sublime, endless moment when who we are has no meaning, when there is no control, only surrender. Our bodies worked beneath us.

Then we crashed down to earth again.

Did I know then? Can I say, truthfully, that part of me understood that this was farewell? Memory is treacherous. The story of our lives is only a story, one that we tell to ourselves as if we still were children. What we carry of our past is no more sacred than a fairy tale. It is bittersweet chocolate, a dark seduction.

I rested for a moment in the hammock of afterglow, warm and pulsing inside her. I would like to say that I felt something like love, but that would be a lie. It was only pleasure. I took a slow, satisfied breath and rolled away, leaving her broken sigh behind me as I sat on the edge of the bed, then stood.

"Stay there," I said. "Don't move. I'll be back in a few minutes." Without waiting for a response I padded out through the kitchen and down the short hallway to the bathroom. The door stood half-open and I pushed it aside as I entered. I ran a hand back through my hair, and I began to hum *The Marriage of Figaro* as I turned to examine myself in the mirror.

The door swung shut, and for a split second I saw Trevor behind me. Then my legs went out from under me and there was the shock of impact as my knee hit the floor, and the panic of breathlessness.

I smelled ozone, tasted leather. I jerked, tore at my throat, pushed against the sink cabinet with my feet. Couldn't breathe. I tried to drive an elbow back into his solar plexus, but he held me too close. His breath was hot in my ear. His arm around my neck squeezed tighter and tighter. A seething blackness seeped in around the periphery of my vision and I thrashed wildly, knowing that I was about to go under. Behind me I heard a thud and a grunt as he struck something—the edge of the cabinet, I think. Still he didn't let go. And the blackness swarmed in, reptilian fractals sucked buzzing into a whirlpool at the center, down into an endless, hungry nothing.

I can't remember the last thing I saw.

Chapter 22
Persistence of Vision

Dean

What came next was a sharp, unrelenting headache. It yanked me awake with vicious suddenness, so that before I knew what I was doing I had cried out and lurched forward. Or tried to. Attempting to move intensified the already overwhelming pain beyond belief — and I couldn't move, anyway, because my hands were bound behind my back.

I couldn't open my eyes, either.

"He's awake." A voice. Zöe's.

Footsteps approaching. Silence.

"Dean?" Trevor's voice, close to me. Above me.

"Sssshit," I groaned.

I heard a snort of laughter. "You really clocked him one," Zöe said.

"Yep. Pretty good aim, too, considering."

"Hey there, buster." Her voice was nearby. "How's the melon? A little tender?"

I took a deep breath. I tried to say something, but it was hard to think through the pain.

"I'm talking to you!" Zöe hollered right next to my ear. I winced, tried to pull away from the sound that splintered the pain in my head into millions of shards. Tears came into my eyes, broke and rolled down my cheeks. "Dick," I heard her mutter.

"Okay, let's do this," I heard Trevor say. A moment passed, then it was his voice next to my ear. Softer. "Dean, my man. This is Trevor.

But you already knew that, right? Listen, I know you're in a world of hurt right now, but I need you to pay attention. I need you to do me a favor. In a minute, I'm going to hold a walkie-talkie up to your mouth, and I want you to say something into it. It's not long, so you should be able to memorize it and say it word for word. Can you do that for me?"

I tried to talk, again, but the words wouldn't come out. Just a low whimper.

"Give him some water," Zöe said.

A moment later there was a glass at my lips. Water trickled down my throat and I swallowed automatically, then again, then I was drinking as fast as I could, water pouring into my mouth and overflowing onto my chest. I gasped when the glass was taken away, drawing in big lungfuls of air. I felt a little better. The pain was still immense, but I could think.

"Thank you," I said quietly.

"No sweat. Now, Dean, it's real important that you say exactly what I tell you to say. No creative substitutions or anything like that. If you don't stick to the script, I'm going to ask Zöe here to play chopsticks on your sore spot. She's an accomplished pianist. Did you know that?"

"I may be a pianist, but at least I'm not a dick," Zöe said.

"Nevertheless, she's more than capable of causing you excruciating pain. In fact, I think she'd relish the opportunity. So you want to be real, real careful. Are we clear?"

"Yes," I said.

"Good. Here's what I want you to say."

A minute later I repeated the words into the walkie-talkie. "Control, this is Big D. Trevor Bailey has been found and is under my supervision. All units stand down. Confirm."

We waited. After a moment, the dispatcher responded. "Uh, confirming that's a termination of Code Red. Subject found. Will notify all units." As always, obedient to the sound of my voice. Without question.

"Further instructions will follow," Trevor said to me.

"Further instructions will follow," I repeated.

"Ten-four."

That was all there was to it. Now the search teams would clear out of Wynant Hall, and the public address system in each building would report that the excitement was over. Students would file into classrooms where, thanks to me, they would retain information at a much higher rate than ever before in their lives. They would listen intently to the professors and ask important questions, all while pursuing the sexually oriented exercise regimen I had prescribed. Most would have no need to take notes. As the brochures promised, our school's renowned deep focus approach to academics removed unnecessary distractions from the learning environment. Primarily the environment of the mind. Within moments, it would be as though none of this had ever happened.

"You see how easy that was?" I heard the hissing sigh of an overstuffed chair being sat in. My office. We were in my office—I could smell the ghost of the incense I sometimes burned here. But I was sitting in a hard wooden chair, probably taken from the kitchen in the apartment upstairs. I tried to move my hands; they were tied together at the wrists, and it took a bit of surreptitious wriggling before I decided that I had been bound with twine and duct tape from the utility closet off the foyer. It was tight. My hands had gone partially numb.

"Look what I found." Zöe's voice came from across the room.

"Hello," Trevor said from the overstuffed chair nearby. "Guess we didn't need to make that trip to town, after all."

"Hot damn," she called. "Check this out. Videotapes. A whole freakin' library of them. And all labeled with names, amazingly enough. Let's see: Amy, Angela, Angelica, April... Gee, I wonder what's on those? Could it be some evidence? Oh, look at that. There's my name, way down at the other end. It's literally A to Z."

"Yeah, I'm guessing these'll be more than enough to put this shithead away for life." Trevor's voice came nearer. "But I still want a confession."

"Me too."

"You're making a mistake," I whispered.

"What was that? Did he say something?"

"I said that you're making a mistake," I repeated, louder. "You shouldn't be doing this. It's not a good choice."

"Hey, asshole." Trevor's finger prodded my chest. "You're blindfolded and we've got our brains back. You can stop with the free advice."

"Do you think that makes a difference?" I said. "Really? Listen to me, boy, I've been doing this longer than you've been alive. I have taken precautions. You cannot seriously believe I wouldn't have planned for a moment like this."

"I guess we'll just have to see what happens when your evil plan meets our evil plan," Trevor said. "In the meantime, seriously, we're not interested in your opinion of us.."

"Just the facts," said Zöe.

"So you can skip it. We ready to roll?"

"Rolling." I heard the click of buttons on my handheld mini tape recorder. "This is Zöe Martin, speaking on the morning of January — what day is this? The eighth? January eighth, in the office of... what should we call you? Dean? Is that even your name?"

"This is Kevin Carlson, university counselor," I said. "I am being held hostage as part of some bizarre and poorly-thought-out scheme by two students —"

I was expecting the blow to my head. I knew it would hurt. But still I gasped in surprise when the pain landed and tightened its fist in my brain.

"This jerk is dumber than I thought he'd be," Trevor said. "Rewind, let's do it again."

"No, let's keep rolling," Zöe said, right behind my ear. I could feel the nearness of her skin, the heat of her breath. "I'm tired of rehearsals and canned speeches. I want the truth. That's the whole reason I'm doing this. So I'm Zöe Martin and I'm here with Trevor Bailey, and we're having a conversation with Kevin Carlson Dean whatever the fuck his name really is. I'm sure it's none of those. I'm..." She stopped to take a breath. "I'm sorry if whoever hears this is offended by my language, but we're in a pretty offensive situation right now. We've just woken up after being hypnotized for the last four months and sexually abused by this man. We have been raped and shot at. We are acting in self-defense to hold this man accountable for what he has done."

"Well, you managed to get just about every detail wrong, Miss Martin," I said. "I suppose you'll hit me again for saying that, since violence is the only approach you seem to understand."

"I couldn't possibly hit you enough to make up for everything you did to me, you sack of shit," Zöe snarled. "Don't tempt me."

"Go ahead, Dean," Trevor said. "I'll just call you Dean for now, until we find out your real name. Tell us all the details Zöe got wrong."

"You haven't been hypnotized and you haven't been asleep," I said. "You haven't been drugged. There has been no abuse and no rape. As for the shooting, Mr. Bailey was in the process of committing grand theft auto at the time. I believe that's a felony. Now you can add abduction, assault and battery to your rap sheets. All of this you claim is in self-defense, yet the only danger you have experienced at this school has been what you brought on yourself."

They both started talking at once. Trevor's voice won out. "We're wasting our time," he said. "Look, it doesn't matter. We've got enough evidence already."

"It's not — about — evidence!" Zöe screamed. I heard the slap first; then sharp heat rushing in to sear my cheek, my ear ringing, throbbing. So that was what it felt like.

"We need to stay focused," Trevor was saying. "Listen to me! I know you want to hurt him. So do I. But we're not safe yet. We can't get sloppy now, all right? Zöe. Zo. I can't do this alone. Remember when you said that to me? I can't do this alone."

She was crying. I heard a guttural shriek of frustration. "Son of a bitch motherfucker." More crying.

I was shocked to find wetness seeping out of my own eyes. When was the last time I had wept? I couldn't remember. A long, long time ago. Years. There wasn't much this time, just a few drops with nowhere to go behind my blindfold. I shook my head to bring back the pain, to keep clear.

The hiss of tape stopped with a click. "All right, Dean," Trevor said. "Enough bullshit. We don't need your testimonial. We know what we've been through—"

"Do you?" I interrupted. "Do you, really? I don't think you have a clue. You should thank me for what I've done, Mr. Bailey. When you came to me you were falling apart, out of control with grief. I helped you get yourself together. I gave you confidence. Look at you now — listen to that swagger in your voice. Do you honestly think you'd have

186

had the balls to confront me like this if I hadn't given them to you?"

There was a moment of silence. I heard Trevor gather a breath. Then he started speaking, slowly. "Look, I didn't ask for anything you gave me," he said. "All right? Yeah, I had a broken heart and I needed help. You didn't give me help, you gave me a brainwash. You didn't give me confidence, you gave me arrogance. And you're so arrogant yourself that you probably don't understand the difference. You get everything you want, don't you? Been doing this longer than I've been alive, you said. You know what you are, pal? You're a fat, balding, dirty old man with too much power who doesn't give a fuck about anyone but himself. That's it. That's all you are. That's all you've got. End of story."

The silence resumed. I waited, but he was done. Zöe didn't say anything, either. I had thought of things to say while he was talking, but for some reason they wouldn't come out now. The stupid tears were pooling around my eyes. It was strange: I didn't feel like I was crying. I didn't feel guilty or ashamed or sad; I didn't feel anything except the pain in my head and the dryness in my throat. My eyes were acting on their own.

And my mouth was talking on its own. "I don't expect you to understand," it said. "I never thought I'd need to explain. They should have found you — the building was sealed off — "

"I was never in it," Trevor said. "That was me who called it in. I ditched the Jeep and took the radio. Made the call when I was over by Fensler, watched everybody go the wrong way, then hoofed it over here. Climbed up the drainpipe and let myself in from the balcony. Pretty easy, considering what I was up against. I'm just lucky you told Zöe not to move. And to ignore me, I think. That helped. All I had to do was put the chamsa on her and wait."

"*Deus ex machina*," I murmured.

"What's that?"

"Latin. God from the machine. Your little magic cliché really screwed things up."

"Takes one to know one, Dean," he said. "You're the biggest cliché I've ever seen in my life. Some teenage wet-dreamer who never had to grow up. What, were you born this way?"

"You little shit," I snarled. "You dare to lecture me about maturity? You think you know the first thing about life in the real world?" My lips were vibrating, my ears felt hot. "You have no idea what I've been through. No idea."

"I see. So you've paid your dues, then."

"You're goddamned right."

Zöe broke in, a note of surprise in her voice. "Look. Look, he's crying."

The tears must have seeped through my blindfold. I could feel them running down my cheeks now, and I couldn't wipe them away. It was so strange. So remote. My own body was beyond my control.

"Okay," Trevor said. "Tell us about it. Tell us what you've been through so we can appreciate the sacrifices you've made. I'm serious, I really want to know. The tape is off. We're listening."

For some reason that made me cry harder than ever. It wasn't that there was anything sympathetic in Trevor's voice, or that I felt sorry. It had been a long time, though, since anyone had wanted to listen to me — wanted it sincerely, with no nudging on my part. Not since...

Not since Gloria.

That day in the park, a lifetime ago. Miss Gloria Daymore and the seedling trees we planted near the sidewalk on that spring afternoon, the scrape of my spade and the smell of damp earth. Talking for an hour, maybe two, with the girl I couldn't get out of my mind. Talking just to talk. I was nervous and hyper-witty; she was relaxed and friendly, laughing at my jokes. She must have known how much I ached and trembled to be in her presence, how terrified I was of embarrassment and how badly I wanted to impress her. She knew and she was kind to me anyway, asking me easy questions and listening to my oratorical responses as if there were nothing in the world she would rather do, as if my words were important. As if I mattered to her.

I found myself starting there, with the story of the park and the riot that followed, the cops and the tear gas and the broken milk bottle in my hand. The crack of the billy club on my skull, my arm swinging blind. Blood gushing over her fingers. The shock in her eyes.

It came heaving out that way, my story, not a thing I could stop once it had started. Like birth, I suppose, all blood and pain and gravity. Vacaville. Spooks. Drugs and madness. Black holes. Shadowboxes.

Nightmare. Needle in the eye.

Then the escape, and the years of wandering. This thing I could do and couldn't stop doing, a kind of freedom that lanced through the tethers of the normal world and left me drifting. No one to answer to, no consequences. An endless vacation.

Until I grew dissatisfied with my rootlessness and decided to settle down. Somewhere I could call home, where I could indulge my passions without undue attention from the world at large. Hence college life. Hence this place, high atop a hill in the sticks of America. My sanctum sanctorum of lovely young women and their keepers. My private theater.

And now, years later, everything was in place. All the kinks worked out, or worked in; a fully functional system of education and entertainment that I had shaped with the power of my mind. Retirement, if you will. A high plateau. A safe place to approach the inevitable end of my life.

"So what, you were just going to leave behind a bunch of sex zombies when you kicked the bucket?" Trevor asked.

"Not at all," I said. "I've been very careful about this. When students graduate, they retain the academic portion of their experience but lose all memory of their sexual history. When I 'kick the bucket', as you put it, a few of my assistants will destroy the records I've kept. Then they'll broadcast a pre-recorded message that will trigger the 'graduation' sequence in everyone's minds. By the time I'm in the ground, it'll be like I was never here."

There was a moment of silence.

"That's sad," Zöe said. "What a waste."

That took me by surprise.

"Really. A waste of what?"

"Everything," she said. "You. All the people you've messed with. Like a stupid video game. It's just—pointless."

"Yeah, well." I smiled. "Don't get all existential on me, now."

"No, I mean... didn't you ever want to do something with your life? Something meaningful? You have this amazing ability. You could've, I don't know, ended world hunger. Or something. Anything, and instead you chose to screw a bunch of women. I mean, why? Why?"

I floundered for a moment. "I—I don't know, Zöe," I said. "I wish

I had a good answer to that question. I guess I just didn't think it was any of my business to interfere. It crossed my mind, don't think it didn't. I could have made everyone on the planet do what I wanted, and I could have forced all kinds of changes for the better. I could have been king of the world, right? But the thing is, kings get killed. And the world is a big place. Look, the two of you managed to get to me, and you're—no offense—a couple of kids. I'm not dumb. If anyone with real power found out what I could do, I'd be a rat in a cage. They'd lock me up and use me, like they did before, only worse. A lot worse. If you think I'm bad now, just imagine what I'd be in the hands of someone with God on his side."

Again, silence.

"I'm not a bad man," I said. "Really, I'm not. I might be a pervert, but I'm not evil. I don't want to hurt anybody. Look, I'm sorry you guys found me out, for your sake as well as mine. That wasn't supposed to happen. If it wasn't for the, uh, thingy you have there—"

"It's called a chamsa," Zöe cut in. "And if it wasn't for this, you'd probably be fucking my ass now."

I smiled involuntarily.

"All a big joke, huh?" She sniffed. "Pretty funny, I guess, if you're in on it. Although it's kinda lame if you're the only one laughing. Has it ever occurred to you, Dean, that you're a chronic masturbator? Someone who's never had a real relationship in his life? I mean, this story you just told us, I don't know whether to feel sorry for you or throw up."

"I'm not looking for pity," I said. "Look, I could lie and tell you I'm sorry about all of this, but I'm not. It's too bad you found out and all, but you're young. You'll get over it. For my part? I had a good ride."

"And now it's over," Trevor said.

I took a deep breath. "Yeah. I kind of figured that."

Chapter 23

See No Evil

Dean

"So. What now?" I asked.

"Well." Trevor cleared his throat. "We can't let you keep doing this. That much is obvious. And we can't trust you to stop it on your own."

"You need help," Zöe said. A sneer in her voice.

"Okay. So how are you going to help me?"

Silence.

Finally Trevor spoke. "You're going to help us, Dean. You're going to get on the radio and tell your uh, assistants that it's graduation day for everyone. Then we're going to take these tapes, and whatever else we can find, and we're going to show them to people who can make sure this doesn't happen again."

I felt a trickle moving inside me. Small, cold and liquid.

"People," I said. "Important people. Powerful people."

"That's right."

"And they'll believe you."

"They'll believe us."

"Right. Of course they will. Evidence, like you said. Lots of tapes and notes." The trickle was icy. Strange, yet familiar.

"Uh huh."

"Then what?" I asked.

"What do you think is going to happen once they believe you?"

"I don't know."

"I'll tell you. They'll cover it up. They'll buy you off or they'll kill you, and they'll stick me in a padded cell with a little hole in the wall, and every now and then I'll have to look through the hole and send a message to someone on the other side. Is that what you want?"

Trickle running down my throat. For a moment I thought I was bleeding inside.

"We can't trust him." Zöe. "He'd say anything now."

"I know." Trevor. "But he's right. This is bigger than us."

"Listen," Zöe said. "All I know is, he turned me and hundreds of girls like me into blow-up sex dolls and that is *not okay*. Whatever else we have to think about, that is the bottom line for me. It's not okay and I can't allow it to go on. You hear me, asshole?" *Crack*. Slap. Heat. The twine holding me to the chair creaked. "I will not allow it."

And at last I knew what I was feeling. Miles away and twenty years later, the blind eyes of Nandita Singh followed me into the darkness and held me fixed in place, held me with nothing more than ordinary human will. Stopped me cold.

For the first time in many years, I felt fear.

In the distance I heard Trevor saying something, then voices moving away. I couldn't focus. Now that I knew I was afraid, it was hard to let in anything else. It wasn't that I was afraid for my life. It was something deeper. Something to do with the disappointment in her voice, in the back, behind her anger. Having been made naked, found out and found wanting. My ugliness pinned to the wall.

"It's time, Dean."

"Time?" I muttered.

"To end it. You said it yourself, you had a good run. Now it's time to move on." I started to make a last, small effort, to say that if they released me I would move on and keep moving, stay far away and never trouble them again. But that was no good and I knew it. Trevor was right: it was time to tie up loose ends.

"Let's do it clean, then," I said instead. "Whatever you have to do to me, I'm asking you, please — don't tell anyone about this."

"About what? The school?"

"Yes, the school. Everything."

"I don't really feel like doing you any favors, old man," Trevor said.

"It's not a favor to me." The throbbing at the back of my head had intensified, probably because of the slap that set me off-balance.

It was getting difficult to think clearly again. "It's... a favor to them. They don't need to know. It wouldn't change anything if they did. Look, I'm going to graduate them right now, all of them. Everybody. Students, faculty, staff, admin, the cops, the people down the hill... everyone's done. They'll go back to being who they were before they met me, and they'll drink too much, and struggle with classes, and break each other's hearts, and maybe they'll earn a degree or maybe they won't. That's what you want, isn't it? Their lives back?"

"Yes..."

"So, you could let that be enough. Or... you could choose to tell them all the truth. But if you think they'll thank you for it, you're mistaken. You'll ignite an atmosphere of paranoid delusion and these people will never be happy again. They'll never feel safe. Always looking over their shoulder in their dreams. That's not helpful. Okay? It's honest, but it's not helpful."

"I hear what you're saying," Zöe cut in with surprising softness. "You're right, Dean. I don't want to cause anybody more grief, and it's fair to ask how the truth would benefit them in this situation. Good intentions and all that."

"Everybody means well," I said.

"I guess we'll just have to trust our instincts," she replied. "I can't promise you anything—only that I'll think about it."

"Fair enough."

"Okay, then," Trevor said. "Let's get started."

Graduation was a simple process, deliberately so. I had streamlined it over the years, setting up subprograms earlier in the year to make the final ceremony as brief as possible. Each year on Graduation Day, all the seniors would file into the handball court and I would walk among them, touching them goodbye with my eyes. By the time I left, they no longer remembered that such a person as Kevin Carlson had ever existed, or that they had played a part in his sexual theater troupe. Each year they walked from the gym over to Fensler Auditorium, where they took their diplomas from Bob Thornhill, the University President, with a smile and a wave to their proud parents. I would stay out of sight, waiting until the last of the cars had pulled away down the hill and all the students were gone—seniors permanently released, underclassmen given a quasi-graduational erasure for the summer: enough to obscure any dangerous memories but easy to lift again in the fall.

By the time Gus gave the word I would have showered, dressed, packed, eaten a meal and be ready to slide into the back seat of the towncar. One of my flunkies drove me to the airport each year and I would catch a flight to wherever I felt like visiting. I'd take a two-month globetrotting summer vacation and come back in early August refreshed, ready to sketch out my plans for the incoming crop of freshmen.

As simple as it was, I had a shortcut for emergencies. So far, there hadn't been any. The plan was that if ever I found myself seriously ill or incapacitated in some serious, permanent way, I could circumvent the whole ceremony with a short broadcast. All I had to do was say the word.

"Dispatch, this is Big D," I said. "Come in. Over."

"Dispatch. Good morning, sir."

"Good morning. Open a channel to all receivers, please."

"Opening. Go ahead."

"Attention, ladies and gentlemen of the police," I said. My key phrase to open access to certain other phrases. A safety measure. "Closing up shop. I repeat: closing up shop. Immediately. Please confirm."

"Confirming, we are closing up shop."

"Make it so," I said with a grin. A small joke.

A few moments later my voice came over the loudspeakers.

"Attention university complete. Attention university complete." There was a pause. "Final graduation day. This is final graduation day. All staff, all faculty, all custodians, all students, all visitors and all residents of Ferngrove are hereby graduated permanently. Assemble all material evidence of contact with Kevin Carlson, also known as Dean. Bring to the front door of the student union within one hour. This is final graduation day. Final graduation day."

Humming silence, then a click.

That was all there was to it.

"They'll be coming in a couple of hours," I said, suddenly weary. "Confiscating all the evidence. If you want anything, take it, but be sure to hide it well if you do."

"Okay," Trevor said.

"Now what?" I asked. "What's your plan? What becomes of me?"

"I've been thinking about that," Zöe said. "I don't feel comfortable killing you and I don't think my boyfriend does, either."

"Boyfriend, huh?" Trevor sounded pleased. "I will if I have to, but—no, it's not something I really want to do."

"And obviously we can't just untie you, or you take off that blindfold and it starts all over again," she went on. "So the answer lies somewhere in between."

"Where, exactly?"

"Well... do you know the myth of Oedipus?" she asked.

Oedipus. The name took a second to register, then I got it. Sudden and cold.

"No," I said, shaking my head. "No."

"I don't see any way out of it."

"Sick," Trevor said. "You're going to stab him in the eyes?"

"Unless he wants to do it himself."

"No. Don't do this," I begged. "Please don't do this."

"Well, I'm not doing it." Revulsion in Trevor's voice. "No way. Give me fucking nightmares."

"I already have nightmares," she said calmly. "I can handle one more, I guess."

"Look, there's got to be another way." I tried to sound calm, but it didn't work very well. "Could you at least knock me out first? I'm — I'm terrified of eye injuries."

"You mean hit you in the head again?"

"I was thinking more along the lines of general anesthetic from Doris in the clinic," I said. "There's an operating room in the back—I don't think you've ever been there. I'll walk you through it. Just give me an injection and I won't feel a thing."

"Painless," Zöe said. "How convenient for you."

"Wait." It was Trevor. "Waitwaitwait. Dr. Graham."

"What?"

"Hang on. I have an idea. No one's looking for Zöe now, are they? Dean?"

"No," I said. "She's with me."

"Right. So there's no problem if she takes a walk over to Hanover Hall."

"Why?" Zöe asked. "You want me to get Dr. Graham?"

"No. C'mere."

There followed a period of conversation in low voices. I heard Zöe asking "Are you sure?" at one point. A while later, I heard the small sounds of someone rising from a chair. Then the door to the foyer opened and closed.

"What's going on?" I asked. "Trevor? What are you doing?"

"Just sit tight," he said. "It'll be a few minutes."

Clearly, that was all I was going to hear from him until Zöe returned. I tried to think of what her trip to Edwin Graham's classroom might mean, but I couldn't imagine what geology had to do with my situation. Geology. Rocks. Knock me out with a chunk of agate? No, there were plenty of heavy objects here in the office. That couldn't be it. But something... something to take away my sight. One way or another, the end was coming soon.

When the answer came to me a moment later, sudden and obvious, my first reaction was gratitude. They weren't doing it this way out of kindness; they were angry and they had every right to be, but they weren't savages. It wasn't in their nature to cause pain. I was grateful for that, grateful that it was kids like them who were taking me down. It would hurt—it had to hurt—but not like a blow to the head or a blade in the eye. I would survive.

Still, by the time Zöe returned, I was trembling. Anticipation does that to you.

More muttered conversation. Footsteps. Running water from the next room. A click. An electronic hum. Then Trevor's breath, his voice beside my left ear.

"You ready?"

I thought he was talking to me, but Zöe responded. "Ready."

"Here we go."

Fumbling at the back of my head. Loosening the blindfold.

It came away and I squinted, blinking my eyes. At once I felt gentle pressure on my eyelids, lifting them, and tape laid across the lifted skin.

I was staring down the bores of two 15-milliwatt, Class 3b laser pointers. Into searing green light that teemed with a poisonous, insectile grain. I couldn't look away. My eyes burned.

"Please..." I croaked. "Hurts..."

A long moment later warm water trickled over my forehead, into my open eyes. It stung and blurred my vision, but soothed some of the agony. I was taking gasping breaths. It seemed that I was screaming now. Vacaville was back, as though it had never left me. The independent voicebox, the primal response to pain.

I tried to twist away, but strong arms held my chair. I couldn't feel my hands anymore. The light ate into me relentlessly, tearing down rods and cones, leaving behind a soft gray drift. Ashes.

Ashes, long after my servants came to sweep up the remains of the temple. Ashes when they carried me from the office into the cold morning and down to a car. The driver forgot who I was not long after we passed the city limits, but he had been a kind man before I met him. He carried me to the next town and dropped me at a motel. Even helped me to my room.

I kept waiting for the smoke to clear. Many days later it did, slightly, enough that I could make out a few colors again. With time, I was able to recognize familiar shapes and steer clear of telephone poles. But the colors swam through a gray haze, blurred fish in a murky pond that flickered away when I held out my hands to them.

Once I tried again, with a woman at a bus stop. I could tell it was a woman by her perfume. I mentioned the weather, then introduced myself, asking her name. She told me, and I had a moment of hope before I suggested that she give me ten dollars. She laughed nervously and said she didn't think so. I nodded and apologized. That was that.

My eyes are gone, but I still have my voice, honed by all the years of intimate conversation. I do radio commercials now in a large city; if you live there, you've probably heard me hawking auto parts and aftershave. I have a second-floor walk-up with central heating and a cat, and once a week a young man comes to cook for me and play chess. I've gotten pretty good at chess.

This is not the story I expected. The abyss below me is still there, although I can't see it now, and the wire I walk seems to stay beneath my feet whether I believe it or not. I have contemplated suicide, but I find that I am in no hurry to follow through. Maybe a day will come when I'll decide I've had enough of this life and end it. Or maybe I'll step out in front of a bus by mistake. Or get cancer. Or maybe I'll fall asleep and forget to wake up, and the young man will find me in bed, eyes closed forever.

It's not up to me. None of it is, anymore.

If you enjoyed this story, you can sign up for a free membership at
ForbiddenFiction.com and discuss it with other readers
and the author at the *Deep Focus* story page
at http://forbiddenfiction.com/library/story/MLC-1.000124.

We do our best to proof all our work, but if you spot a text error we missed,
please let us know via our website Contact Form
at http://forbiddenfiction.com/contact.

Author's Notes

Deep Focus began as a short story called "Point of View", which I published under another pseudonym on the Erotic Mind Control Story online. Any list of acknowledgements must begin with a bow to Simon bar Sinister and the forum he has maintained for so long with such integrity. At the EMCSA I found inspiration, both as an onanist and as a writer, to explore the possibilities of literary kink. I'm grateful to the community of readers and writers there who gave me feedback and encouragement as the short story began to develop into something larger.

The portion of this story which draws upon the actual events of May 15, 1969, for inspiration is in no way meant to diminish the very real tragedy of the death of James Rector or the struggle over People's Park. Additionally, the portion of this story that takes place in Vacaville State Prison draws upon historical events for inspiration, but is not intended to be a factual rendering of them.

For those interested in further research into the CIA's experiments with mind control and the MK-ULTRA program's presence at Vacaville, I recommend *The CIA's Greatest Hits* by Mark Zepezauer, Odonian Press, 1994; *Operation Mind Control* by Walter Bowart, Dell, 1978; and *The Search for the Manchurian Candidate* by John Marks, Dell, 1979.

About the Author

M. L. Caufax writes and breathes and does other necessary things in lovely Northern California. Under other names, M. L. has published poetry, reportage, and somewhat less scandalous fiction. In addition to writing smut and remaining anonymous for professional reasons, M. L.'s enthusiasms include singing, playing guitar and ukulele, experimenting in the kitchen, typography, etymology, cephalopods, social justice, live theater, old paperbacks, and puzzle-boxes.

About the Publisher

ForbiddenFiction.com is a publisher devoted to writing that breaks the boundaries of original erotic fiction. Our stories combine intense sexuality with quality writing. Stories at ForbiddenFiction.com not only arouse readers through sensations, but also engage them emotionally and mentally through storytelling as well-crafted as the sex is hot.

ForbiddenFiction.com is also designed to be a social reading environment. You'll have fun even if just reading the latest post each day, yet you will have the chance for so much more. Readers and authors can be part of ongoing discussions of specific works and individual authors as well as more general topics.

Sign up for a FREE Membership today at ForbiddenFiction.com.